1971

HOUSE OF EXILE

HOUSE of EXILE

A NOVEL BY

Joseph E. Coyne

THE BRUCE PUBLISHING COMPANY

MILWAUKEE

Joseph Coyne
Is Also Author of:

"The Threshing Floor"
Published in German as:

"Spreu Und Weizen"

Library of Congress Catalog Card Number: 64–22862

For My Children
Susan and Joseph

[v]

HOUSE OF EXILE

CHAPTER ONE

THE last obstinate stars were fading from the morning sky as
the priest emerged from the monastery on River Street. He
paused for a moment on the cracked concrete sidewalk to button
his coat, speculatively raising his eyes toward the glow in the
eastern sky. The sun would soon be up over the city of
Darrington, in south central Massachusetts.

Alert-eyed in spite of the early hour, Father Massimo Nadi
gave a vague wave of greeting to the policeman sitting in the
patrol car, waiting to drive him to St. Camillus Hospital.

He had dressed hurriedly after getting the emergency call and
now he stood securing the top buttons of his cassock as he
breathed the fresh morning air. He savored the heavy smell of
lilac coming from the copse of bushes beside the old monastery
building and the myriads of them in the "no-man's-land"
between the monastery and the Jewish cemetery.

Officer O'Gara raced the cruiser motor impatiently as the
priest pulled open the door and got in, knocking his biretta
from his head in spite of his great care in ducking as he slid onto
the seat. O'Gara's grim face told him better than words that
the injured man whom the call was about was in serious
condition.

A police car was always available to take him to either of the
city's hospitals when a priest was needed. Father Massimo's good
friend, Sergeant Muldoon, had seen to that. This morning's call
from the hospital had come at 4:30.

At the hospital, O'Gara hurried with the chaplain through the doors of the emergency ward and to the room where the interns and nurses were working over the injured man. One of the interns, Andy Lambert, glanced up and pointed to a crucifix tattooed on the man's arm. Apparently that was the only indication they had that he was a Catholic.

"He was crushed by a freight car," said Andy.

The chaplain bent low over the weathered face. The man's eyes were wide radars of pain as Father Massimo whispered, "I'm a priest. Do you understand? I'm going to give you absolution — if you are willing — "

The man eyes flicked in recognition and his hand moved, a nurse suddenly seizing it as though she thought he would put it to the mangled mass that was his stomach, but instead he had been groping for the priest's hand. He found it and held tightly as the words of absolution were whispered over him.

A moment later the fingers relaxed, releasing time and extending to eternity. The priest, accompanied by Andy Lambert, walked from the room.

"We did our best, Father. He didn't have a chance."

The priest glanced at the young, crop-haired intern. "He had the chance that counts, Doctor."

The intern looked away uncomfortably. "Anyway, I'm glad the police called the monastery after they saw the crucifix tattoo."

"Then it is not too strange to imagine that the crucifix saved him, Doctor."

"No, Padre, not at all," Lambert said with a wry smile. "But I am wondering what the outcome might have been if the cop had seen the other arm first — the tattoo of a woman entwined with a reptile."

Father Massimo left the emergency ward and went to the chapel on the third floor, where he said Mass every morning for the Sisters and any of the nurses and doctors on the staff who cared to attend. At the vesting bench in the little sacristy he saw that Sister Alexius had set out vestments for the day, Tuesday, June 7, a ferial day free of any feast on the liturgical calendar. Anticipating his wish, the Sister had prepared black vestments, aware that he always said a requiem Mass when the ordo of the diocese permitted. This morning it would be a Mass for the man who had died a few minutes before.

A half hour later, the intern was coming down in the elevator, his night's duty done, when the elevator stopped at the third floor and Father Massimo stepped in, his biretta on his head and his coat over his arm.

"Well, Doctor, I hadn't expected to see you so soon."

"Welcome aboard, Father. One?" Lambert grinned.

"One? Oh, yes. I'm going out. That is your meaning." He watched for the intern's nod; then said, "But I did plan to look you up before I left. I'd like you to try again to examine Bishop Dworjanski." The priest chuckled, putting up his hand at the sign of protest on Andy Lambert's face. "I know, Doctor, I know — he has locked his door on you, insulted you, turned you out quite unceremoniously — "

"But you think I ought to turn still another cheek." Andy grinned. "OK, Father — for you."

Andy Lambert had known the priests at the monastery for almost a year. Shortly after he joined the staff at St. Camillus the Sister administrator had asked him if he'd give medical attention to the exiled priests at Archangel Monastery. It was an unusual procedure, but Dr. Barnhardt, head of the medical staff, and a good friend of Bishop Hickey, had recommended the service for the indigent priests at the monastery. Since then Lambert had been called a number of times to attend Stefan Dworjanski, the old Polish bishop; Father Largo, who had more ills than Lambert had been able to diagnose, diabetes among them; and Father Maximilian, who was almost deaf and had vision in only one eye.

"I'll stop by this afternoon," Lambert said. They got out of the elevator, the intern motioning the priest ahead of him in the corridor where the day workers were streaming toward the cafeteria for breakfast.

Andy Lambert liked the Father superior of Archangel Monastery, probably because he never looked as though he were imposed upon no matter what hour he was summoned to the hospital. The priest appeared to be in his mid-fifties. His short-cropped black hair was amply peppered with gray. His excellent white teeth flashed when he talked and his rather prominent nose actually looked as though it had been smashed by a gun butt, as Father Edmund, the English priest, claimed.

The Britisher was full of information about the superior, some of it undoubtedly accurate. He said Father Massimo had once been secretary to the papal nuncio in Warsaw and when the nuncio withdrew during the Nazi invasion, Father Massimo had stayed until the nunciature was bombed, when he moved eastward with the refugees and later became the apostolic administrator of a Polish diocese replacing the local bishop, who was shot. Father Maximilian, the German, had once whispered to Lambert that the superior had been in a concentration camp, a report he insisted was true in spite of the fact that Father Massimo would never confirm nor deny it.

After a light breakfast with Dr. Lambert, the superior left the hospital on the heights and stood for a few moments on the ramparts, a little park with an ancient cannon and a few words of dedication to immemorial heroism on a greened bronze plaque. Below near the river and on the fringe of the city's business district was the monastery which had become a popular shrine with the Catholic people of Darrington. It was convenient for Mass and confession on weekdays but, since the monastery was not a parish, there was no congregation; and Bishop Hickey had made it clear to his people that they were expected to attend Sunday Mass in their parishes.

Father Massimo had little idea why he had been dispatched from Rome to take charge of the heterogenous house of exiled priests. The Father general had informed him that it would be

[4]

a temporary task and when he first saw the old house he hoped the Order's general was right. It was easy to put faith in the local story that the house had been abandoned by one religious order after another as damp, drafty, and architecturally unsound. But the exiled missioners had righted what they could and endured what could not be repaired.

The priest walked down the hill, acknowledging the greetings from the children on their way to school and from the overly plump Mrs. Fitzpatrick who jiggled like a bowl of gelatin as she swept her sidewalk vigorously.

"Good morning, Father," she gasped.

"Buon giorno," he said, smiling and bowing a bit as he hurried on to avoid conversation with the woman who was forever buttonholing one of the priests to get a theological opinion on her invalid marriage.

He came to the old red-brick building and pushed open the gate to the walled garden. At the far end Father Maximilian was pacing and reading his breviary, determined to carry out the letter of his priestly role even though he'd been excused from reading the Divine Office because of his eye condition.

It had been Father Maximilian's peculiar mission to smuggle the Order's most precious relic out of East Germany when he had received a visa to travel to America for an eye operation. The relic was the Holy Shirt of Mail which tradition said the Venerable Bruno Von Barth, founder of the Brunite Order, had worn day and night for more than forty years. It was a heavy, homemade piece of armor of chain mail which Bruno's biographer said had more than once saved him from assassination.

When the Communists realized that the relic had been taken from the chapter house at Meissen and worn by Father Maximilian under his clothing when he left the country, they let out a whoop of dismay. Their vitriolic debates in the UN failed to impress the delegates who knew that the Communists suffered more from the loss of prestige than they did the loss of what they called a "treasured antiquity."

The Communist protests had a side effect they hadn't counted on. The cause of Venerable Bruno, long dormant, had been revived in Rome; there was talk of resuming the process for his beatification, and demands came to Archangel Monastery that the relic be displayed. Father Massimo had seen it but once, and that was not in Meissen but here in Darrington when Monsignor Lawrence Brady, rector of the cathedral, took him down to the crypt where the deceased bishops were buried and where Bishop Hickey had ordered the Holy Shirt kept when the Communist agitation was at its height.

But now it was to see the light of day again. Rome and Bishop Hickey had given consent and tomorrow it would be carried in solemn procession from St. Mary's Cathedral to the monastery.

The German saw Father Massimo and hurried toward him and together they went into the house, the nearsighted and deaf old man seeing nothing incongruous in his insistence on carrying out his chosen role of Father porter by holding the door open for the superior. He had contented himself with the humble position even though in Meissen and throughout the Order he was known as a theologian and had lectured at many Brunite colleges and institutes. But now he was not well qualified even for the job of doorkeeper, since he was usually the last, not the first, to hear the doorbell.

When Father Massimo arrived in Darrington he had found the exiled priests gathered, some of them from Europe and others from missions in China, India, and Africa. He found them to be men of divergent and sometimes conflicting personalities. His orders concerning Bishop Dworjanski were still quite obscure. He had been left with the impression that there was some danger in the task, but from which direction it might come he was not sure.

In the chapel, British Father Edmund was concluding the last Mass of the day. He had been a missionary in India, in a town near the Chinese frontier and had been requested to leave the country when he found himself on the wrong side in the Goa seizure. He was generally suave and almost as worldly-wise as he imagined, but given to uncharitable remarks about Bishop Hickey, whom he said had never quite appreciated the prestige the exiled priests brought to his diocese. It was a particularly unkind remark, Father Massimo thought, in view of the fact that the Englishman should be aware that the bishop was more disturbed by than pleased with their presence.

Father Massimo left his coat and biretta in his office near the front of the house and stood looking up the long, rather precarious staircase that led to the cavernous second floor.

The staircase had undoubtedly been an elegant piece of carpentry in its day, but now was reinforced with an unhandsome row of metal posts.

Father Massimo was wondering if he was too early to expect a cup of coffee, when he heard Father Georgio's booming voice from the kitchen door.

"Pax tecum, Father Superior!"

The Father commissario stood with his elbow holding open the door to the kitchen, a large white apron nearly covering the wide expanse of his soutane. His great black beard hung like a rabat on his enormous chest. He was known in the Order as one of its most successful missionaries and had established several hospitals for lepers in South China, a work for which he had been decorated by the national government and condemned to death by the government in Peking. But when they came to arrest him they learned that he had taken a boat and rowed the 50-odd miles to an island off the Vietnam coast.

The great fatherly affection Father Georgio had for everyone was evident in his blustering face. Even his somewhat noisy abuse was taken in good spirits by all of the exiles. Blunt and explosive as he was, he had proved to be the unifying force among the expatriates.

He wiped his face now with an expanse of his apron, but the gesture failed to banish his perturbation.

[7]

"I have great patience, Father Superior!"

"It's well that one of us has," said the superior, hoping he didn't appear too unconcerned about the big Croat's complaint. Complaining was one of the few satisfactions he enjoyed in return for all the work he did in the house.

"Come," Father Georgio said forcefully, a command that the superior would have felt compelled to obey even if the big bearded cook hadn't held the door open authoritatively and motioned him into the kitchen.

"This is a terrible thing to happen in a religious house!" he boomed. He strode to the table and picked up a ham bone which had been picked clean. "This was to be our lunch, Father Superior! What do you say to that?"

Father Massimo smiled with relief. "Can you make soup with it?"

"Nothing fit to eat can be made with a ham bone!"

"What about pea soup? I heard Father Edmund say it is quite palatable."

"Talk is cheap," said the cook. "Our English brother can dispense advice by the yard but when it comes to work he can't get back to his books soon enough. I've yet to see him come into the kitchen to offer his services. Even if he'd volunteer as a pearl diver."

"Pearl diver?" said the perplexed superior.

"Dishwasher," replied Father Georgio with a shake of his head at the superior's ignorance of ordinary expressions. The big Croat in his two years in America had collected a variety of terms which remained unfathomable to Father Massimo, most of them from the tradesmen he encountered at the market or the back door. He was pleased with his acquisition of what he called an American polish.

"There must be some food you can prepare, Father," the superior said.

"We have beans!"

The superior nodded in resignation. Beans it surely would be.

There was row upon row of New England style baked beans in the cellar, all from the bounty of Les Dames du Bon Secours. The good ladies under the direction of Mrs. Daisy Doolan, had a food collection for them twice a month, and as much as they hoped for a change of diet, the exiles found that nine out of ten cans were baked beans.

In the little clinic across the hall from the kitchen Father Columba's musical Irish brogue rumbled on soothingly as he gave the Spaniard, Father Largo, his daily insulin shot.

"There you are, Padre, oiled for another day." The big white-clad missioner stood back, his weathered, freckled face looking like a relief map of one of the bleak China coast islands he had known in his twenty years of missionary odyssey.

He knew that the little Spaniard trusted him and often told him that he was his only friend in Darrington — his only friend anywhere. Father Largo was a partisan of San Juan de la Cruz and had been a bit overwhelmed to learn that the Irishman knew San Juan's *Dark Night of the Soul* in Spanish, English, Cantonese, and Gaelic.

Father Columba had been in Hong Kong in the mid-1950's when he first heard of Father Largo. He himself was recovering after three years in a frozen Manchurian prison and had been ready to board a ship for the Philippines, when he heard that a Spanish priest, a member of the Brunite Order, had disappeared from Chienchio mission and the alarm of the Communists indicated he might be alive and free. If so, his escape had been miraculous for he had been sentenced to death after confessing to crimes against the people's government.

Not until the Irish priest arrived in Darrington did he hear of Father Largo again. The apostolic delegate, disturbed that a Brunite priest had apparently slipped away from federal authorities in San Francisco, had wired Father Columba to ask if he knew of such a man. From then on the Irishman had watched the news, and eventually heard that the Spaniard identified himself at a parish rectory in New York City after a trip across the country. Father Columba had hurried to New York and brought the erratic priest to Darrington, much to the dismay of Bishop Hickey.

Father Columba doubted that his Spanish brother would ever be entirely rational again, except at unexpected moments. His actions since coming to the city had caused Bishop Hickey to forbid him to celebrate Mass, although he did give in to the extent of allowing the Spaniard a dry Mass, a *Missa Secca*, without the elements of bread and wine.

Father Largo felt cheated and when the opportunity presented itself he disobeyed the edict. Turbulent nightmares disturbed his sleep — and the sleep of everyone in the house — as he carried on his endless discourses with San Juan and Madre Teresa.

Just this morning Father Columba had heard the Spaniard stumbling around in his room in the dark, muttering to himself, and finally when he heard the loose knob on his door rattle the Irishman knew he was on his way downstairs to attempt to offer Mass. Father Columba had been patient with him when he found him vested and ready to go out to the altar. After taking the chalice and host away he had conducted the little priest through the prayers of the Mass. Tears ran down Father Largo's cheeks but he made no protest. However violent he might be on other occasions, he never protested when he was apprehended at the altar.

"Now, how about a walk in the cloister for some fresh air?" said Father Columba.

"Fresh air!" exclaimed the Spaniard. "Do you think I live for fresh air. I have my show this afternoon and I'm not at all sure which of my paintings I want to display."

Father Columba smiled, wondering if the show would come off. They had tried to arrange showings of the wary Spaniard's work before and he had backed out at the last moment, with no one quite able to convince him that changing his mind was not a very acceptable excuse.

[10]

This afternoon's show was the doing of Mother Evariste-Marie, superior of Beau-Joseph Convent across the street. The local "coming out" of the artist was but one phase of the afternoon that the good Sisters had arranged and was actually only an appendage to the farewell ceremony they were giving for Father Constant, the Lithuanian, who had been assigned as curate at St. Smaragdus parish in Cohagansett.

Bishop Francis Hickey, as he took a breath of fresh air in Monsignor Brady's lush flower garden beside the old red-brick cathedral, suddenly remembered with some discomfort that he had promised to attend the Spanish padre's art show. He must remember to take his checkbook with him.

The bishop of Darrington was an early riser and usually got out on the grounds as soon as possible before the monsignor got his radio going full blast so as not to miss the news while shaving. The rector always got out of bed apprehensively, as though he were fully prepared for the possibility that the floor might not be there when he put his feet down. No dawn came that didn't find him prepared to hear the news that the Reds had blasted the world to bits. It must have been reassuring simply to hear the static while he located his station.

Francis Hickey wondered if his increasing preoccupation with the past was an indication that he was approaching his dotage. During these strolls before his morning Mass he had found himself thinking more frequently of Leonard Foley, the rotund and jolly bishop who had sent him to the seminary more than forty-five years ago and had ordained him in the midst of World War I. The gentle bishop had reluctantly allowed Father Hickey to go off to Europe as a chaplain and had welcomed him back with tears in his eyes just a year later.

"I prayed for you every day, Francis," he had said as he clasped an arm around the priest's khaki-clad shoulder. The dear old bishop had made Francis his secretary and constant companion in his remaining years.

[11]

They had gone together to Chicago in 1926 to the Eucharistic Congress. There, in a hotel suite, as the congress was closing in Soldiers' Field, Leonard Foley lay gasping on his bed. Hickey held him up trying to make it easier for the bishop to breathe while they waited for the doctor.

Leonard Foley's last request was simple and unselfish. He had a brother who had been drinking himself to death for thirty years. The bishop knew he had encouraged his brother in sending him money. And almost his last breath he was asking Hickey to follow the case to its grim conclusion.

"Look after him, Francis. He won't be much trouble." His best hope for brother Jim was that he'd die in a clean bed with his senses anointed and the sacraments conferred; and, after that, burial in the family lot.

When he had said it, and had heard his secretary's agreement, Leonard Foley seemed quite at peace.

"I've heard, Francis," he whispered, "that it's a sign of God's favor to die in an alien land."

"This is only Chicago, Your Excellency, and far from alien," Hickey had said.

But then Leonard Foley gave him a look that said he would defend to the death his contention that it was alien and strange.

Perhaps it was. Perhaps all the world was alien, for in a few minutes Leonard Foley would be winging it to his true country.

"Let me have my way one last time, Francis," the dying man gasped, not without humor. "We'll have eternity to split hairs."

What a man he had been, and what a friend: gentle, compassionate, and beloved by all. His funeral was a mass demonstration of that affection, the biggest Darrington had ever seen.

The great bell in the cathedral tower, sounding the morning *Angelus*, startled Francis Hickey from his thoughts. He closed his unread breviary and hurried through the Gothic cloister under the massive apse of the church, aware that he was late for his Mass.

The bishop found Father Redmond, his secretary, awaiting

[12]

him. Paul Redmond was a young, cherubic-looking intellectual — black-haired and ruddy-faced and almost as well versed in Canon Law as Gasparri himself.

Father Redmond had prepared the chalice and had the bishop's vestments laid out for him. In the corner at the wine cabinet the altar boys were rattling the cruets as if to inform him that they were on time. The bishop began to vest, and as he let the stole fall uncrossed he was reminded of its symbol of jurisdiction and authority, and wondered if he had lived up to the high standard set for him by Leonard Foley.

The bishop wished he could think of himself as a man of compassion and prudence. But there had been times when his prudence provided more weight than ballast. When provoked to intemperate decisions by politicians or newspapers he frequently took no more than twenty-four hours to decide against consulting his diocesan consultors.

He had been caricatured in the local press as a clerical Teddy Roosevelt — the crozier his big stick, and beauty pageants his target. It had started because he ordered Catholic girls to withdraw from the local beauty contest put on by the Cohagansett Municipal Association. He had sailed into the organization with the comment, "Beauty can never be determined by a tape measure!" From then on the epithet of "Watchdog" was pinned to him, but instead of resenting it he had taken it as his own badge of fidelity.

The bishop was of average height, healthily rotund, quick of step, and shrewd of eye. His sparse stubble of iron gray hair was his way of adhering to the military regimen since his chaplaincy days in World War I.

He had shown compassion, if not prudence, he'd been told, in taking the exiled Brunite Fathers into the diocese.

But if it was an impetuous decision, he could excuse himself with the thought that the exiles had infiltrated rather than arrived openly.

Actually, Hickey thought, it was a *fait accompli* the moment he had laid eyes on the genial, weathered face of the Irish Father Columba. Then before he quite grasped what was happening, the missionaries were descending on Darrington as weary travelers to an inn.

The aged Polish Bishop Stefan Dworjanski, who was now determined to officiate at the procession tomorrow, had proved to be the most disturbing of the exiled missioners. Hickey had first heard of him one day in March, more than a year ago, when an excited call came from the stationmaster at the depot who informed Father Redmond that an old priest had just got off the train from New York and demanded to see Monsignor Le-Vecque. Catholic though he was, the stationmaster had never heard of any such monsignor.

Father Redmond guessed immediately who the new arrival was. He knew, though he had neglected to inform his bishop, that Father Columba had invited the Polish bishop "for a visit."

They hurried to the railroad station and there, sitting on a bench, his dejected appearance seeming to indicate that he had reached the end of the line, was Stefan Dworjanski.

His heavy-featured face was grim as he looked at the Bishop and Father Redmond. He rose ponderously.

"Monseigneur l'eveque — ?"

"Hickey," said the bishop.

"Ickee!" he repeated. He greeted them in French, then said quite distinctly in English, as though it had been rehearsed tirelessly, "I am in your hands."

Not long afterward inquiries and then directives began to arrive from Rome concerning Stefan Dworjanski. The cardinal prefect had been instructed by His Holiness to request that Bishop Dworjanski be given every consideration because of his age and the precarious state of his health. The cardinal prefect felt obliged to inquire if Bishop Dworjanski had received the recent communications from the Congregation. The cardinal prefect had been exhorted by His Holiness to obtain assurance that Bishop Dworjanski would reply soon.

[14]

But it was not until Father Massimo arrived and had spoken firmly to Stefan Dworjanski that the requests of Cardinal Vincenzo Agazarini were complied with.

From the first, the number and variety of these letters dismayed Bishop Hickey. They were firm, cautious, and usually apprehensive. Invariably they were threaded with meanings that the American bishop grasped only partially.

Bishop Hickey went out to say his Mass, confident that he would be able to drive the concern about Stefan Dworjanski from his mind during the Holy Sacrifice.

But as he reached the Te igitur, praying for the peace, unity, and safety of the Church, and for those who governed her, the bishop thought again of Stefan Dworjanski. Surely he was an orthodox confessor of the faith if anyone was. The presence of the Polish bishop in the diocese drew Hickey back to a dramatic chapter of history. With Hitler's rise Dworjanski had become a critic of the dictator's racism and pagan doctrines, and with the Nazi march into Poland Dworjanski became an international figure, a man of legend with his fiery sermons against the invaders. Dragged from his pulpit he was carted off to a concentration camp, to be freed briefly by the Soviets, only to be promptly arrested when he turned his powerful voice against them. Tried for crimes against the people, he was banished to an unknown prison. Kept from his See of Grajewo for more than fifteen years he had become a symbol to the world of unremitting fortitude.

Francis Hickey took an unusually long time with his thanksgiving after Mass, kneeling in the sanctuary while Father Redmond offered his Mass.

He remembered clearly the international tension as the news broke suddenly on the free world in the fall of 1960 that Stefan Dworjanski had escaped from his Soviet prison, and, after a flight across the Carpathians, he appeared to have been swept from the rocks to the whirlpool as he suddenly appeared at the door of the Polish embassy (where he presumed he had friends) in Prague, Czechoslovakia, only to be turned away by the terrified diplomat. There was a period of forty-eight hours of suspense and then the news came that he had found refuge in the French consulate in Bratislava.

Momentarily he was safe, but with Vienna and freedom only some thirty-odd miles away, the world was anxious for his deliverance and the Soviet for his surrender.

Months passed while the Communist press raged and the French government surmounted crisis after crisis. Then, quite abruptly, black headlines across the world told of the death of Stefan Dworjanski there in the consulate.

The wire services presented to the public pictures of the casket for Dworjanski being carried into the consulate. In a magnanimous gesture the Communists said they would permit a motor-cavalcade escort for the funeral procession back to Grajewo, but secretly, suspecting a ruse, they placed a heavy guard around the coffin as it was carried out of the consulate. They had been informed that Dworjanski was within, alive, and would be rescued somewhere on the road back to Poland.

There had been a ruse, but not the suspected one. As the crowd surged around the consulate, Stefan Dworjanski slipped out among the mourners, and within an hour crossed the frontier into Austria. The next morning, in a magnificent gesture of defiance he celebrated a Mass of thanksgiving in the Cathedral of Vienna.

Great crowds escorted Stefan Dworjanski to the railroad station and gave him a hero's departure for Rome. But the hero could not accept the comfortable exile and secured from the Pope permission to make a world tour condemning Communism. But as he landed in New York he learned that the permission had been withdrawn. Rome had decided it would be best to keep silence and the angry and somewhat rebellious Dworjanski found himself with no place to go.

It was then that Father Columba sent one of his typically

generous telegrams inviting Stefan Dworjanski to visit in the diocese of Darrington for as long as he chose. In the fifteen months he had been at the city he had seldom ventured from the old monastery, remaining aloof and uncommunicative when Francis Hickey tried to talk to him.

After a time Hickey learned that Dworjanski was writing his memoirs, and though the Polish bishop seldom left his room, he was fully aware of the unusual interest in his manuscript. A leading magazine wanted to publish it, and there were rumors that a book publisher had offered a fortune for it sight unseen. But when news of the literary work reached Rome, Cardinal Agazarini, much alarmed, sent to Francis Hickey a directive that he see to it that no one was to read the manuscript before the cardinal prefect himself. His Holiness was determined, Agazarini said, that neither priests nor people still behind the Iron Curtain would be endangered by revelations in the Dworjanski memoirs.

Rome was concerned and so were the neighbors, particularly Archbishop Nicholas Shannon, bishop of the nearby diocese of Concord, who delighted in his title of archbishop ad personam. He had complained to his friends in Rome that Hickey had done nothing to honor him (what honors could be added to such a life? Hickey had wondered), and continued with his worrisome comments long after the cautious Cardinal Agazarini had reminded him that his Concord jurisdiction encompassed 1200 square miles, no more, no less.

The feud between Hickey and Shannon went back to the Spanish Civil War when Shannon had won great public popularity for himself by denouncing Franco (undismayed that he had found himself practically alone in his attitude among the hierarchy). Only in recent years did he admit that the regime of the Caudillo was better than a Communist government.

Father Redmond was in the sacristy unvesting after his Mass when Hickey came in from his thanksgiving, which had turned out to be more of a reverie.

"Did you time me this morning, Bishop?" said the young secretary with a wise smile on his face.

"Time you?" said Hickey absently. "No, but I'm sure you have slowed down to a respectable pace. Twenty-five minutes is a good average for a low Mass. But I should take some corrective measures myself. I was thinking and not in a properly recollective frame of mind for my thanksgiving."

"About the art show this afternoon, Bishop. You wanted me to remind you — "

"My checkbook — don't let me forget that. Mother Evariste-Marie would never forgive me — nor would the wild Spaniard — if I neglected to buy one of his paintings."

Steve Halidon studied his bearded image in the bathroom mirror of his Victorian-style room in the once elaborate Phoenix Hotel in Darrington. He had chosen the hotel for several reasons. It was only a few blocks from Archangel Monastery, it had a bar, and the management didn't care how disreputable guests appeared as long as they paid their bill.

Halidon rubbed his grizzled jaw then bent and dashed cold water in his eyes, daubing them dry as he studied the five-day growth of whiskers. They itched and probably would itch more before he got his job done at the monastery. He had looked disreputable before, quite a number of times in his somewhat happy, often haphazard life — but never deliberately.

He had been at first angrily opposed to the assignment his editor, Dev Shanley, gave him. He wasn't a political or religious reporter. In an age of specialists, Halidon prided himself on being the *New York Chronicle's* top spot-news reporter. Disaster reporter would be more apt. He had just recovered, with a fast and furious weekend in the Catskills, from a torturous and nerve-wracking ten-day vigil over three entombed miners in the Pennsylvania coal country. It had turned out to be a wake.

Shanley had conceived the idea, in one of his celebrated flashes of genius, that Oliver Newman, the ex-Communist and now fervently devout Catholic, had something more than a chat in mind in his proposed visit to the exiled missioners in Darrington.

"He's up to something," Shanley had commented; then a few days later added, "I think it's that relic they smuggled out of East Germany, Steve."

Halidon had picked up Shanley's trick of extending a piece-meal conversation over days and weeks, and several days later (having boned up on the Holy Shirt of Mail and the rather frightening mystic who had worn it, a subject that a news magazine had thought important enough to devote several sardonic columns to) Steve plunked himself on Shanley's desk. "I think you've hit it, boss. Newman does have a definite interest in the relic. He studiously avoided getting into the harangue the Russians made over it in the UN, but in two of his books he mentions it."

Shanley's eyebrows hardly moved. He fingered through some yellow copy he was editing. "I see you did your homework — you read *The Star Spangled Penitent* and *God Did Not Forget Me*, Newman's epics of his romance with divinity."

"Yeah, I liked the way he gave the impression that he and God share top billing and the rest of us are DeMille extras."

With Steve committed to pursue the story, Dev had conceived the idea of his posing as a tramp to get admission to the monastery and Halidon had reluctantly quit shaving. Yesterday he had packed, putting in with his Madras suit the worn outfit and shoes he had picked up in an East Side tailor shop on the proprietor's pledge they had been fumigated.

Halidon, settled in his mauve-decade quarters in the Phoenix, had spent the after-dark hours Monday night prowling outside Archangel Monastery. The three-story red-brick building (with a cornerstone date of 1869) was little credit to Bishop Francis Hickey who, Halidon had learned, was known as a brick-and-mortar bishop. A long flight of limestone steps led up to the main entrance to the monastery chapel from the street. A few yards beyond was the door to the residential part of the building, a door flush with the sidewalk. The monastery could also be entered from the rear through a service alley with the Jewish cemetery on one side and a Protestant church and parsonage on the other.

As Halidon was inspecting the stumblebum outfit he was going to wear when he applied for admission to the monastery, the telephone on the marble-top table beside the bed jangled. He picked it up and heard Shanley's voice.

"Steve? How's that for promptness? Nine a.m., right on the button. How do you look?"

"Like hell — "

"Good . . . I've finally got a plane time for Newman — Saturday, 2 p.m. That will give him more than a week in Darrington before his lecture Sunday, June 19."

And today was only June 7. Good Lord, he could have a beard like Peter Ustinov by that time, Halidon thought.

"Have you made contact with the foreign priests yet?"

Halidon chuckled. "I've done some observing and picked up some helpful information. The weekend would be the best time. Most of them go to hear confessions in the city's parishes on Saturdays and usually stay overnight to help out with Sunday Masses. The English priest is always assigned to St. Peter in Chains — The Irisher, Padre Columba, goes to St. Lawrence O'Toole Parish — and the Central European beaver, Georgio, to St. Andrew Babola — "

"You got a look at them then?" Shanley cut in.

Halidon laughed. "No, but I got a cup of coffee from the wife of the Baptist minister who lives next to the monastery. They're very friendly — the priests and the Baptist minister."

"This ecumenical spirit is a wonderful thing, Steve — "

"But they've only got to the stage of exchanging baked beans for blueberry pie and hot biscuits so far."

"Any start is a good start — "

Halidon laughed. "That's good, chief. Why not have it

embroidered into an antimacassar for your Aunt Fuzzy? By the way, what kind of an expense account have I got? The reason I ask, I thought it might be a nice touch if I bought you a painting by Father Largo when I attend their art show this afternoon."

There was a long pause; then Shanley said, "Fine. Go ahead. Anything up to fifty bucks. But chalk it up to your booze bill. It would take me all day to explain to the old man how you happened to buy a religious painting."

He listened remotely as Dev Shanley rambled on about the publisher's eccentricities. One of them had been a flirtation with the cult of Oliver Newman — after the latter had given up being a Communist, of course.

Newman was an Englishman who had worked briefly as a college professor in the United States in the early 1930's and had become an American citizen. In the late 1930's he was deeply involved in various anti-Fascist movements and (although he had afterward been discreetly obscure about causes and his sponsors) went to Europe in the summer of 1939, just in time to be swallowed up in the whirlpool of war. After an intensive probe by various U. S. embassies and consulates, it became evident that Newman had vanished.

There was speculation but no evidence of what had happened to him, until the summer of 1947, when he reappeared at a displaced persons camp in West Germany. Newman told the story, widely believed, that he had been arrested by the Nazi SS at the outbreak of war, was sentenced to serve in a labor battalion, and found himself in Poland where he was eventually liberated by the advancing Russians. Why he hadn't tried to, or been allowed to, leave the Russian zone immediately, Newman never explained, not to Halidon's satisfaction anyway.

It was almost ten years after his return to the United States, and after he had been received into the Catholic faith by Bishop Bryan McAuley, that Newman told what he admitted was the whole story. The unexpected fortunes of war had confused him — muddied his sense of values. He had no reason to feel a

[21]

traitor or ashamed that he had chosen the Soviet credo and bowed his neck in the direction of Lenin's tomb. His feelings were no different from any American's. The Russians were our allies and had come into the war in time to claim their share in battering down the Nazi dream from that of a thousand years to a pitiful decade.

Newman said disenchantment set in when he really grasped the Communist grand design. He confessed and repented and received the profuse blessings of the Congressional committee for turning in his friends who were still in the party, and to clinch the whole remittance bit he told how he had become a convert to Catholicism. The Church received him in the person of the elegant and eloquent Bishop Bryan McAuley.

Dev Shanley was still talking, Halidon realized remotely. He had a way of mentally recording the essential points so he could play them back later. For an editor who regarded brevity as sacred, Shanley took an exceedingly long time to say little. At length he got to the point, but so casually that Steve almost let it slip by.

" . . . convinced of it. This trip to Mexico clinches it as far as I'm concerned — "

"Trip to Mexico? Whose trip?"

"Oliver Newman's," Shanley said impatiently. "He's scheduled to travel with a pilgrimage from New York City to Mexico City on Monday — June 20 — the day after his Darrington lecture. It's supposedly one of those pious trips to the shrine down there — "

"Guadalupe — " Halidon said.

"Oh, you've heard of it! You know quite a bit about your religion for a nonpracticing member, Steve. Anyway, it looks as though Newman has one final job to do for his comrades before he gets out of the country."

"Can't the U. S. government extradite from Mexico?"

Dev Shanley chuckled coldly. "Before they're aware of what he's up to he could be in Cuba."

"And beyond our reach — "

Shanley grunted. "I hate to think of it — and maybe we can do something if you get a foot in the door at the monastery. Keep in touch."

The editor had hung up and Halidon ruminated through his luggage looking for his flask while he thought about the task Shanley had dumped in his lap.

Their speculation about Newman's real objectives in visiting the monastery was, after all, only speculation. The facts which led them to speculate could be mere coincidence — his lecture trip to Darrington — the fact that the holy relic which the Communists were so anxious to recover was there — the fact that Newman had mentioned the relic several times in his various books — the presence at the monastery of Stefan Dworjanski, who had announced to the world that he would never bend his neck to a Communist overlord in his native country nor conciliate with the atheistic system.

From what he had read of Dworjanski, Halidon knew the old bishop was a man of incredible strength of mind. His spectacular escape had earned him worldwide attention as a living symbol of defiance. The periodic potshots at him since his escape, appearing in the Red press, indicated that they hadn't forgotten him and were undoubtedly concerned about what he might reveal in his memoirs.

Shanley's opinion to the contrary, Halidon felt that Newman was after something other than a relic. Undoubtedly the Communists wanted to get the Holy Shirt back to its niche at Meissen all right, but from the way they had dragged it out into the open at the UN, Halidon was convinced that they wanted to accomplish their illegal end by legal means, in this case.

Content with his deductions, Halidon poured himself a drink and stretched across the great old-fashioned bed to review the other points Shanley had brought out in the phone conversation. He had said something about the columnist Mark Curtain — one of the men whom Newman had denounced before the Congressional committee.

Curtain was found with a bullet in his brain at his country retreat a few hours after Newman had exposed him. And Dev Shanley had hinted that a new angle was opening in the case. ". . . I hear they've been up to his place at the lake in Ross county. It would be interesting to know if the FBI has new evidence on how Curtain died — and who was with him when he died!"

Halidon closed his eyes, trying to sort out the bits of information he had stored away about Curtain's death. There had been intimations before that someone might have been with Curtain when he died — that another hand than his had held the automatic to his head.

Dr. Lambert called at the monastery that afternoon as he had promised and the superior led him upstairs to Stefan Dworjanski's room. At the old man's response they entered and Father Massimo gave the usual greeting.

"Pax tecum, Your Excellency."

"Et cum spiritu tuo," the bishop replied with asperity as he arose ponderously from his leather chair before the gas grille that had been installed for his comfort in the old fireplace. His large, almost bald head wavered expectantly as he stared at them from under heavy-lidded eyes. His once huge frame stood like a pathologist's skeleton under his loosely, hanging soutane. His plain gold pectoral cross swung like an impatient pendulum from about his neck. "You have come for another look at the Polish cadaver, Doctor?"

It was the type of half-serious reproach the superior expected. "We want to make sure you are in good health, Monseigneur. We hope you will be with us for a long time. For my peace of mind I hope you will allow Dr. Lambert to examine you — if you are to walk in the procession tomorrow."

Dworjanski's eyes flashed at the priest, momentarily annoyed; then his heavy, colorless lips parted in the vaguest crease of a smile. "Oh, that is the bargain, Father? If I don't submit to this physical scrutiny you will deny me this chance to honor your holy founder."

The superior smiled blandly, giving a slight continental shrug, "You are a bishop. The most I can do is recommend — "

Dworjanski sighed. "Yes, I am a bishop — but doomed to be one *in partibus infidelium*. That would be a suitable append-age to my title, but I believe Leo XIII did away with the term many years ago." He moved his shoulders in resignation. "Have your way, Doctor. But do not expect too much."

Leaving the intern alone with the bishop, Father Massimo went downstairs, his eyes brightening pleasantly as he saw Julie Nealy awaiting him in the corridor. He saw the armload of books and suddenly realized that his request for a book on sociology had been multiplied perhaps a dozen times by the requests of the other priests, none of them realizing she had got phone calls from the others.

Julie worked at the branch library up the hill from the monastery and they had made asking for books an inexcusable habit simply because they knew she would stop by their chapel sometime during the day. She was a beautiful girl, but handi-capped by a lame leg, that had apparently given her a feeling of inferiority.

The priest hurried to Julie, taking the books from her. "My dear child! One of these days you must tell us to go for our own books. This is a terrible imposition. And I'm afraid I'm the worst offender."

Julie smiled. "It was silly of me to stand here holding them."

Father Massimo regarded her affectionately as she walked along with him to the library where he set the books on the huge mahogany table in the middle of the room. They talked together casually about Father Largo's art show and the de-parture of Father Constant to the seashore parish. He told her about the farewell dinner Father Georgio planned for his little Lithuanian brother that night. "It's a surprise — even to the menu."

[25]

"I wish I could be here," Julie said, "but I suppose it's an all-bachelor affair." She smiled up at the superior, amused that he was quite unaware that he was holding her hand as they paused at the entrance to the oratory.

He released her hand in sudden embarrassment and watched her go out to the chapel for a visit. He tried now, as he had at other times, to rationalize his feelings about her. His affection for her was something more than pity. To be lame wasn't such a great misfortune that he had to pity her — but he and the other priests did have a tendency to dramatize her misfortune. And worse than that, they imagined she came so often to the chapel because she was lonely. Father Edmund, of course, hazarded the guess that she was praying for romance to come into her life. That was all Father Georgio — her fierce partisan — needed. He began to pray blindly that she would get a husband soon and at times he became more demanding than prayerful with good St. Joseph.

Praying was good, the superior was sure, but after months of it he had begun to wonder that if God had put the idea into their heads he must also have made available a practical means of bringing it about. With that in mind he had kept an eye open for the right young man for Julie and during the past few months had just about settled on Dr. Andy Lambert.

Father Massimo was still standing at the oratory door when he heard Dr. Lambert hurrying along the hall toward him. He gave his report on Stefan Dworjanski in a brief and perfunctory way. "I think he can get through the procession tomorrow. He's in fair physical shape for a man in his eighties. It would do more harm to precipitate tension — precisely what we would do if we forbade him the activity tomorrow."

"I think that's what we all wanted to hear, Doctor. Thank you."

Julie Nealy had arisen from the pew and had given the priest a quick smile as she dipped her fingers in the holy-water font and walked away toward the door that led to the street.

"Poor kid!" Andy Lambert said.

"You know her?" said the priest, a little dismayed.

"No — no. I meant the limp. I always pity someone like that particularly when you realize that the chances are if the parents had been sensible it could have been corrected."

In the cloister behind the monastery the priests were enjoying the warm sun of early June, Father Columba darning the community's socks and murmuring an ejaculation of the Litany of the Saints with each stroke of the needle while Father Dmitri, a bit absently shot back the *ora pro nobis* as he dug his trowel into the ground and pushed himself back on his haunches. The black-bearded Moravian was a fierce-eyed man of sixty, tall, lean, and hard from twenty years in the African missions.

He let down the folds of his soutane which he had tucked into his belt while working with his flowers. He had the habit of counseling his brother priests to take up gardening as a hobby that kept the joints loose and developed faith and patience. But the pessimistic Father Edmund told him his garden project was doomed to failure. "Flowers can't grow without manure and where will you find it in a nation of motor cars?"

Father Edmund raised his eyes in annoyance from his breviary as the litany exchange intruded on his devotions. "I thought we had agreed that everyone would be quiet while I recited my Office. If I had my way we'd chant the Divine Office in choir as our venerable founder recommends for an established Brunite house."

Father Columba's sun-baked wrinkles spread into a genial smile. He was accustomed to the Britisher's complaints. There was always the Jewish cemetery to pace in and read his Office if he wanted to be alone.

The Irish priest was the best known of the missioners in Darrington mainly because he wore a white soutane, which was the usual Brunite habit for tropical climes. He had continued wearing white in Darrington only because on sight of him when he arrived in Darrington the English priest had immediately dubbed him the "Irish Pope." The derisive comment was enough to make Father Columba stick to white.

The English priest arose, groaning as he straightened up, pushing a thin wisp of yellowish gray hair from his pinkish brow. "Bones a Becket! My sacroiliac!"

Father Largo, who sat cross-legged cleaning his brushes, looked up innocently at his English brother. "What kind of language is this, Padre? You should have speech lessons if you want to be understood in America." He drew the fine hairs of a brush through his fingers. "I tell you something, Padre. If you want to learn the Engleesh good you listen to me. I come to this country on an American sheep — first class! You're damned tootin! And when I land here, I say to myself, this is the place for you, hombre! Across the desert I travel — gringo style! Madre de Dios! Those truck drivers! I never know how pious thees gringo is."

The Britisher hurried from the cloister with the Spaniard scurrying after him, flailing his brush under his nose, leaving Father Columba (with his litany finished) time to think about what the little Lithuanian priest, Father Constant, would use for luggage when he departed for Cohagansett Thursday. He had arrived in Darrington with only a blue canvas bag slung over his shoulder and his visitor's visa clutched in his hand as though he thought he had to show it at every transportation terminal. But the duffle bag would never do for the trip to Cohagansett. He would have to let the missioner use his suitcase. It was constructed mostly of cardboard, but what it lacked in material was made up in craftsmanship.

The Lithuanian was a man without a country and without existence as far as the Communists were concerned. He had spent almost all of his priestly life in a concentration camp in his native country and had been garroted and thrown into the

[28]

river when he persisted in hearing confessions and giving spiritual consolation to his fellow prisoners. He had survived the plunge into the freezing river and had been taken by fishing boat to Sweden where, on his recovery from pneumonia and the garroting, he had applied for readmission to Lithuania. But the Communists said he was an imposter, that the real Father Constant had died from religious austerities.

On arrival at the monastery, where the Father general had sent him a year ago to recover his health, he had insisted on showing the other exiles the scar left on his neck by the garroting wire as though proof was needed that he was not an imposter.

The Lithuanian had not been long in Darrington when he got himself in trouble through his persistent attempts to do good. The most recent episode occurred a few weeks ago when Father Constant had volunteered to help serve meals to vagrants at the Kingdom Come Gospel Mission down near the waterfront.

His compassion had been aroused at the sight of the little slavey who did all the mission work while the Prophet Moses Earnshaw sat in a halo of cigar smoke in his sanctum, emerging each night to conduct rousing evangelical rallies and afterward baptizing his converts in the bathroom adjoining his office.

When Father Columba had followed Father Constant one day and caught him in the act of dispensing soup he had protested that he was doing it for the madam. Madam! The Irish priest had been in many ports of the world and the term was a universal one. A madam presided over a brothel, not a soup kitchen.

The Irishman had found the prophet a difficult man. With evangelical thunder he had denied fatherhood of the madam's infant son, his wrathful words following them as they ran from the gospel mission, Father Columba certain that he had never heard so much biblical geography entwined with firm pledges of damnation.

But at least the health authorities had been alerted, even though it had been done at the cost of scandal in the neighborhood, which made Bishop Hickey realize that he had to remove the Lithuanian from the scene of his indiscretions. Madam Earnshaw was taken to the County Hospital to be treated for tuberculosis, and Prophet Moses was led off to jail, loudly calling down recriminations on the Lithuanian, as he heard the charges read against him. District attorneys across the country wanted him and Darrington officials were more than precipitate in signing extradition papers.

During the early afternoon Father Largo's paintings were carried across the street to Beau-Joseph Convent and hastily arranged in the garden under the supervision of Mother Fidelia, aide to the superior, Mother Evariste-Marie, who was on the roof of the convent caring for her homing pigeons. During her more than fifty years in Darrington the aged Mother Provincial had raised hundreds of pigeons, a hobby she shared with another nun in Quebec City. It was through use of the pigeons that she kept in touch with the motherhouse in the Canadian city. But she had never found anyone in Darrington who was interested in her birds until Father Constant came along. When she learned that he was going to Cohagansett she decided to have the priest take two birds with him to the seashore to keep in contact.

Mother Evariste-Marie came down from the roof to find the others assembled for the formal farewell to Father Constant. Mrs. Daisy Doolan, La Grande Dame of the Bon Secours Society, made short work of the ceremony of handing over the purse of money to the Lithuanian and wishing him Godspeed.

She had plunked the sack of coins into the little priest's hand and hurried away to the convent garden where the art display had been set up. She had warned her friends to bring their checkbooks and (sight unseen) assured them the Spaniard's paintings and sketches were as Catholic as might be expected from the brush of a man who had seen the heights and depths.

Darrington's Mayor Billy Huggins was there. He liked everyone to call him Billy, the name he'd been christened with, he said — christened not baptized, as though he had been launched instead of redeemed.

The mayor greeted Bishop Francis Hickey with a "Howdy, Bishop!" as he strode across the room and clapped him on the arm.

"Thinking of buying some art, Billy?" asked the bishop cheerfully.

Billy took another quick and doubtful glance at the pictures, "I was hoping to see something Eyetalian, Bishop."

Hickey breathed a sigh of relief as Huggins left to greet Judge Jameson, who had a reputation as a relentless foe of bicycle and tire thieves.

Fathers Massimo and Columba were helping themselves to punch at the refreshment table when they were approached by the mayor.

Huggins shook the superior's hand vigorously as he introduced himself. "I'm glad I ran into you, Father. We just rented out the City Hall auditorium to this ex-Communist fellow. His agency has your place on the top of his list as local patrons. What kind of a joker is he?"

"Communist?" exclaimed Father Columba.

"Ex-Communist," corrected Huggins. "He must be clean — prominent Catholic and all that," Huggins said. He was thoughtful for a moment. "Wasn't this the guy who was investigated by Congress a few years ago?"

Father Massimo nodded. "He wrote books about it."

"If you know him he must be OK," Huggins said confidently.

The superior drank his punch without confirming the mayor's opinion.

The art show appeared to have been a success and (much to the surprise of everyone) Father Largo enjoyed the experience, basking in the admiration of the art lovers. It was not until he got back to the monastery that he realized his paintings were all gone and he would have to make a fresh start.

Mayor Huggins' comments about Oliver Newman had only renewed in Father Massimo's mind the realization that he had to do some serious thinking about the notorious convert. And as if to give irrefutable confirmation that Newman was coming, the priest, on returning to his office after the art show, had found a letter propped up against the pen stand on his desk as though it had been placed there by someone who knew it demanded special thought from the superior. Undoubtedly it had come in the afternoon mail and had been placed there by Father Maximilian.

The superior had read it and now he stood staring at the polite words, the veiled words of Oliver Newman, requesting the privilege of visiting the monastery to interview the exiled priests and write articles about them.

This was the letter he'd been waiting for — the visit he had prepared himself for. He knew what he must do. He had discussed it all with Cardinal Amalfi almost two years ago in Rome. He had accepted the cardinal's commission — yet, at the time neither of them had any positive idea that Newman would ever reveal himself.

Father Massimo had never discussed with the other missioners his principal concern as superior of the house. Yet there were times when he had the feeling that Father Columba suspected something, when he wondered aloud why all of them but the Father superior had been forced by adversity to seek refuge in Darrington.

They knew that Father Massimo had had a secure place as librarian of the Brunite Institute in Rome. There appeared to be no logic to uprooting him.

But in Darrington, as in Rome, life had been peaceful so

far, so peaceful at times that he had, ironically, looked forward to the danger Cardinal Amalfi had warned him to guard against. But he had faced danger many times in his imperiled life during the war in Poland. It seemed like a reckless bravado now to remember how determined he was to stay in Poland when the firewalls of war closed in from the east and the west.

And now, quite as eagerly, he would watch for the arrival of Oliver Newman. He wondered if he was too confident in his certainty that Newman wouldn't remember him. Newman would be amazed to know that Father Massimo had seen him — on three occasions to be exact. But only once had they met face to face for a brief exchange in the corridor of the Ministry of Information in Cracow.

There was no reason why the Russian intelligence officer should remember Father Massimo Nadi, apostolic administrator of Kzalineka. After twelve years it was unlikely that one would remember one face out of those of several hundred nationals who had to be questioned and searched before they could leave Poland.

Father Massimo folded the letter and tucked it in the sleeve of his soutane as he rose from his desk.

The memory of his departure from Cracow was far enough away in time and space so that the superior could recall it without too much dismay. Perhaps Venerable Father Bruno at least had found the ignominy of it satisfying to his anchoristic spirit. Father Massimo had left Poland poorer than he came, with despair in his heart and nothing but a few books in his briefcase. They had confiscated his chalice and torn his vestments to shreds looking for hidden documents.

On his arrival in Rome he had submitted his report on his administration of the See of Kzalineka to the Congregation of the Council. Within a few days he had been summoned to the office of Cardinal Frederico Amalfi. But it wasn't to question the report. It was complete enough, so complete that it had stunned even the rather crusty old cardinal who had suffered indignities of his own at the hands of the Fascists. He had only wanted to see the priest who had been so inventive as to aid Allied fliers in their escape from Poland by salvaging from parish records the birth certificates of young Poles who had died early in the war and giving these identities to the fliers. Later the procedure had worked as well in helping some of the Jews to survive.

Cardinal Amalfi allowed Father Massimo to return to his work at the Institute which he had left eight years before. The time passed peacefully and the priest had thought that he was forgotten, when one day he was summoned again by Cardinal Amalfi. When he was escorted into the great baroque room that had once been the library of the prince of Tivoli, he saw the old cardinal seated behind the ponderous desk, his heavy-lidded eyes hardly moving as he watched the priest's progress across the mosaic floor. The meeting was informal and it appeared for some time that the cardinal merely wanted some excuse to reminisce aloud.

"My mind stores up bits and pieces," the cardinal had said, "perhaps because I remember my mother picking over her pitiful treasures. Well, I remember you, Father Massimo, and your Order which is trying to find new roots. There's a little band of Brunites in America. Perhaps you've heard. I have talked to your Father general and he agrees they need a shepherd.

"I remembered you particularly because news from Poland reminded me. The man Bransk, whom you have so good a reason to remember, is now a man born again — and like so many of the reincarnate he has a new name — Newman. Ironic, is it not? It need be no surprise to you that he has adopted the holy Faith and is broadcasting many profound and revealing things about his evil past. But, strangely, there is no word from him about the years you and I are so familiar with. I would like to get closer to this man. I would like to know if someday he will talk about Poland . . . about Krostok Fortress. . . ."

The superior stood in the hall of the monastery, trying to ease the tension within himself before he went out to the cloister to join his brothers for a few minutes before the dinner bell rang.

It was surprising, exhilarating to realize how strength surged through his body at the prospect of Newman's arrival, and how fond and suddenly possessive he felt about the monastery.

Fathers Dmitri and Georgio were at their maps (which they had secured from the Russian embassy) absorbed in the vari-colored pins with which they were devising a theoretical grand strategy for the evangelization of Russia.

The commissario hurried off to watch his pots on the stove and Father Edmund took his place at the wicker table, an amused smile on his thin lips as he watched the new deployment in the fanciful work of dividing once holy Russia into provinces and dioceses (although they were always careful to point out that they had no intention of inconveniencing any Orthodox prelates who were willing to adopt the Filioque and the principle of *primus inter pares*).

There seemed to be no harm in the game, as long as it remained a game, although at times it appeared that the Moravian was itching to get at the work of converting the Communists and might indeed lose the precarious balance between hating the sin and loving the sinner. The fierce look in his eyes gave the impression that he was more in a mood for lining them up against a wall rather than at an altar rail. Father Maximilian was particularly unhappy about their scheme of entrenching themselves in Leningrad and renaming it St. Petersburg.

"What are your plans for the clergy?" asked Father Edmund. "Will they be celibate?"

Father Dmitri shrugged and pulled a green pin from Kiev replacing it with a bright red one. "I think Kiev deserves a cardinal's hat. What do you think, Father?"

"Red does seem appropriate," said Father Edmund.

Father Dmitri stuck the green pin in his sleeve and glanced up. "Celibacy should come gradually, I think. Bishops do not marry anyway, so that provides the good example."

Father Edmund chuckled. "It always seemed to me that the bishops should have been granted the privilege of marrying — not the lower clergy. But I suppose the Holy Synod sees their mistake now. It will be interesting to hear what Oliver Newman thinks of your scheme. Perhaps he will have some data of his own that will be helpful."

"I know what he will tell you," Father Largo said. He came to the table and looked down with hostile eyes at Father Massimo. "He will tell you they are waiting for you with open arms! And when they have closed on you — prepare to die! Wait until they *sheep* us off to Russia."

"You will never go to Russia," Father Massimo said. "I promise you, Father Largo."

"What then are all these preparations — this Bolshevik coming to instruct us?"

The superior smiled patiently, relieved as he heard the dinner bell in the hall. The exiles got up and hurried off toward the refectory and Father Massimo waited as the Irish priest inserted the needle in the socks he was mending and stood up.

The Irishman looked questioningly at the superior as they entered the house. "You continue to amaze me, Father Massimo. There was a moment when I thought you were going to tell Father Largo that Oliver Newman wouldn't be permitted to come here."

Father Massimo smiled cryptically. "I'm sure there are some things to be learned from this man."

The superior paused at the passage to the chapel, allowing Father Columba to go ahead of him to the refectory. The chapel was deserted, or appeared to be, but he had thought so on other occasions only to be startled by coming upon someone huddled against a pillar, half drowsing, half praying.

At the altar the superior stood studying the glass and silver reliquary which Bishop Hickey had given them to house the Holy Shirt of Mail. It was safely secured to the floor and its glass parts, the manufacturer had assured them, were burglarproof. There were but two keys, one for Father Maximilian, who had worn the holy relic under his clothing when he left Meissen, and one for Father Massimo.

The relic, which tomorrow would be carried here from the cathedral, was an undergarment made of chain links, which had been worn for more than forty years by Venerable Bruno. That collectors trusted in its authenticity was verified by the fabulous offers that had been made for the Holy Shirt. The Communists, of course, had offered nothing for it except threats and indignation.

On his way to the refectory the superior was confronted by Father Georgio who pushed out the kitchen door with an elbow as he dried his hands on the great white apron that encompassed his portly frame.

He greeted the superior jovially. "We have something nice for a change for tonight, Father Superior — roast lamb, onions — creamed just the way you like them, beet greens with tender little beets and plenty mashed potatoes."

The superior smiled agreeably. "I'd just as soon have a rest from potatoes, Father, for my own tastes."

The commissario shrugged. "Well, it's not easy to please everyone. Padre Dmitri could eat potatoes all the time and never complain. This morning for breakfast he has them!"

Before going on to the refectory the superior peered into the kitchen to see that Father Edmund was helping out as he had been assigned, even though he had complained loudly that he had been ordained to offer bread at the altar, not slice it in the galley.

Father Massimo stood at the head of the table, nodding to each as the exiles took their places. There seemed to be a reflective sadness in their faces at the realization that they were losing Father Constant.

[37]

Even Bishop Dworjanski, who preferred to dine in his room, came down to dinner and had agreed to give his episcopal blessing to the departing priest. Watching the exiles gather around the table, Father Massimo thought how like a little college of cardinals they were with their varied nationalities, temperaments, and loyalties, yet bound together by their profession in the Order founded by Venerable Bruno and by the apostolic Faith.

They said the grace and sat down, all except Father Largo, who had been waiting impatiently to read them a passage from St. John of the Cross. His inflexible devotion to the Spanish mystic who had courted the stake in following St. Teresa on the hard road to Carmelite reform, was accepted tolerantly by the missioners. But Father Edmund sometimes expressed the opinion that their Spanish confrere should cultivate some of San Juan's virtues, such as humility, humor, and stability.

But it was the others who had to work at the virtues when Father Largo observed challengingly that surely the refectory was the proper place to hear from San Juan de la Cruz. He had reminded them that it was in the Calced Carmelite convent in Toledo that the saint had been imprisoned for nine months and it was in the refectory of that house that he was taken each night to eat bread and water sitting on the floor.

Those of the group who had come to Archangel Monastery unclear about the details of St. John's life had long since had the details filled in for them.

Father Massimo sighed. Perhaps they would never know exactly what had happened to Father Largo after he disappeared from his mission in China. He had told a story of fleeing into the hills with some of his flock when the Communists took over their village. But one by one the faithful abandoned him and he wandered alone, his books and his vestments secured to the back of his burro. He had no idea how long or how far he had traveled when he was found by a group of monks, presumably Buddhist monks, though Father Largo never identified them as such. He had the fixed idea they were an heretical band of Christians who had severed themselves from apostolic authority.

Father Largo's conversations since coming to Archangel Monastery caused grave doubt that he any longer had an understanding of his priestly character. His mind wandered between past and present, sometimes engaging in loud and turbulent harangues with his esrtwhile Buddhist hosts, whom he called captors. At other times he would angrily denounce King Philip of Spain and the Nuncio Sega whom he blamed for the imprisonment of San Juan almost four hundred years ago.

Father Largo also was forever writing long and excited letters to the Congregation of the Oriental Church urging a restoration of discipline among the Burmese monks and demanding that an apostolic visitator be sent from Rome to bring them to obedience. The letters, of course, never left the house — nor did the Spaniard, unless one of the priests was with him.

The priests ate in silence, averting their eyes as the Spaniard paused to stare at one or the other as he read from the writings of San Juan. Father Massimo often murmured a prayer of thanks that none of the exiles had the misfortune to be Portuguese as had been the archvillain of San Juan's life, Padre Jeronimo Tostado. Even his impressive string of titles (Consultor of the Holy Inquisition, Vicar-General and Commissary for Spain and Portugal, and Provincial of the Calced Carmelites of Catalonia) failed to save him from Father Largo's wrath.

The Spaniard finally finished the lengthy passage and sat down to probe his cold meal with a suspicious fork.

The Englishman glanced at the well-worn volume of St. John's works and said with a loud sigh, "I never knew of any other man so stubborn about putting his shoes back on."

There was a disapproving look in the remote eyes of Stefan Dworjanski as they came to rest heavily on the Englishman, "To be discalced is one way of keeping your feet on the ground."

CHAPTER TWO

At ten o'clock the next morning the bells of St. Mary's Cathedral tolled solemnly for the start of the procession. The candles of the acolytes weaved with the ritualistic tread of the marchers as the organ burst forth in the vibrating throbs of the Palestrina processional.

Bishop Francis Hickey set his violet biretta firmly on his head as he assumed his place at the episcopal throne in the sanctuary to await the removal of the relic of Venerable Bruno from the vault under the high altar.

The bishop was quite satisfied to take a passive part in the day's ceremonies. His function, as his secretary Father Paul Redmond so often remarked, was merely to preside. His was neither to do nor die, but simply to engage in the heavy looking-on; and for the occasion he was robed in the cumbersome *cappa magna*, every bit as burdensome as its name implied. But the job of carrying it was shared at the moment with two angelic-faced and devilish-eyed altar boys who at times gave the impression that they were airing a rug instead of bearing a train. But the bishop, to tell the truth, found their attitude refreshing.

Stefan Dworjanski stood across the sanctuary, his face impassive as always, seemingly unaware of the feeling of concern that the functions of the day might be too much for him.

Bishop Hickey had sent his car to the monastery to pick up the Polish bishop but the convenience he had provided had not made the old man a bit more approachable. On entering the cathedral sacristy to vest for the ceremonies he had maintained his remoteness by merely bowing his head vaguely and murmuring a perfunctory greeting as he went to the prie-dieu for a brief prayer before the sacristy crucifix.

The front pews of the cathedral were lined with officials of the city in their morning suits, Mayor Billy Huggins looking uncomfortably out of his element, as the bishops passed by on their way to the altar.

Bishop Hickey had been surprised to hear, less than two hours ago, that Monsignor Brady had invited Archbishop Nicholas Shannon and the retired Bishop Aime Thibeault to add the dignity of their presence to the occasion.

At breakfast, Monsignor had fidgeted through his egg and, after making a few acrimonious remarks in the direction of Father Redmond who was perusing the morning paper while waiting to be served, addressed a speculative cough in the direction of Bishop Hickey. "I thought it would be nice to have four of the foreign priests act as chaplains to the visiting bishops."

The bishop tried to repress his surprise even though he never failed to be amazed at finding Monsignor starting at the middle, or perhaps somewhat toward the end, when he had something to confess. It was his usual device to present a consummated fact.

"I wasn't aware that there would be visiting bishops, Monsignor."

The rector nervously battered the empty eggshell in his egg cup. "I wasn't sure that Archbishop Shannon and Bishop Thibeault could come until late last night."

Hickey shrugged in dismissal and when he glanced at Father Redmond he saw the amusement on the secretary's chubby face. And after a moment the bishop himself saw the humor of it. The rector had his way but he'd gone through purgatory in having it. He had paid for his stubbornness in inviting

[41]

Shannon when he knew the Concord prelate wasn't particularly welcome. But possibly the rector had a right to have guests, and the headaches that went along with them.

And he might have thought that Shannon would have his little chat with the exiles during the procession and go away content that they were happy in Darrington.

When the bishop came to the sacristy he found Shannon and Thibeault there. He greeted them politely, inquired about Thibeault's scrofula which provided a medical excuse for his nervous temperament, and complimented Shannon on his robust appearance.

Francis Hickey had been disturbed to hear that his hospitality to the exiled priests had earned the concern of Nicholas Shannon. But his act in giving refuge to Father Columba was an impulse of the heart that he couldn't foresee would lead to the present establishment. The Irish missioner was the first to arrive in Darrington still weak from his imprisonment in Manchuria. He had been told that passage money and a ship awaited him in Boston for the return home to Ireland. But he never quite got to Boston. He was carried from the train in Darrington on a stretcher, a stranger in the city and with a high fever.

He was at the mercy of fate, but the bishop had intervened, paid the missionary's hospital bill, and when Father Columba had recovered from pneumonia he was invited to stay at the cathedral rectory until he was able to travel.

Then, before Francis Hickey realized what was happening, Father Georgio had arrived and, almost on his heels, Father Largo.

The Spaniard, with his wild and erratic ways, disturbed the whole house and kept Monsignor Brady on edge. But Father Columba calmed the Spaniard while Father Georgio defended him fiercely, finally eliciting from the bishop the comment that if he didn't take Father Largo in he supposed no one else would.

With the arrival of Father Edmund, who to Monsignor

Brady's dismay recommended that the exiles be formed into a cathedral chapter, the bishop, finding no more rooms available in the house, offered the exiles the use of the monastery.

He might never have known how vehemently his hospitality was resented if his good friend, Bishop Bryan McAuley, hadn't informed him.

It was through McAuley's good offices that the bishop first learned that his generosity was referred to by Shannon as "gestapo methods."

At the moment Bishop Hickey was chary of Shannon's motives in coming to Darrington for the exposition of the relic. Shannon was known to frown on such things and even used rather severe language in denouncing what he termed "Compostellan pilgrimages." Shannon was a strict liturgist and, with much hilarity, had been quoted far and wide as warning his clergy against deviations from the Latin rubrics to the extent that not even an "Amen" was to be said in anything but Latin.

Aime Thibeault was the retired coadjutor bishop of Rutland, a post to which he had been appointed some thirty years ago with the right of succession to Bishop Blaise Wallenburger. In those days, as well as in these, Wallenburger was a sickly man, momentarily expected to expire. The tale was told that his vicar-general had got Thibeault out of bed in the middle of the night at least a score of times over the years to inform him that Wallenburger was dying.

Having bounced back from the brink of the grave, Wallenburger invariably recommended the efficacious effects of Extreme Unction which he had received, all told, upward of twenty times. The post of coadjutor had proved to be a frustrating one for the impatient Thibeault, and after thirty years of playing footsie with the dark angel he determined to resign his nebulous post, confiding to friends that he was more exhausted by the waiting than Wallenburger was by his labors and his chronic illness. Thibeault accepted the post as professor of history at the archdiocesan seminary. The peace of seminary halls obviously agreed with him more than the vicarious bouts with the specter the words *in extremis* evoked.

Bishop Hickey felt a tug at his train and when he drew his eyes away from the visiting bishops who stood across the sanctuary he saw that the altar boys were trying to steer him into the end of the procession that was leaving the church.

Father Georgio had carried the relic of Venerable Bruno up from the crypt, his massive frame vibrating as he strode across the sanctuary and deposited the relic on a platform to be borne by four uniformed knights.

The procession emerged onto the portico of the cathedral and Bishop Hickey found himself abreast of Bishop Dworjanski as they waited for the knights to make the precarious descent of the steps with the relic.

In the sudden glare of sunlight the translucent flesh of Stefan Dworjanski's face had the sheen of great age. He was a large-framed man, with but a sparse covering of flesh on his once giant body.

Bishop Dworjanski's face was impressive and medieval under the tall, peaked miter. He was vested in the heavy cope and his hands clasped, fingers upward, were encased in white gauntlets. At that moment, his reserved, enigmatic eyes gave Dworjanski the look of a warrior prelate of old going forth to face the enemy.

The platform supporting the relic weaved precariously as the knights descended the steps. There was a look of alarm on the face of Monsignor Brady, who had the place of honor before it, but was ready to scamper out of the way if the metallic garment, suspended on a cross frame, should topple toward him.

The procession streamed out across the square, girls in white dresses, altar boys in black and red robes, groups of parish organizations, and the diocesan clergy.

Father Columba, who, with the superior, served as chaplain to Archbishop Shannon, was delighted to find the archbishop such an affable companion. It was flattering to realize that Shannon knew all about the exiled priests, and though he had never seen them before, was able to identify the others as they walked in the procession.

"Do you expect to return to the missions, Father?" asked the archbishop.

Father Columba laughed heartily. "Don't be so ready to offer me up, Your Grace! I've put in twenty years in China — and not one year of peace the whole blessed time."

"We cannot expect to have peace in this world, Father. If a man isn't in turmoil outside, he's fermenting inside," said the archbishop. "Even among the clergy there's more restlessness than you'd imagine."

"Restlessness probably accounts for a good deal of our mission activity," said Father Columba placatingly.

"Either that or ulcers," said Shannon.

"I don't think I've ever had an ulcer, Archbishop."

Shannon looked at the Irishman grimly. "If you had one, you'd know it, Father."

"What is the cure, Your Grace?" asked Father Columba.

"If I knew of one I'd have packaged it long ago," said the archbishop.

No one enjoyed a friendly little chat with prelates more than Father Edmund, but he was always surprised that they talked of everything under the sun except holy religion.

He found Bishop Aime Thibeault's distraction to be more palatable. The bishop had an unexpected predilection for the spiritual fringe benefits to be derived from pilgrimages and various devotions not in the Roman ritual.

Aime Thibeault had seen all the shrines, or nearly all of them. He somehow always forgot about the body of St. Francis Xavier in Bon Jesus Cathedral in Goa.

"That's in India, isn't it, Father?" asked the bishop.

That was somewhat right the Englishman said. But the exact status of Goa was vague in his mind.

"But I thought you were at a mission in India?"

Father Edmund laughed. "I was never quite sure. We were on

the border — at times, but that changed almost as frequently as the guard at the frontier. There was almost a cosmopolitan atmosphere in the village, a customs post, a Chinese warlord presiding from his mountaintop over our heads, and a British garrison not far away — or more correctly a British officer with a squad of colonials. Later when the British pulled out, a fierce-looking Indian took charge. The place where I was was called Sochique and among missioners there we enjoyed a sort of protocol. A Dr. Tester was the dean of the corps, an Anglican priest — as they style themselves — a delightful fellow who couldn't get it through his head why I couldn't take over for him when he absented himself on his semiannual trips. He was quite willing to fill in for me, and more than once put me on the spot by offering to celebrate Mass for me when I was laid up."

Bishop Thibeault shook his head.

"I managed," said Father Edmund. "Anyway, Dr. Tester, on one of his trips, went to Goa and there viewed the procession in which the body of St. Francis Xavier was carried through the streets. He said he was horrified that parts of the saint's body had been carted off. I was rather embarrassed, for I hold no brief for cutting up holy cadavers. I'd much rather, for the sake of good taste, that they'd left the poor man's body intact."

Aime Thibeault smiled forbearingly. "You're much too sentimental, Father. The saints have given themselves to the Church. It may parcel them out as it pleases."

A sour sigh came from the Britisher, and Father Maximilian, who was escorting Aime Thibeault on the other flank, tuned out his hearing aid judiciously.

After a moment's pause the retired bishop headed pell-mell into a discussion of the merits of first- and second-class relics. And Father Edmund, clamping his jaws together rebelliously, wondered what the good bishop would have to say about the Holy Shirt of Mail, which he would undoubtedly get to sooner or later. Father Edmund felt that the Church was happily cautious about giving its stamp of approval to some of the holy souvenirs to which were attached highly suspect mystical occurrences. For his own part, he fervently hoped that the unexplained events legend attributed to the Holy Shirt would remain unexplained.

It was Steve Halidon's first glimpse of Stefan Dworjanski, but there was no possibility of mistaking him. The massive, inscrutable features had been on the front pages of too many newspapers in the past few years. People lining the route of the procession to the monastery broke into spontaneous applause when they recognized him, but he was as unmoved by it as he had been by the persecution by his enemies.

Halidon turned from his position among the crowd across the square from the cathedral and walked in the direction of the monastery. He moved along through the crowd until he came to the far end of the square.

There was a greater gathering of people here where the procession would pass close as it curved around the monument. A truckload of photographers and newsreel cameramen were parked at the corner.

The movie cameras turned as the end of the procession moved by, close to the corner, following it. The news photographers scrambled down from the truck for close-range shots of the relic and Stefan Dworjanski. Halidon smiled in amusement. Hundreds of shots would be taken but few would ever see beyond the darkroom. He was about to move away through the crowd when he saw a man pushing back from the range of the cameras. He had turned his face once, a startled expression in his eyes, then he shouldered his way out of range.

Halidon edged back beside the truck, trying to get another glimpse of the man. But there were too many people moving now, some of them hurrying along the sidewalk toward the monastery.

Halidon laughed aloud, dismayed that he had so ill-prepared

himself. It had just never occurred to either Shanley or himself that he didn't know what Newman looked like. It would have been a simple thing to get a cut of Oliver Newman out of the library. Now he'd have to work a bit harder for it.

He started away, then turned, glancing up at the cameraman getting his equipment together. The television station letters on the camera were unfamiliar, undoubtedly the local station.

"Hey, Mac — " he shouted up to the cameraman.

"It's Fred," the man said, winding cable around his hand. "What do you want? A dime for a beer?"

Halidon laughed. "This foliage is just for color. How can I get some of your film?"

"Knock me over the head — that's one way."

Halidon pulled himself up on the side of the cab. "I'm serious. I want to see some of that film."

"See it?"

"Yeah, just see it. I don't want to keep it — or peddle it to your competitors — "

"How bad do you want it?" the cameraman asked rubbing his fingers and thumb together.

Halidon pulled out his billfold and selected a ten-dollar bill. He slapped it into the man's hand.

"Come over to the studio in an hour and I'll run off the whole shebang for you. Fourth floor — Wheatley Building."

If he was right Halidon reflected — if it was Newman he'd seen — why had he arrived in Darrington several days before his itinerary indicated he would?

Halidon located a drugstore and went in, thumbing through the telephone directory for the address of the Wheatley Building. When he'd viewed the film — and if his guesses were right — he'd call Shanley to find out where Newman was alleged to be today. Quite obscurely between lectures somewhere, probably.

The crowds which followed the procession to the monastery overflowed into the street as Father Georgio carried the relic of

Venerable Bruno to its place in the sanctuary. At the altar, Bishop Dworjanski intoned the *Te Deum*, his powerful voice echoing through the chapel and carrying to the throng outside.

Francis Hickey, presiding from a canopied chair, could see how the overwhelming voice might have alarmed the Communists. When he had been free to speak he never spoke of conciliation. "The Church of God does not bargain with the devil," Dworjanski had cried. "The blood of persecution purges it, but it damns you!"

The world had seen Stefan Dworjanski, through his bold words, as a symbol, a rather frightening symbol, of the Church Militant. He was a man of another age and, for a moment, Francis Hickey was startled to realize that it might be the age of the future instead of the past. Dworjanski had come living from the tomb of his imprisonment, an angry resurrection which dismayed both friend and enemy.

But he was safe here at Archangel Monastery, if it was safety he wanted. Holy Michael the Archangel, patron of this house, from immemorial days had been the angelic protector of the Church. His statue, armed for battle against the powers of darkness, stood across the sanctuary, sword in hand, Satan squirming at his feet.

The statue had once been one of the many which cluttered the cathedral, but years ago, when the Sisters of Our Lady of Egypt occupied the monastery and were looking for a statue of the patron they had chosen, Bishop Hickey had given them the gaudily painted plaster figure during one of the absences of Monsignor Brady.

The chanting of the *Te Deum* stopped suddenly and there was an exclamation of dismay from Monsignor Brady. At the altar Stefan Dworjanski had crumbled to his knees and might have collapsed altogether except for the supporting hands of Father Massimo. A moment later Father Columba hurried to him with a chair. The Irishman and Father Georgio lifted the bishop into it and carried him out.

"Just like the Pope!" exclaimed Father Edmund under his breath.

The superior spoke calmly to the congregation, dismissing them, then hurried from the sanctuary. He was in time to see the priests carrying Stefan Dworjanski up the stairs. The superior hurried to his office and summoned Dr. Lambert.

Father Massimo waited with Bishop Hickey in the lower hall, his apprehension ill-concealed. Bishops Shannon and Thibeault had been ushered into the library to await word on the Polish prelate's health. They hurried to the door of the room as they heard the doctor coming downstairs, listening anxiously as Andy Lambert gave his report to Bishop Hickey: " . . . a slight stroke, but next time it could be fatal. If he were more cooperative we could do more for him. He refuses to go to the hospital."

Shannon and Thibeault looked at each other in alarm and withdrew further into the privacy of the library, thankful they would be going home very shortly. Archbishop Shannon was shaking his head and wondering where Stefan Dworjanski might be buried — "when he died, of course," he added hastily when Aime Thibeault's brows lifted in shock.

There was a disturbance at the library door and the two prelates turned in time to see a small, swarthy priest catapulting toward them. "Excellencies," cried the Spaniard. "San Juan de la Cruz sent you, no? You will bring my case to the attention of the nuncio?"

Both stared at the Spaniard in dismay and Father Massimo came quickly to Father Largo but his hand was pushed away.

"Help me!" Father Largo cried, "They take away all my rights! I am not even permitted the consolation of my Mass!"

Archbishop Shannon's alarmed eyes were on Father Massimo. "I'd like to help you, Father, but this isn't my diocese."

Father Largo clasped Shannon's hand, "One word to Ormaneto and pronto — I am out — libre!"

Shannon sighed relievedly as he saw Bishop Hickey hurrying across the room toward them. Father Massimo put a restraining hand on the Spaniard. "I hope your Excellencies will excuse Father Largo. He is not himself today."

Bishop Hickey took Father Largo's arm patiently. "You have had your say now, Father. His Holiness the Pope knows all about your case and has asked me to give you sanctuary. I'm sure you don't wish to return to your native land with the generalissimo still in power — not after the hard things you have said about him and the regime."

"He is a dog!" cried Father Largo.

"But top dog at the moment, Father."

Father Largo looked at the bishop, a shrewd smile puffing his face. "Will you allow me my Mass if I stay?"

Bishop Hickey tried a placating tone: "You have so many other things to be doing, Father. You still have your breviary to read — and you have your painting." Hickey turned to the other bishops. "Father Largo is an artist, I'm sure you've heard. His painting of the Holy Family adorns my study. And I'm certain you noticed his mural of Pentecost over the altar of the chapel."

Nicholas Shannon was at ease again. "I'd be delighted, Father, if you'd paint a mural for my cathedral."

"I will — certainly, Senor Obispo, if you have a cathedral worthy of it!"

Hickey watched as Father Massimo led the Spaniard away, then turned to his confreres, hoping his placid smile assured them that he was being a reasonable jailer for this unfortunate, but difficult priest.

"I had no idea you had such problems to contend with, Bishop," Aime Thibeault said.

"What is this about a *nuncio*?" asked Shannon. "Doesn't the fellow know that the representative of His Holiness in Washington has only the rank of apostolic delegate?"

"You heard him mention Ormaneto?" Hickey chuckled. "Well, for a moment he was translated to the age of Teresa of Avila and St. John of the Cross. He has developed a great devotion for St. John — so much so that at highly irrational moments he lives in that period of history."

"It must be trying for Father superior," said Aime Thibeault.

The bishop nodded: "Particularly when you realize that he sometimes thinks poor Father Massimo is the Carmelite Superior Jeronimo Tostado who imprisoned his hero in the priory at Toledo. Father Largo disappeared from his mission in South China in 1952 and wasn't heard of again until he appeared at Saigon five years later. He told of being held captive by Burmese monks, and of his eventual escape by a rope hung from a high window. But Father Massimo surmises that this is part imagination — taken from the life of St. John who escaped in a similar manner from his cell at Toledo."

"If I remember," said Aime Thibeault, "St. John broke his leg in the fall because the rope was too short."

"So did Father Largo," said Hickey.

"The same story then," said Nicholas Shannon.

"But not the same rope, I don't think," Francis Hickey said.

Francis Hickey's most steadfast and newsy pen pal was Bishop Bryan McAuley of Utica. Hickey had finally resigned himself to the probability that their antitheses of personality and interests had drawn them together. The friendship had been prolonged only by the fact that they met infrequently and that Hickey was careful to make restrained replies to McAuley's bits of provoking news and comments.

At the moment Hickey was disturbed at his friend's request that the red carpet be rolled out for Oliver Newman when the ex-Communist arrived in Darrington for his lecture. McAuley had written several letters in this vein — the latest awaiting him when he returned today from the procession — smoothing the way for Newman. He had even made the presumptuous request that Hickey introduce Newman to the foreign priests.

The bishop arose from his desk, drawing down the violet sash over his stomach as he went to the row of long Gothic windows

[52]

which faced the street from his second-floor study. He fingered the heavy plush drapes absently, wishing he could feel objective enough to reply to McAuley in the tone the request deserved.

McAuley wrote that Newman would like to meet the foreign priests and that Newman was especially anxious to call on Bishop Stefan Dworjanski.

Dworjanski wouldn't be happy about it, the bishop knew. He had let his distaste for interruptions be known more than once when Hickey had made a call.

Hickey was concerned about his Polish confrere. He had yet to understand fully the meaning of the several communications from Rome concerning Dworjanski. But one thing at least was clear. They wouldn't permit Dworjanski's memoirs to be published until they had been thoroughly scrutinized by prelates of the secretariat of Extraordinary Ecclesiastical Affairs.

In perspective Hickey realized that Bryan McAuley had been singularly interested in the memoirs for several months and had probably divulged some of his interest to Archbishop Shannon. Undoubtedly McAuley would have liked to translate Dworjanski's memoirs but ignorance of the Polish language was one of the few unfinished facets in this ecclesiastical diamond.

The bishop turned from the window and glanced vexatiously at the huge portrait in oils of McAuley which hung in the place of honor over the fireplace. In merrier moments he had chuckled over the thought that it was a more appropriate location than he had first imagined.

He had met McAuley for the first time when they were making their *ad limina* visits to the Pope in 1938, and were passengers together on the *Queen Mary*. McAuley knew his way around Europe and conducted Hickey to the best hotels, which Hickey had no taste for; and saw that Hickey ate the best food, which proved to be even less appealing.

In Rome, while they waited their turn for an audience with Pius XI, McAuley led him on a merry chase up holy stairs and down into even holier caverns. He knew where all the impious deeds of the past had been done and where some of them had been undone. But God alone knew why McAuley was preoccupied so much with the past when he was so obviously a child of the present.

They had, however, struck it off pretty well. McAuley said he was impressed with Hickey's refusal to be overcome with things immemorial. He even appeared to take great enjoyment in personally presenting Hickey to His Holiness, who remembered McAuley but had no memory at all of Hickey — who had talked to him for a half hour five years before.

During the next year or two Hickey had felt a little tingle of prestige at the realization that he was a friend of the distinguished bishop of Utica. Whenever McAuley felt the need of a little vacation he packed a bag and entrained for the Seaview Hotel at Cohagansett so he could be near his friend.

Francis Hickey smiled reflectively as he studied the portrait. He was uncomfortably aware of the deep velvet eyes looking down at him serenely from under a wide ivory brow. McAuley made an elegant figure among his coterie of friends: theologians, canonists, liturgists, and a vast court of surmisers.

Hickey turned to his desk, quite abruptly aware that he had been uneasy about McAuley's friendship for some months. Perhaps it began with the very sound lecture McAuley had penned him on working out a *modus vivendi* with Nicholas Shannon. There had been a series of admonishing letters, provokingly studded with bits of conversation he had had with Shannon which McAuley must have known would annoy. But the letters invariably ended with the admonition against making any unconsidered retorts.

He had to think that McAuley meant well, but Hickey wondered if that might not be the worst instead of the best thing he could attribute to his friend.

Contented with his conclusions, the bishop lighted a cigar. He hadn't wanted to see that McAuley was a lightweight in a world of heavies. Was it little wonder that most of the bishops found it amusing when McAuley was persistently mentioned as a likely candidate for a red hat?

Hickey picked up the latest letter from McAuley, looking rather dismally at the coat of arms at the top and aware of the good rag content of the paper. It was as though the sender was satisfied the letter would be preserved. It was long and so far had been informative.

He was still perusing the letter inattentively when Father Redmond tapped lightly on the door and entered. He came to the desk with the usual secret and disquieting smile on his tiger-turned-to-butter face. The bishop had learned early that Paul Redmond's knowledge, or more specifically his store of information, was boundless. It was pleasant having someone around him who knew everything, or thought he did. Francis Hickey freely admitted that he himself didn't. Honorary degrees in philosophy and letters had added nothing to his education but he hoped that bishoping it for thirty years had.

Redmond's supply of facts, figures, and biographical data had proved useful and he seemed to be precisely the bright young man that the bishop needed, sometimes. But at the moment Hickey was unhappy about his secretary, a quite sudden pang that had come over him as he perused McAuley's latest missive which, toward the end, and quite casually, mentioned the name of Cardinal Gasquet: "Of course you know by now, Francis, that His Eminence has purchased the Whitaker estate at Cohagansett. . . ."

Hickey was sure that McAuley was rather gleefully aware that he didn't know about it even though it had happened within the range of his diocesan radar. There had been rumors that a cardinal was visiting at the resort but until this moment he had no particulars, in spite of the presumed efficient inquiries of Father Redmond. Until McAuley mentioned the name Gasquet, Hickey had only a vague idea which cardinal it might be. The first rumor indicated it might be a Canadian, but the fact that there were three of them only confused the matter.

Hickey became aware, when Father Redmond cleared his throat for the third time, that he wanted some attention. The bishop looked up.

"We have a telegram from the cardinal's secretary, Bishop," Father Redmond said.

"He's made contact then?" Hickey said.

The secretary smiled. "He's been making contact with you for weeks. I'm speaking of Cardinal McBride. He wants to know if you're going to be able to make it for the dedication of the seminary wing."

"Oh, dear," Hickey said, "didn't we answer that yet? It will mean rearranging my confirmation schedule — and incidentally upsetting the plans of several pastors and the Lord knows how many parents."

"Everyone's going to be there," said the secretary.

"I'm sure of it," said Hickey. "They won't miss me. I imagine there'll be a bigger splash of red than at a powwow of the Communist Internationale." Hickey glanced at McAuley's letter again. "But I thought you meant we'd heard from the Canadian cardinal."

"He's at Cohagansett," said Father Redmond uneasily, "I'm sure of that. But which place he has rented —"

"Purchased," said Hickey.

"Oh," said Father Redmond.

"I have the information from Bishop McAuley, which almost makes it *de fide*. We now seem to have it pinned down as Cardinal Gasquet."

"Gasquet? The last I heard about him he was on a tour of pontifical seminaries."

The bishop chuckled. "I'm surprised at you, Father. That was six months ago."

"I do have the information that he has a magnificent limousine," the secretary said, "but so far only the chauffeur has been seen. Perhaps we can find out that way."

"I certainly don't want you pumping for information at filling stations. Perhaps the cardinal will inform us when he's ready. He may be ill for all we know. I imagine it would be my duty to call on him, but not until he officially informs us that he's in the diocese. It would be imprudent of me and probably socially fatal to impose on his privacy. If he intends to do anything of an ecclesiastical nature I'm sure he's informed on the intricacies of canon law — probably better than I am. But as it stands, I'm bound to honor what I must presume is Cardinal Gasquet's desire to remain incognito during his stay at Cohagansett." The bishop folded McAuley's letter.

Father Redmond said he'd get the telegram off to Cardinal McBride, and went out, closing the door quietly.

The bishop was disturbed, but being disturbed was but another occupational hazard with bishops. Yet, at the moment, Francis Hickey wondered if he didn't get more than his share of annoyances. He had to admit the slight he felt that Gasquet didn't even bother to inform him that he was in the diocese.

Hickey wondered if he was being too sensitive, if he was beginning to take things, oftentimes trivial and obscure things, much more to heart than a sensible bishop should.

But Cardinal Gasquet was becoming an increasingly important figure in the new pontificate and had proved an effective troubleshooter for His Holiness as well as a versatile linguist who could be dispatched to any part of the world with the assurance that he'd make himself understood.

But it was unlikely that such a small matter as the fate of the exiled priests would be his concern, unless Archbishop Shannon was able to pull more strings than Hickey realized were available. Shannon had tapered off somewhat in his remarks about the missioners being detained unwillingly in Darrington, and it was more than a year since he had let out a blast about the old monastery being unfit for human habitation, but he could have resorted to more discreet channels.

Hickey had thought it best not to reply to Shannon's comments, partly because he was right about the building. But the exiles had worked hard at making it livable, so much so that Hickey felt he would welcome an inspection.

Content for the moment with the thought that Cardinal Gasquet was probably not even aware of his existence, the bishop ranged his mind for some stored-away details about him. Almost half a century ago Andre Gasquet had been vicar apostolic of a remote and frozen vicariate apostolic in northern Canada. An accident ended his activities there and he was summoned to Rome and given a leisurely benefice as chaplain of the motherhouse of a French-Canadian order of women. He had remained there, quite forgotten, until the Pope raised him, amid much consternation, to head one of the congregations and placed a red hat on his singularly unhandsome head.

Now he was at Cohagansett and there was not the slightest indication of why he had chosen it as a place of retreat. It would appear that Gasquet was doing precisely what he seemed to be doing, enjoying an hermetical vacation.

The bishop rose from his desk and had picked up his breviary when Father Redmond appeared at the door again, this time to announce the Doolans.

Daisy swept into the room. "Dear Bishop Hickey!" she cried, advancing toward him with an alarming eagerness. She clutched his hand and made a swipe at his ring with her too-red lips. The bishop breathed a prayer of gratification that she hadn't attempted to genuflect, not in that tight skirt.

"We hoped we'd find you in, Bishop!" she exclaimed.

Francis Hickey smiled grimly. He would have hoped differently if he had had time for even a furtive wish. But now he could do nothing but greet them affably.

As J. Dalton Doolan clasped the bishop's hand, Hickey noticed that the man's face was more mottled than usual and his bulbous nose looked as though it might be excruciatingly sensitive.

"We always seem to be dropping in on you unannounced, Bishop," Doolan said.

[58]

Francis Hickey smiled ruefully as he conducted them to a group of comfortable chairs near the windows. "You seem to be among the few in the diocese to have taken me at my word when I said, many years ago, that I would always be at home to anyone who wished to call on me."

Doolan laughed. "I'm sure the people are afraid of you, Bishop. The only time they see you is when you're rigged out in your fancy doodads."

The bishop felt there was little point in attempting to explain to Doolan that in his countless rounds of confirmation tours he had met nearly everyone in the diocese and made himself as approachable as any priest could in the confessional every Saturday.

"Daisy just had an idea," Doolan said. "We were picking up some bric-a-brac for the beach house and Daisy got an idea of how to spend some more of my money."

"Oh?" said the bishop.

"I'm afraid it started with a criticism," Daisy said, and when she saw the bishop's frown she hurried on to explain. "A friend of ours — not of the faith — happened to see the procession of the relic to Archangel Monastery this morning. He thought the relic perfectly horrid — artistically speaking, much like something you'd see in Spain or Mexico."

Hickey smiled, relieved that her complaint was nothing serious.

"Well," continued Daisy, "our friend thought the Holy Shirt of Mail looked too much like a skeleton hung up on a rack and it surely could stand to be cleaned up. Then, just an hour ago, when Dalton and I were looking at some marble lawn pieces, the solution came to me."

Hickey raised his weary eyelids apprehensively, doing his best to restrain his annoyance as the woman pressed forward with her inspiration.

"The relic could be fitted to a marble statue, executed by some great sculptor. I had in mind to commission a statue of Venerable Bruno if the price is reasonable."

[59]

"The price might be reasonable, Mrs. Doolan," said the bishop, "but I'm afraid I wouldn't be — nor would the mission priests, who like the relic as it is. The relic itself doesn't matter at all. It's the reminder it provides of the holy founder of the Brunites, who, it now appears, will be beatified — thanks partially to the Communists who have once again made his a *cause celebre* owing to their intemperate activities. Bruno put a lot of holy living into that shirt. I wouldn't remove one layer of sweat and mortification."

Daisy passed off the bishop's comments as gracefully as she could and launched into a summary of the plans for her daughter Maryanne's wedding.

Maryanne's upbringing was one of the few things the Doolans had to their credit as far as Francis Hickey was concerned. She was an intelligent and unspoiled girl, though how it had been brought about (unless by the singular intervention of the Almighty) he had no idea. Hickey had the impression that if it hadn't been for Daisy's social pretensions Maryanne would never have become engaged to Huntley Winslow Wood III, a North Shore socialite. But at least the boy was taking instructions in the Faith from Father Galvin and would be baptized before the wedding.

The bishop listened inattentively as Daisy rambled on. He had hoped for a minute, when they had spoken of spending some of Dalton's money that something would be said about a contribution toward the renovation of the cathedral. Doolan had dwelt with considerable detail on his tax burdens and the bishop had wondered if he was searching for a tax loophole to relieve his burdens for the fiscal year.

Over the years, starting with O'Boyle's Folly, otherwise known as St. Finbar's Church named for Hickey's predecessor, Finbar O'Boyle, the diocese had made Doolan's acquaintance to the tune of some thirty million dollars. It was disquieting to realize how long he had watched J. Dalton Doolan's pursuit of the dollar. Doolan had started out making red bricks in the pottery

[60]

with immigrant Armenians for ten dollars a week. He might be there still except that his sister Delia went to work as a maid in the home of Sumner Seaton, Sr., the contracting tycoon.

Sumner, Jr., didn't allow Delia to get her hands very toil worn before he marched her off to the altar. In no time at all Dalton was a bricklayer, then a foreman, then a member of the firm, and eventually a partner when old Sumner Seaton died. It was not long until Dalton was something of a corporation sole when he convinced his brother-in-law that there was business to be had in building Catholic schools and churches simply by letting the Doolan name predominate.

The abundance of cash had made it easy for Daisy to pursue culture, and Dalton had tagged along, reluctant at first, but eventually acquiring a taste for hobnobbing with people he unfortunately regarded as his betters. Daisy, however, remained stoutly and loudly Catholic, sticking conscientiously to the letter of Church discipline. The bishop felt that if it were possible to gain paradise on technicalities she'd make it. She had founded her club, Les Dames du Bon Secours, for the very purpose of storing up merit with the celestial bookkeeper.

"We'll see you at the wedding — if not sooner," Daisy said airily. "Poor Father Galvin appears doomed to miss out on all the festivities. The poor man is having his purgatory on earth with his arthritis."

"I'm convinced it's gout," said the bishop, "not arthritis or rheumatism."

"My father died of gout," Doolan commented.

"I hope you won't tell Father Galvin that," Hickey said. "Anyway, I'm sure the medicos have a fancier name for it now. It's too bad Father Galvin doesn't trust doctors as much as he does his sister's home remedies. From what he tells me, she has an abundant supply of them. I've been unable to convince him that the diet Clara Galvin provides is slowly finishing him off."

The Doolans were making for the door when suddenly the

feather which stood like an exclamation mark atop Daisy's hat quivered as she remembered something.

"I nearly forgot the real news, Bishop!" she cried. "We hope to have His Eminence officiate at Maryanne's wedding!"

"Which Eminence is that, Mrs. Doolan?" asked the bishop warily.

Daisy came toward him, peering into his face curiously. "We thought you'd know, Bishop."

"If there's a cardinal anywhere on the diocesan premises he hasn't notified me."

"Oh . . . but surely you'll soon be," was all Daisy would say.

With a feeling of relief the bishop saw them to the door and when he returned to his study he found Father Redmond awaiting him.

"What did they want this time, Bishop?"

"I'm not quite sure. We ran the gamut — from theology to gossip."

"I thought they might have heard about Cardinal Gasquet's visit to Cohagansett. And, knowing Daisy, I'm sure she'd want to lionize him."

"Badger would be the better word," said the bishop.

Fortified with proof that it was Oliver Newman he had seen this morning during the procession, Halidon ate a leisurely supper and waited in his room at the Phoenix Hotel until he knew Dev Shanley would be at home.

He dialed direct and in a moment heard Shanley's somewhat rasping voice on the wire. "Something go wrong, Steve?"

"No — something is right, maybe too right. Newman is already here, days ahead of schedule. . . ." He told Shanley the events of the day, concluding with his visit to the local newspaper office to look at a picture of Newman and further glimpses of him on the newsreel film.

"You mean you didn't know what Oliver Newman looked like?" cried Shanley, somewhat irked.

"I do now. I'd like to know why he arrived so soon."

"I've been keeping tabs on his movements, Steve. Tonight he has a lecture in Stamford, Connecticut. He's been over in Jersey the past few nights. Stamford clears up his slate until Saturday when he has reservations on the afternoon plane for Darrington."

"He would have had time then to drive here from New Jersey last night," Halidon said. "And while I've got you on the phone, Dev . . . you said something yesterday about Ross County. I missed your point though. The only connection I can make between that and Oliver Newman is Mark Curtain's suicide."

"My guess is that's the right connection," Shanley said. "The FBI boys have been up at Curtain's place on the lake. If my sources are right they're about ready to decide that Curtain didn't commit suicide. The grand jury is going to sit up there next week."

"And Newman and Curtain were friends."

Shanley laughed cynically. "Curtain never really had any friends. He was too objective a columnist."

And ended up the way nearly everyone predicted he would — with a bullet in his head. But when he was dead it was a little too late to more than surmise which of his enemies had evened things up. Officially it was ruled a suicide. Curtain had been alone at his cottage that weekend, as far as the sheriff had been able to determine.

When Newman, during his testimony before the Congressional committee, named Mark Curtain as one of the men he had worked with in the Communist underground, Curtain took the easiest way out. It was a veritable confession. His death was timed too close to Newman's revelation for anyone to believe it was anything but suicide.

But there was a time element that had never been considered too important. Curtain had apparently gone to his lake cottage on Friday and was seen by no one until Monday night when the sheriff, accompanied by FBI men, went to the cottage and found Curtain dead. That morning Newman had named Curtain as a Communist, but the medical examiner said the columnist had been dead for more than twenty-four hours, possibly longer.

"Dev — " Halidon said.

"Yeah, I'm here. I was thinking — "

"About the convenience of tight lecture schedules?"

"I don't get you."

"I mean Newman's schedule. It seems as though he finds it to his purpose to announce exactly where he's going to be. You remember he was registered at a Washington hotel when Curtain died. And today he's probably registered at a Stamford hotel, presumably some two hundred miles away from Darrington."

"Good Lord, Steve! You think he was going to make a try at Dworjanski today?"

"A shot from the crowd — why not? Assassins have worked that way for centuries. He might have done it except that the television camera turned on him — "

"Why Dworjanski, Steve — "

"Maybe he has orders to get the old man — "

"And then steal the relic?"

"I don't think the Communists give a damn about the relic," Halidon said. "My idea is that they just wanted to be indignant and righteous about it while it served their propaganda purposes."

"You think Newman is going to get the bishop?"

"I do now, Dev. If you saw his face — I never saw a man so frightened. But he'll only do it when he's officially someplace else, some place within driving range."

"And tonight he's undoubtedly back in Stamford — probably giving his lecture right now. He'll wind up about 10 p.m., but even a dedicated Red wouldn't have the stamina to make another trip to Darrington and back tonight — but he's apt to make another foray anytime. You'd better get to the monastery."

Halidon laughed, "Oh, just like that! You usually have to take vows to get into a religious house."

"I vowed you would," Shanley said. "That's enough. Still got the beard?"

"Yeah — and I hope the first thing the priests hand me is a razor."

Benediction closed the first day of exposition of the relic of Venerable Bruno. Father Massimo, removing his vestments in the sacristy, was pleased that there had been no disorder, no overzealous efforts to touch the relic.

The superior came to the library and found the others assembled, all except Bishop Dworjanski and of course the unwearied Father Georgio (who had caught his usual forty winks at Benediction) and was now out closing the oratory for the night.

Taking advantage of the big Croat's absence, Father Edmund said something should be done about his snoring at services, but the superior smiled placidly, content to make no decision. The snoring was no worse than the Englishman's sighs of exasperation. And, in any case, the snores were probably heard by no one but his immediate neighbors since Father Columba (the jack-of-all-trades) was at the organ and managed to time his most resounding chords to the Croat's improvisations. Father Georgio, even in sleep, was a binding force in the house and sometimes brought a smile even to the taciturn face of Father Maximilian.

His boisterous affection frequently proved an embarrassment, markedly so in the case of Father Edmund. The reserved Englishman shuddered at the way Father Georgio gave him a bear hug and a loud smack at the bestowal of the kiss of peace at high Mass.

Father Massimo learned only sometime after his arrival in Darrington that his appointment as superior had been the cause of dismay to Father Edmund. The Englishman had assumed that he would be appointed superior and had commented to Father Maximilian that he was qualified for the job since he had served once as a prefect apostolic in India, which gave him quasi-prelatial rank, even though it was later revoked.

Father Edmund would, of course, have been chagrined to learn that Father Massimo knew the Englishman had asked, "Why does an Italian always have to be the big cheese?" when he'd heard Father Massimo was on his way to Darrington.

Undoubtedly he was just as happy now that he didn't have the responsibilities of the house. He was much happier writing his lectures and giving days of recollection for lay groups throughout the diocese. He was pleased too with his weekend assignment assisting the parish priests at St. Peter in Chains Parish.

It was a fashionable parish, one that fulfilled Father Edmund's whim to rub elbows with people who could grasp his message. The pastor, Father Benson, had told the Englishman that his sermons on the liturgy provided a much needed intellectual element in the parish.

"I'm speaking on the Mozarabic Rite again this Sunday," the Englishman remarked. "There's an example in it for us Latins, you know."

Father Dmitri was unimpressed. "Myself, I always talk about sin. I think the people want to know these things. At least my people at St. Cyril's do."

"They've been rubbing elbows with sin all week," retorted Father Edmund. "On Sunday they want to hear something uplifting. I'm sure they'll all be inspired to learn that those poor Catholics who were Islamized by their conquerors in Spain somehow managed to keep the Faith — but with a few interesting innovations of course — such as circumcision."

"You think this is wise?" asked Father Dmitri anxiously. "It seems to me these people — Mozarabs, you call them, I think — were corrupted if they adopted this practice."

"Nonsense!" laughed Father Edmund. "It has nothing to do with morality."

"I don't think the pastor there will like it," said Father Dmitri cautiously.

[66]

Father Edmund looked at the Moravian indignantly, "I had no idea you were such a prude. We are men of the world, are we not?"

The Moravian's look indicated that he felt his confrere was too much of the world, and as Father Edmund looked to the others for support of his opinion, the bearded priest strode from the room with a mumbled "good night."

Pushing his limp wisp of yellow hair back from his forehead the Britisher looked to Father Columba, his natural (though more friendly) rival in his garrulous battles with the world, the flesh, and the liturgical innovators. The Irish priest seldom let any of Edmund's invidious remarks go unchallenged but his thunderous replies (which could never quite dispel the humor in his eyes), was only another indication to the others of the camaraderie between the two.

Father Edmund's barbs were usually aimed at Irish Catholicism, with the implication that the Gaelic liturgy was tainted with Druidism, but fortunately he had never lectured on this theme at St. Peter in Chains Parish, where the Irish there had not yet found out just how insular he really was.

Liberal in matters where faith, morals, or patriotism were not involved, the Britisher refused absolutely to go along with the ex-cons tag that Father Columba had pinned on the exiles. The Irishman had said it seemed appropriate since most of them had spent time in concentration camps of one sort or another.

They had all returned to their preoccupation when there was the noisy clatter of wooden beads in the hall, and Father Dmitri bobbed his head in the door to tell them there had been an automobile accident nearby. If he was not mistaken he had heard there were some injuries.

The superior closed his book and hurried from the library. "You had better come along too, Father," he said to the Moravian. The superior got his coat from the office, making sure his stole was in the pocket, and went to the corner, where a crowd was gathering. In the distance police sirens wailed.

Father Massimo excused his way through the onlookers and saw a car encased about a lightpost and another one overturned on the sidewalk.

A man was emerging from the car which was against the post. As he backed through the broken window two men assisted him to a supine position on the ground in spite of his protests that he was all right.

Father Massimo came to him, putting one knee down on the pavement. "Are you a Catholic?" he asked.

The man stared at him angrily. "What a hell of a time to be asking me questions like that!"

"Well — you must be all right," Father Massimo said, with a smile. He stood up wondering if there was someone who did need his attention, when he heard a shout.

"Here, Father! This man's unconscious!"

There was an arm waving to him from the sidewalk and Father Massimo hurried over to the man sitting propped against the brick wall of the building. He was poorly dressed, his face bearded, and at the moment a trickle of blood ran down his nose.

Father Massimo knelt down, a bit fearful this time to ask the man if he wanted absolution. He shook his head and looked at the priest dazedly. Then suddenly he grinned.

"Who are you?"

"Father Massimo — from Archangel Monastery nearby. Are you all right?"

The man continued shaking his head, but in a moment the priest realized it was more in amusement than stupor.

"A man can't even walk the streets safely anymore," he muttered. "I was an innocent pedestrian. The car came right up on the sidewalk after me —"

Telling the bearded man to stay where he was until the doctors arrived, Father Massimo hurried to the overturned car where another victim was being laid on the pavement. The superior saw that he was no more than a boy. He had a broken leg; that was certain, and probably other injuries from the gasps he emitted in his semiconscious state. The priest quickly made the sign of the cross over him and murmured the form of absolution.

Father Dmitri hadn't been far behind the superior. It appeared to him that he had given up too easily on the first man, who appeared to be a person of some education. It was too bad that his vocabulary didn't seem to match it. Such language! he thought, thankful that it was directed at the other driver and not at him.

The man tried to move but Father Dmitri held him down firmly. "Stay where you are," he said. "You can never tell when there are broken bones."

The Moravian turned to see Father Georgio looming over him and through the crook in the big Croat's arm he saw the inquisitive face of Father Edmund.

"Are you going to watch the man die?" cried Father Georgio. He dropped heavily to his knees and produced a flask from his belt. "Here, drink this — brandy. It will revive you," he said as he cradled the man's head in his big hand and forced the flask to the man's lips, ignoring his protests.

"Be calm, my good man," soothed Father Edmund. "A little drop won't harm you —"

The wail of sirens drowned out the man's shouts of dismay and then Father Georgio felt himself knocked off balance as the injured man scrambled to his feet and began to run.

"The poor fellow is delirious!" cried Father Edmund, as he watched a policeman rescue the man from his ill-considered flight.

"Intoxicated," the policeman exclaimed as he grappled with the man. "You can smell it on him!"

The injured were loaded into ambulances and Father Massimo went along with the unconscious youth to St. Camillus Hospital.

Father Massimo was in the waiting room to get a report on

the condition of the young man when a policeman approached him.

"Father . . ." he began nervously, "there's a complaint that one of your priests gave one of the drivers liquor — "

"Liquor? You must be mistaken, officer. I'm sure none of the priests know the men involved —"

"I mean after the accident," said the policeman impatiently. "A man named Wadleigh Thorne — a pretty important citizen — claims liquor was forced on him while he was in a dazed condition."

"I'm not sure I understand his complaint, officer," said Father Massimo.

The policeman breathed impatiently through his nostrils. "He's been arrested for drunken driving. He's screaming his head off down at police headquarters."

The priest sighed. "Well, I will have to inquire. It sounds like Father Georgio. . . . If the man is right I will have the priest who is responsible go down to your police headquarters and set things straight in the morning."

"I guess that will have to do, Father."

The policeman went away and after a few minutes Father Massimo became aware of the young man sitting two seats from him in the waiting room. It was the fellow who had been knocked down by one of the cars. He was very thin and his clothing had seen better days.

He got up, smiling at the priest as he moved to the seat beside him. "Have you got any cigarettes, Father?"

The priest groped in his pocket and took out a pack. "You were the man involved in the accident?"

"Just a bystander — but the police dragged me along when I told them I saw the whole thing."

"Oh, how did it happen?"

"I told the police. Looked like one of the cars tried to beat the light at Central Avenue and — I don't remember the other street —"

"River — perhaps."

"Yeah — that was it. I'm a stranger in town. I wouldn't have known Central Avenue either except that I was on my way to Archangel Monastery."

"Yes — ?" the priest said uneasily.

"I heard through the grapevine that a guy could get a meal there if he happened to be down on his luck."

Father Massimo looked at the young man and asked, "You are hungry?"

"Haven't eaten since yesterday —"

"Oh, my — we must do something about that. Our house wouldn't be a good place at this hour of the night. But perhaps I can get something for you here. One moment."

He went to the desk and spoke briefly to the nurse on duty. He returned. "The young lady said if I took you to the cafeteria — it could be arranged. Come."

They entered the long room, where a tray was prepared. When Father Massimo saw the man comfortably seated he returned to the emergency ward. An hour later as the priest came through the waiting room again the shabby young man was still there. He got up and joined the priest at the door.

When they were outside he spoke. "I didn't get a chance to thank you, Father."

The priest nodded uncomfortably. "I have been thinking about you. You have no place — no work?"

"I'm a knight of the road —"

"Knight of the road — ?"

"Hobo."

"Hobo," said the priest. "Oh, I see, this is like a gypsy?"

"Something like that."

Father Massimo studied him covertly. He seemed to be shivering in his threadbare coat. "Where will you go tonight?"

He shrugged, then grinned quickly at the priest. "I heard there's a jungle somewhere along the riverbank."

"Jungle?" said Father Massimo, puzzled.

[71]

"You don't know much of this jargon, do you, Father?"

Father Massimo smiled. "I've been here only about a year. I have much to learn."

"Well, there are several kinds of jungles. There's the business jungle — work; the animal jungle, like Africa, and the hobo jungle — peace, but a heck of a lot of insecurity."

"I wish I could help you, young man."

"You can, Father."

"Yes, I think I can. I'll write a little note to my friend Sergeant Muldoon. I'm sure he'll put you up for the night."

"No, thanks. Cops don't like guys like me. Can't you put me up somewhere at the monastery — just for the night?"

Father Massimo sighed. He knew of no place he could provide for the man — and he knew little about him, not even his name. He walked on in silence.

They came to the monastery and Father Massimo looked at his watch. It was after 10 p.m. Chances were everyone would be asleep, with the exception of Bishop Dworjanski who worked all hours on his autobiography, and possibly poor Father Largo, to whom night and day were the same.

"Perhaps it would be all right if you came in," he said. The young man followed him quickly and watched while Father Massimo closed and locked the door.

"You have a place where I can sleep?"

The priest looked at the fellow uneasily. "I'll put you in the library. There's a leather couch. You should be comfortable." He showed the stranger to the library. Then, snapping on the light, he turned with a faint smile. "Don't be alarmed if you hear someone wandering around during the night. It will be Father Largo. Well, make yourself at home. I'll get you blankets. . . ." The superior started from the room, then turned. "One thing more, I must lock you in. It's a reasonable precaution, I think you'll agree."

Father Massimo went upstairs for the blankets and a few minutes later when he came to the library with the blankets across his arm he was dismayed to see that the young man had gone.

He put down the blankets and hurried through the other rooms, but found no sign of the stranger. He had been sure for a moment that he could find the man in the kitchen helping himself, but when the superior looked he sighed in relief that the Father commissario's larder was undisturbed.

In the darkened chapel heavy shadows hung about the arched vaults of the ceiling and the confessionals, shadows which moved with the flickering of the red sanctuary candle burning before the Blessed Sacrament.

But somehow the sanctuary seemed safe with the massive plaster statue of St. Michael the Archangel standing with his sword on the neck of the bat-winged devil at his feet.

The superior turned quick, anxious eyes toward the relic of Venerable Bruno. It was there still, safe in its locked reliquary. The superior had been unhappy about having the relic on display after all the publicity and the incredible estimates of its value.

For himself, Father Massimo regarded the Holy Shirt of Mail as a symbol of eccentricity and he trusted good Father Bruno would now, certainly, appreciate his sentiments. But for a moment he wondered about the relic's significance. Perhaps he was getting soft. To abhor the means used by the venerable founder to discipline his body was surely an indication that his own spiritual discipline was softening.

Turning his thoughts impatiently from the relic, the superior hurried from the chapel, aware that he had much more immediate problems to worry about than the encrusted relic and the need of penance its presence evoked.

He found the door to the cloister at the rear of the house ajar. The stranger had taken his leave this way, Father Massimo felt sure. Perhaps it was the thought of being locked in the library that had frightened him. It would be too secure a prison for his gypsy spirit.

CHAPTER THREE

As THE first light of morning found the dusty basement windows of the monastery Father Largo was revealed, sitting on a crate, his soul rapt in ecstasy. Time meant even less than usual to the priest as he steeped himself in every detail of the vision.

It must have been two hours ago that he came down to the cellar to get wine for Mass. A rustling noise caused him to flash his light into the crypt. He had felt not a ripple of dismay as he peered in through the bars and saw his *saint* asleep on the straw, a tattered black cassock drawn about him. He forgot all about the wine as he sat with his hands clasped together, his old, tear-brimming eyes blinking happily. This was the way San Juan de la Cruz wanted to be remembered, in prison where he had endured torture and persecution, for out of it had come his imperishable works, his unique masterpiece for Spain and for the world.

Father Largo had prayed that some day his devotion to St. John of the Cross would be rewarded with a visitation, but he thought that at best it would be a quick glimpse. He had held little hope that this holy man whose case had long ago been closed in Rome and in eternity, and who certainly had little in common with men of this worldly and self-indulgent century — men who filled their stomachs instead of their hearts — would care to return among them for long.

After he had assured himself that he wasn't dreaming, Father

Largo had pushed open the grille door to the crypt where, perhaps a century ago, the cloistered nuns who had lived here had prepared niches in the wall for coffins; but none of them had died during their brief stay and the vaults had never been used.

Father Largo had sat, watching blissfully, and after a time, when his eyes got used to the dark, he put out his light and sat quietly, breathing as softly as he could so he wouldn't wake the saint of his dreams.

It seemed to Father Largo that San Juan's snore had the roar of eternity to it. He would not wake the saint. He had waited too long for this apparition to do anything now that would drive San Juan away. The priest was certain that the saint had never been allowed to sleep so peacefully in his cell in Toledo. But then, with a great rustling of straw, the figure moved and Father Largo wondered if his stare had prodded the saint from his sleep.

The brittle straw crackled as the figure stirred, his hand rubbing his grizzled jaw as he drew himself up. He winced with pain and when he turned his face to the light the priest saw the bruises and discolorations on his unexpectedly youthful face.

He opened his eyes, suddenly drawing back in alarm as he saw the priest. But then he smiled quickly. "You startled me. I couldn't think for a minute where I was."

The old priest gasped, muttering to himself. These saints! God denies them nothing. They need not even crack a book and in an instant they can speak any language as well as the greatest scholar.

San Juan de la Cruz, who probably never had need or occasion to speak English in his whole lifetime, now speaks it perfectly — at least a sentence or two.

"I'm Father Largo," the priest said. "You wouldn't know me. I'm only a humble priest — less than a priest, if you must know the truth. They will not even permit me to say my Mass." He studied his visitor's face expectantly. "My only consolation is that you have been denied your rights too, Mio Santo!"

"I've heard of you. Father Largo, you said — "

"Oh!" exclaimed the priest, marveling. It was good to be known where it mattered. He began to think how inspiring it would be if the other priests might have a chance to talk to this glorious saint. Perhaps that was his intention in appearing in such humble surroundings and in a torn and ragged cassock — not even the Carmelite color that he had earned with so much suffering — but black which they had forced him to wear at Toledo to shame him.

Father Largo came close, studying the saint's face. At least someone had been merciful enough to patch up his wounds.

"I am stupid, I know, but did you say you have heard of me?"

"Yeah," he replied, pointing upward with his thumb.

Father Largo gasped, then slowly he laughed with satisfaction. "Up there — Si? Well, perhaps they were expecting me. I came very close several times. I know it was you who was watching over me those times! *Fuera de broma!* They had it in for me, those Communists! Even the Holy Inquisition, which you have good reason to know was far from holy, had never devised such devilish tortures. Then I fell into the hands of those peculiar monks in Burma. They thought I didn't catch onto their insidious plot! They would ensnare me in heresy! If the Holy Office only knew how far they have strayed from orthodoxy. I did my best to reform their liturgy. But this is in the past. I forgive them, as I know you forgive those who persecuted you."

Father Largo would have sworn that the saint laughed as he spoke. "I think we should get one thing straight, Padre. I haven't the slightest idea what you're talking about."

"Oh, my!" said the priest in distress. "If you spoke that way to Padre Tostado I do not wonder that you got in trouble with the Church authorities. But you have been canonized, so I assume that the Holy See finally saw fit to put its seal of approval on your life. . . . Perhaps they ignored some of your comments."

Father Largo sighed, thankful that San Juan had not been

[76]

required to testify at his own canonical processing. The priest sat watching his visitor rapturously, tasting the tears of joy which ran down to his lips. He could hardly wait to hear San Juan speak in Polish to Bishop Dworjanski, Italian to Father superior, and perhaps even Gaelic to Father Columba.

The saint seemed in no hurry to move. If the priest weren't looking at him through a haze of awe he would have wondered about the amazement on the man's face as he began to comprehend the situation.

"You will at least forgive me, my dear blessed one, for disturbing your rest. It would be brash of me to think you came here to discuss the merits of your life with me, a miserable priest. But there is something you want to do — something I can help you with — "

"It should be the other way around. I'd like to help you while I'm here, Padre."

"Help me!" Father Largo cried. "It is I who should be at your service — after the terrible things you endured! Do you suffer much?" Then, before the man could speak, Father Largo came to him and looked closely at the bruises on his face, touching his fingers to the wounds. "We will care for you and have you in good shape for the convocation. How long is it? I have forgotten the date of your arrival at Almodovar."

"Almodovar?" the word came from the saint's lips like an invocation from the Litany. Father Largo drew his hands together in a gesture of enchantment. "Ah, Si! Almodovar! What pleasant memories it must hold for you! It was there that the shoes were put aside forever! You have no idea, Blessed Juan, how often I have traveled with you to Duruelo, Alcala, Avila, Medina, Toledo — "

"Holy Toledo!" Halidon exclaimed almost without thinking.

Father Largo drew back, his hand prayerfully joined and his face ecstatic, "Holy Toledo! Forgive me! I thought you would have only sorrowful memories of that place. But it was the scene of your glory — your suffering — your vision of the Virgin! Your

[77]

writing was done there — *La Flama de Amor Viva!* Yes, perhaps it is after all holy Toledo!"

The saint leaned back against the wall, quite wearied by the memory apparently. "I am wearying you," Father Largo said. "You look starved. I'll bring you food, and then I hope you will allow me to take you to Father superior for an audience. Or perhaps he should come to you. I wonder if *audience* is the proper word. But you must bear with me, Mio Santo. I am not too familiar with celestial protocol. One more thing I would like to know — if it is your pleasure to tell me — how long you will stay. I hope, too, that we can induce you to accept more dignified quarters."

"This is all right. I don't want to trouble anyone. I'd feel better about it if I could help out. Maybe I could wash dishes."

"Wash dishes!" cried Father Largo. "The hands that have written *Dark Night of the Soul!*"

Father Largo stood for a moment, smiling contentedly. This was his saint all right! The humility proved that. For a moment the priest thought that even he himself might volunteer to wash dishes one day. He smiled happily at his vision, quite reluctant to leave. Perhaps he would never see San Juan again once he left him. But he had a duty, one of the few they allowed him these days — and even for that he had to beg, to be allowed to carry the wine from the cellar to the sacristy. It was his part of the Mass, a very humble part which he pretended to himself was very important. Without the wine there could be no Mass.

He went to the row of shelves and selected a bottle, dusting it carefully. To Father Largo it was already sacred and he held it with veneration as he went up the steep steps.

He smiled secretly. It was still very early, too early for anyone to be about. Perhaps he would have time for a Mass before they came looking for him. If there was any day in his life when he should be allowed to celebrate Mass it was today.

Father Superior Massimo was hurrying down the stairs from

his room when he saw Father Largo emerge from the cellar. He let out his breath in relief. He was on time, after all. He had awakened at his usual hour, had said his morning prayers, and prepared to go to the hospital for his Mass. In the hall he noticed that Father Largo's door was ajar. A quick look into the room confirmed his fears.

Now, as he saw the Spaniard scurrying toward the sacristy, the bottle of wine under his arm, the superior followed, and found Father Largo making a search of the cabinets, undoubtedly looking for a chalice.

"Pax tecum, Padre Largo," the superior said.

The Spaniard whirled, in his alarm forgetting the usual response. Then he smiled secretly, his olive eyes bright. "Buenos dias, Father Superior. You are up early. I didn't expect you. I went to the cellar to get wine for Mass. The Fathers will be needing wine for Mass, I'm sure."

The Superior looked toward the glass doors of the cabinet where the wine was kept. The lock Father Dmitri had put there was still secure, the bottle inside more than half full. "There's plenty of wine for today, Father."

The Spaniard shrugged, "Well, tomorrow they will need more. Perhaps there was no need for me to get wine today. . . ."

Father Largo's eyes brightened with excitement as he came close to the superior. "I was compelled to go down to the cellar this morning — compelled — almost as though I knew he'd be there!"

"He?" repeated the superior, aware that he had done a bad job in trying to conceal his alarm.

"I talked to him," the Spaniard said. "You will be amazed, Father Superior! These artists are all wrong. He looks very little like the paintings we see. He is very thin — his face somewhat bearded — perhaps taller than we thought — but I cannot be sure."

Father Massimo tried to be calm. He was not sure yet who the priest imagined was in the cellar, but he himself was quite certain that it was the stranger he had admitted to the house last night. So that was where the man had disappeared to. It was a relief to know that he didn't have to spend the night outdoors.

"Is he young, Father Largo?" asked the superior cautiously. "Does he have a thin face and black hair?"

Father Largo nodded quickly. "Si, si! I marvel that you know! But when you hear him speak, then you will be convinced, as I am. But it puzzles me that he speaks this English. You'd think he would know that we could converse better in Spanish — but perhaps he wants to forget the past."

"Are you sure we're talking about the same man?"

"You don't believe me?" cried the Spaniard.

"Certainly I believe someone is there," said the superior. "I admitted him to the house when he came last night looking for refuge."

"You!" cried the Spaniard. "It was you who let him in!" Father Largo laughed secretively. "He didn't choose to reveal himself to you then. Come, I will show you." He grasped the superior's sleeve and led him toward the cellar stairs. They went down the steep flight and came to the crypt.

Suddenly Father Largo spread his arms, glancing tremulously into the corner where a rectangle of light fell upon the figure crouched on a bed of straw. The superior peered over his shoulder at the man in an old discarded cassock pulled on for warmth. Undoubtedly the straw was the packing that had come around the new statues. Father Dmitri should have burned it, but with his pack-rat instinct he probably expected to find some use for it, perhaps for a crèche at Christmas.

The superior relieved his anxiety with a sigh, and Father Largo smiled at him, then whispered, "I too was fearful that he might be gone. I imagine the great theologians would be astonished to learn that the saints require rest."

"Father," the superior said with annoyance, "don't you think you have carried this far enough?"

[80]

Father Largo raised flashing eyes to his superior. "You must be quiet! Blessed Juan is sleeping. Besides, you cannot blame me if God has determined to send San Juan de la Cruz to comfort us in our exile."

"Juan de la — oh, my goodness!"

"We are providentially honored to have San Juan de la Cruz as our guest. I think it is your place to see that he is treated befitting his rank."

The superior felt the blood surge to his head and he groped for the pillar for support. "St. John of the Cross!"

Father Largo smiled perceptively. "You're overcome, Padre. So would I be, except that I knew if I was ever visited by a saint, it would be San Juan."

Father Massimo looked at his watch. "I must get to my Mass." He hurried back toward the stairs.

The Spaniard followed, tugging at his superior's robe. "For me, Father, would you say a Mass of thanksgiving?"

The superior waited until he got back to the sacristy, where he stood waiting for Father Largo to catch up. "You are making things very difficult, Father. We all know of your devotion to the saint, but to believe that he should come here. This is the twentieth century."

"Time!" said Father Largo. "What is time to the saints? Do you think time is impassable? Faith is the important thing. Padre, neither you nor I could have seen him if we did not believe. You must let him know that you are pleased that he is here."

The superior went out to the hall and took up his coat from the bench. He wondered if he went peacefully to his Mass at the hospital he might find that Father Largo's obstinate determination that the stranger was St. John of the Cross might be forgotten.

Father Largo tugged at his sleeve again. He looked at the little Spaniard compassionately. He was sure that some day the priest would have a genuine vision of San Juan, but he was just as sure that it would have to wait for eternity.

"Father Superior, we have a great privilege! This is a good solid visitation! Did you hear him snore?"

The Father superior smiled. "We'll talk about it later, Padre. I want you to go to your room now while I'm out of the house."

The Spaniard shrugged. "OK, Padre. You're the boss." He went up the stairs and Father Massimo waited until he heard the door of the Spaniard's room close.

He left the house and as he walked toward the hospital he was afraid it would take an even greater miracle than the one Father Largo was now certain had befallen them to disabuse the Spaniard of the idea that he had been visited by St. John of the Cross.

That afternoon they said good-bye to Father Constant and watched him get into the Reverend Gillis' station wagon. The minister had volunteered to drive the missioner to the bus depot for the trip to Cohagansett, where he would become the curate of Father John J. Galvin.

As the little Lithuanian scrambled into the old car, placing the borrowed suitcase under his knees and holding the box with the two homing pigeons on his lap, he promised he would send them a letter soon via the pigeons.

Afterward Fathers Columba and Edmund crossed the "no-man's-land" to the Jewish cemetery to stroll and read their breviary. But the Englishman always went to the place a bit warily since he often ran into Rabbi Silver who had a way of clucking his tongue that made the priest feel he was wearing out the path. Certainly the rabbi could not believe that they were responsible for the depredations of nature that had toppled headstones and heaved open the doors of the vaults.

The rabbi stood at the top of the path now as the priests approached, his hands behind his back and his beard twitching ominously.

It was the beard that had fooled Fathers Georgio and Constant

[82]

the first time they had seen the rabbi, shortly after their arrival in Darrington, as they were pacing on the sidewalk early one morning before Mass. They stared at the approaching rabbi and then at their own beards. Thinking it was another exile arriving they ran toward him.

The rabbi had raised his hands in alarm, quaking in outrage as the priests came abreast of him.

"What do you want with me?" he cried.

"We've come to welcome you."

The rabbi drew away, anger in his watery eyes.

Father Constant nudged his companion and seized his beard as he pulled him down to whisper to him. Father Georgio gasped, "A thousand pardons, Rabbi. We thought you were a priest. They have been coming on occasion from the Communist countries — "

"I am an American citizen," said the rabbi. "I have every proof — "

"You will pardon me, Rabbi, but you don't look like an American."

"You are some kind of authority on this?" said the rabbi. He looked them over tranquilly for a moment, then he drew his hands behind his back and strolled away.

Now the usually intrepid Englishman held back, allowing Father Columba to go ahead to bear the brunt of the conversation with Rabbi Silver if there had to be one.

The Irishman laughed, slapping his companion on the arm. "We may as well face up to it. And perhaps we can find some common ground with him, as our commissario found with the Baptist preacher. After all, the rabbi is our closest kin — biblically speaking. Pius XI said that spiritually we are all Semites, if you remember."

"Don't mention the papacy," said the Englishman. "The Reverend Gillis said the rabbi has a blind spot as big as that billboard at the corner as far as the Vatican is concerned."

"Evidently he's had an unfortunate experience with a priest."

[83]

"Our bearded companions, you mean?" said Father Edmund.

"Even before that, I'd surmise. And from the way he's bearing down on us it evidently isn't only beards that annoy him."

"He'd be in a predicament if it was."

Rabbi Silver stood squarely in the path with the apparent purpose of cutting off their exit from the cemetery.

"Good day, Rabbi!" boomed Father Columba. "I'm glad I encountered you today. I've been meaning to get a new suit of clothes and I noticed in the directory that there is a tailor by the name of Silver on Central Avenue."

"Ah, yes! My brother!" The rabbi came close and put his hand on Father Columba's white soutane. "You want something white to go with this?"

The Irishman laughed. "No, I wear black underneath. As you might suspect — white outside, black inside."

Rabbi Silver laughed appreciatively as he groped in his vest pocket for one of his brother's cards. "Tell Solly I sent you. He will take good care of you. He has excellent material — the best!"

Father Columba thanked him as he and his companion edged past and hurried on toward the cloister. The Englishman turned after closing the gate, his voice breaking indignantly: "You compromised us out there! Black and white, indeed!"

"I spoke only for myself. It was plain for him to see that you are all black."

A few minutes later Father Massimo came out from his afternoon stint of hearing confessions in time to see his Irish brother crossing the street to conduct the 4 p.m. Benediction for the Sisters.

The superior went into the kitchen and had started to lift the pot of hot coffee from the stove when it was snatched from his hand by the burly commissario. "You go sit down," he ordered in the stern tones assumed in his area of command. "While you are superior here I wait on you. If our positions were reversed I would expect the same service. And — as you surely know — it could happen. I was a superior once."

Father Maximilian came scurrying into the kitchen and the big Croat sighed and poured another cup of coffee, meanwhile commenting that he already missed Father Constant, whom he feared was ill-prepared for the beach-resort atmosphere where men and women were usually driven a little mad by the pounding of the waves.

Father Massimo had been wondering all day what he would tell his fellow priests about the man in the crypt. They had all been so busy helping their Lithuanian brother get ready for his expedition to the seashore that they had missed the implications of Father Largo's comments about the encounter he had had in the basement with San Juan de la Cruz. The superior wondered if he might hope that the stranger would leave before another day dawned.

Quite abruptly Father Massimo realized that the old German was holding him with his one good eye and smiling secretively. But what it meant, he wasn't sure — perhaps only that he was able to tune out the Spaniard when he had rambled on at lunch about his vision — or perhaps it meant he had been to the crypt and had seen that the vision was something quite substantial.

The speculation ended abruptly at the indignant cries of Father Edmund coming from the corridor. They hurried out to the hall and found the outraged Englishman trying to disengage himself from the tenacious grip of Father Largo.

"I will not go to any musty cellar to see your wraith, my dear Padre! You may invoke all the Spanish invective at your command, but I refuse to be a party to this hagiological nonsense!"

The superior handed his coffee cup to the cook and drew the Spaniard away from the irate Englishman. The latter stood back indignantly.

The Spaniard was quickly calmed by the superior's soothing words and scampered upstairs to his studio, commenting that it was just as well that his English brother was an unbeliever.

[85]

Even skeptics were of some use, he said, if only to prove that they were in the minority.

They watched him go, the superior feeling an increasing sympathy for the priest who felt content with his unique vision. It would take more reasoning than the superior could muster to convince Father Largo that he had deceived himself.

The superior felt an inward thrust of conscience that he had allowed the Spaniard to think that he actually had a heavenly vision. His only satisfaction was that if such an event did occur St. John of the Cross could be in no better hands than Father Largo's. The Saint had suffered cruelly during his imprisonment and had the stripes to prove it. St. Teresa had been moved to remark that Juan would have fared better at the hands of the Moors.

Father Massimo was grateful that the other priests hadn't yet reached the point of investigating Father Largo's claim, but when it dawned on them that their Spanish brother was determined about it, even Father Edmund might want to have a look at the cause of Father Largo's ecstasies; and after that he would probe aloud, he would speculate, hazard possibilities, and presently he would arrive at a probability.

He would have to make good use of the reprieve granted him, the superior knew. There was little consolation in the thought that superiors before him had problems as onerous. Father Casimir, the second Father general of the Order centuries ago, had been given custody of a deposed antipope and had been forced to permit the wild old man to live out his life issuing bulls of excommunication against everyone connected with his plight, including Father Casimir himself.

Venerable Father Bruno had been a cause of strife and controversy during his lifetime. On his death the townspeople of Barth drove out his monks and left Father Bruno's corpse to decay in the collegiate church. But when they unlocked the church after a week they found the body uncorrupted, and when they cast it into the sea it returned again and again on the tide.

[86]

With the swords of the Graf's soldiers at their necks they repented, carried the corpse to the church for burial, and carried his cause to Rome, where, after two hundred years, he triumphed over the eccentricities of his life and was declared venerable.

Father Massimo smiled as he realized how Father Bruno might have felt waiting a month for burial and two hundred years for the title of venerable, and perhaps two hundred more before the pope would venture to count him infallibly among the saints.

The superior was thankful that his own worldly trials could not possibly be so prolonged. One of them might be terminated quite abruptly if he was firm enough.

With the decision made he hurried to the cellar, and when he looked through the grille the man was standing at the window looking out through the bars as though he were quite at home viewing the world through bars.

The door ground rustily and Halidon turned as Father Massimo entered.

"Oh," he said, a quick smile of relief on his unshaven face, "it's you."

"Sit down," Father Massimo said quietly, "I think we should talk."

The man grinned. "It will be a pleasure to talk sensibly for a change, Father."

"I still know nothing about you — not even your name."

"Steve —" he said, "Steve Halidon."

"And you are a gypsy?"

"You said gypsy. I said hobo."

"I suppose you had no choice — living this kind of life?" Father Massimo asked.

Halidon shrugged. "Are you going to tell me it isn't normal?"

Father Massimo smiled faintly. "There is no normal — Mr. Halidon? — yes. A priest learns this — often with much praise to God. He has created an infinite variety of persons — each different — each puzzling sometimes."

"And it makes a priest's work that much harder — puzzling out these individuals."

"We expect a man to be truthful — particularly in the confessional. If he is not, then it is quite hopeless."

"Count me among your hopeless cases then, Father. I haven't been to confession for years."

"You are of the Faith then? That relieves my mind."

There was a sardonic smile on Halidon's face. "You think there's hope for me — is that it?"

Father Massimo shook his head, "My thoughts were selfish. I was thinking of ourselves — the priests here — the oratory — the sacred mysteries we guard from profanation."

Halidon smiled slowly, his big hand rubbing his grizzled jaw. "If you were worried about all these things last night — when you let me in — you must have had a nervous night, Father. I'm sorry."

"I slept little last night, I assure you. But I am used to sleeping with one ear cocked. As you perhaps have observed, Father Largo is — irrational. Turbulent nightmares disturb his sleep and the sleep of everyone else. But the quiet nights are often as alarming. When one does not hear, one imagines. At times his nocturnal visits to the oratory are harmless — but sometimes he attempts a Mass."

"He told me that — and quite a lot about his Saint. I wasn't asleep when you came down with him early this morning." There was a quick look of embarrassment on Halidon's face. "I can see you're in the habit of humoring him."

Father Massimo smiled. "You, too, humored him. It was kind of you. But I'm not sure it is the merciful thing to do — for either of us."

"He's going to trap me in one of these sessions. I know very little about saints."

"You will learn about this one." Father Massimo laughed. The priest was silent for a time wondering how he could induce the man that it would be best to leave. But there was something

[88]

Halidon had said that intrigued him and aroused his compassion, and in spite of his better judgment he felt the impulse to probe further. God's ways were invariably inscrutable. If the providential hand were at work here, the superior knew he would be rash in trying to foil it.

Perhaps with the help of Father Largo some of the eternally sensible spirit of St. John of the Cross would rub off on this man. His kindness in humoring Father Largo revealed that he was not insensitive. Perhaps the conscience was beginning to prick a bit already.

Halidon stood under the window, his hands thrust deep into his pockets, his face thoughtful. It was a face, the priest thought, full of the wisdom and the discontent of the world.

Without turning, Halidon said: "I'm sorry I forced myself on you last night, Father. It didn't occur to me then that you might not be allowed — by the rules of your Order — to have a lay person in your monastery."

"There is nothing wrong with having a lay person — male — in the house, but at the moment I'm concerned about our own position as guests in this country, and in this diocese. If you could give me your assurance that you have no evil intent — "

Halidon laughed abruptly. "Good Lord, Father Massimo, do you think I'd desecrate the altar — or rob you — or murder one of you?"

"I must think of every possibility," Father Massimo said, "and those were among them. But now that you have mentioned them they seem quite absurd."

"Thank you, Father."

The priest turned to the grille door. "If you are to be a guest I suppose I must treat you as one. I'll bring you a cot and blankets — but coffee and something to eat first."

Halidon glanced ruefully at the priest. "I'd like to shave, Father — and use your facilities."

"Facilities?"

"Head — toilet — "

"Oh — it never occurred to me. There are 'facilities' at the front of the cellar. As for shaving, I think you had better clear that with Father Largo."

"Is the charade part of the deal?"

Father Massimo smiled sardonically. "The transition from sinner to saint becomes you — and the beard seems to be part of it."

CHAPTER FOUR

FATHER MASSIMO had finished his Mass in the hospital chapel the next morning, and as he unvested he wondered about the meaning of Dr. Lambert's pacing in the hall outside the room. The young intern was usually much too busy to wait, even impatiently, for anyone.

The chaplain folded his vestments and put them away, then knelt for a few moments in a brief thanksgiving, made so by the impatient glances Dr. Lambert was giving him. He came out, hoping his smile was placating enough.

"I've been meaning to ask you, Father," the intern said. "The police were annoyed with us the night before last, the night of the accident. You remember the fellow with the gash on his forehead? — the poorly dressed fellow? They said we shouldn't have discharged him without their OK. Actually we didn't. He just walked out."

"I remember him — yes. Is he wanted for something?"

"Apparently. He witnessed the accident and both drivers want him to testify. The emergency ward secretary said she saw this fellow talking to you."

Father Massimo nodded. "He talked to me. He had no place to go and asked if we could put him up at the monastery."

"And you did?" Andy exclaimed.

Father Massimo nodded. "I had no alternative. And now he seems to be pretty well entrenched."

"He's still at the monastery?" Andy asked with some annoyance in his voice. "But you know nothing about him!"

The priest looked at the intern placidly. "He's all right. I talked to him. He means us no harm."

"But the police should know he's there."

Father Massimo smiled. "I'm not sure that I understand. The young man who is our guest tells me that he is the innocent victim in the accident."

Andy smiled. "Both drivers are men of some prominence. If they weren't I don't think the police would be interested."

Father Massimo smiled wanly. "I'm uncomfortably aware of the importance of one of them — Wadleigh Thorne. He appeared satisfied when Father Georgio made a deposition that he had forced some brandy down the man's throat."

Andy laughed. "I heard he was furious when he was arrested for drunken driving."

"From what the police told Father Georgio when he was at headquarters, Mr. Thorne has a record for careless driving. Apparently his social position has protected him so far."

They reached the door and Father Massimo paused to adjust his biretta.

"Have you time for a cup of coffee with me, Father?"

The priest glanced at his watch. "I promised our guest I'd bring him breakfast — and I was also wondering, Doctor, if you would come and look at his injury."

Andy Lambert nodded, a puzzled look on his face. "You said you would bring him breakfast? Is he ill?"

Father Massimo smiled ruefully. "Perhaps I will have coffee with you, Doctor. There are some things you will be interested to hear — about our guest at the monastery and about Father Largo."

When he returned to the monastery Father Massimo went in through the front entrance from the street to the oratory. It was crowded with worshipers as it had been the past two days since the relic of Venerable Bruno had been carried from St. Mary's Cathedral.

Father Maximilian was at the altar and had reached the Consecration of the Mass. The superior knelt in a rear pew, watching attentively as the German priest focused his huge reading glass on the page of the missal then bent low over the altar as he enacted the dual Consecration, first the bread, then the wine — symbolic of the two natures of Christ, and symbolic too of the historic fusion of these natures in the earth-rending wonder of the Redemption.

Father Massimo raised his eyes, wondering if even now he comprehended the veiled Divinity. It was pride that made him think that he might even begin to unravel what God meant to be unfathomable.

Faith must suffice.

But there were other things that would take something more than faith to accept. The man in the crypt, for example.

Father Massimo got up quickly, genuflected, and hurried through the passage to the house. When he came to the kitchen he found coffee prepared, and in a few minutes he had a tray ready and carried it to the basement.

Halidon, resting comfortably on the cot, his back supporting a pillow against the concrete wall, raised his eyes expectantly as Father Massimo entered the crypt.

"Buon giorno, Padre!" he said pleasantly.

The superior smiled in spite of his annoyance. "Good morning, Mr. Halidon." He put down the tray on the box. "I prefer to converse in English."

Halidon pushed forward on the cot, sniffing at the coffee and hot rolls. "And plain English, probably," he said with a grin.

"Where were you this morning? I came down quite early — four o'clock. You weren't here. When I was ready to leave for the hospital at five-thirty you were back again and sound asleep."

"I'm sorry if I disturbed you, Father."

The superior rubbed his chin reflectively, thinking how easy it would be for Halidon to slip out, leaving the back door latch

[93]

off so he could return at his convenience. "I want to help you — if you'll allow me to. I've been thinking much about you since you've been here. I had the thought that I might speak to some businessmen I know about giving you a job."

Halidon had begun to eat. He shrugged, his mouth full, then asked quickly. "What sort of job?"

"I'm not sure. What can you do?"

"I'm not prepared for any kind of work."

The superior sighed. "If you don't find employment the devil will find some for you. Perhaps he has already. One of the men involved in the accident blames you. He has made the claim that you can vindicate him."

Halidon laughed briefly. "If I vindicated anyone it would be myself."

"Let me be honest with you, Mr. Halidon. I am letting you remain here because you gave me no choice."

"Do the police know I'm here?"

"From what Dr. Lambert tells me the police aren't too much concerned, but perhaps pressure will be put on them by this man — the driver — to find you. You have no idea, Mr. Halidon, how long — if imperfectly — I have searched my conscience. It is wrong perhaps to permit Father Largo to believe he is experiencing a rather prolonged vision. Yet, if I put you out now you will most certainly return to the nomad life."

"I had no idea you were taking this so seriously," Halidon said.

Father Massimo smiled faintly. "I must take it seriously. I'm sure when His Excellency learns that I have encouraged Father Largo in his fantasies, I will have much explaining to do — many excuses to make to my conscience, to the bishop, and to my Father general. I will truly have no excuse, only that of a momentary weakness that made this *vision* possible. Perhaps eventually I will look quite the fool and my only defense will be that I'm a poor foreigner — a priest too long sheltered in my library to realize the duplicity in the world." Father Massimo shrugged unhappily. "You see, Mr. Halidon, I'm searching for excuses because I can find no justification for giving you shelter. My only excuse is weakness."

"Is it wrong to be merciful, Father?"

The priest looked at his guest for a moment. "That is the only thing about this situation that has given me any content. But I find that my better judgment rebels against it. I have motives that are not altogether unselfish. Like the other priests here I had hoped for a period of peace."

"I'm sorry, Father. I guess I thought that priests are always perfectly content and at peace."

"It's impossible to be content when we see there is so much to be done and so little indication from men that they want God's work perfected."

Halidon laughed hollowly. "Everyone has his own idea of perfection. I'm sure you wouldn't care for mine. But my hopes are practical, Padre, where you want only the unattainable."

Father Massimo nodded, uncomfortable under Halidon's amused scrutiny. Eternal life was an improbable prospect when viewed from a merely material standpoint.

"Do you think it's an unreasonable desire that God has placed in us?" the priest asked.

Halidon shook his head impatiently. "It makes my own impractical dreams seem very reasonable." He put down his empty coffee cup, took out a cigarette and lighted it slowly, then stood up and stretched. "I have the impression that you've been preaching to me, Father Massimo."

There was a remote smile on the superior's face. "As every priest since the morning of Christ I have sown much seed on barren ground."

"Are you sore at me, Padre?"

Father Massimo moved to the door of the crypt. "Angry, you mean? No. I would be disturbed if you reacted favorably — because I'd be sure it was a pretense." He went to the door, then turned.

"I'll bring you some books to read. Under the circumstances the *Ascent of Mount Carmel* by John of the Cross might be appropriate."

"Father Largo gave me the book," Halidon said.

The superior smiled ironically. "It will do you no harm to read about this saint. You will surely be amused to see that he was a wanderer, much like yourself, and something of a trouble-maker for the established order."

Father Massimo was emerging from the cellar a few minutes later with the tray and had turned from closing the door when he heard a chortle of dismay from the cook.

"Father Superior! What is this you are doing?"

He handed the tray to the commissario, trying to be as calm as possible as he spoke. "The saint must be fed."

It was apparent from the apoplectic flush on the big Croat's face that he had so far taken Father Largo's claim of a vision rather lightly.

"Is this poor Father Largo's idea?" gasped Father Georgio.

"No. It's my idea," the superior said calmly. "I'm sure he wouldn't think of anything so practical."

Leaving Father Georgio holding the tray, the superior went upstairs to his room to put away his coat and when he returned he found Father Columba standing with his hands on his haunches eyeing the superior with his best medical look.

"I think you should let me take your temperature, Father."

The superior laughed and conducted Father Columba ahead of him into his office. "There is nothing to be alarmed about. The man in the crypt is very real. He is — without a home — at the moment. I agreed to allow him to stay with us for a while. I brought him a cot and blankets — so he will be quite comfortable."

"We could give him a room — "

"Yes, we could. We could have before Father Largo settled on his idea that saints are determined to be uncomfortable."

[96]

Father Columba was still eyeing his superior warily when they heard a clatter of beads and Father Maximilian appeared at the door.

"A gentleman. He wants to speak to you. I directed him to the library."

Father Massimo thanked the Father porter and hurried to the library. The visitor turned from his browsing at the large table. He was a young man with short-cropped red hair. His smile was engaging and a little secretive.

"I'm Kevin Byrne — and I assume you're Father Massimo?"

The priest nodded and indicated a chair. "Please. I rarely have visitors so early — "

"I know." Byrne smiled. "I hope I'm not upsetting your routine. It was an impulse — actually. I'd heard that the Fathers here were of various nationalities and I thought it would be just the thing for my purpose."

Father Massimo smiled, wondering a bit as he took off his biretta and placed it on his table. "What would your purpose be, Mr. Byrne?"

"I'm going abroad this fall — and suddenly I realize I have very little knowledge of the languages."

"And you would like to acquire some?"

"Yes — I'd be glad to pay for a period of instruction. I thought if I had some French, German, and Italian — "

"Quite an order!" The superior laughed. "But we may be able to accommodate you. Possibly I could take on the task myself — "

"That would be wonderful! When can we start?"

Father Massimo studied the young man's face. It was open, bland, and at the moment reflected pleasure at the ease with which its owner had accomplished his mission.

"Would tomorrow do? Perhaps in the afternoon?"

"Fine — yes."

Father Massimo stood with a reflective look on his face. "Have you any background, Mr. Byrne?"

The red head's eyes were startled, but then he smiled quickly.

[97]

"Oh, you mean in foreign languages. I've forgotten almost everything I ever learned."

The superior walked toward the door. "I'll do what I can. Perhaps you should leave your address — in case I cannot keep these appointments."

Kevin Byrne nodded. "I'm staying at the Essex Hotel."

He shook hands with the superior and went out through the passage to the chapel. Watching him go, Father Massimo wondered if he hadn't too readily accepted this stranger as a student. But he was curious to discover just what the young man was up to.

Kevin Byrne found his exit blocked by the people leaving from Mass. He waited until the line had nearly passed and had dipped his fingers in the holy-water font when he became aware of a slim white hand beside his own.

The hand drew away quickly and was raised to a young woman's beautiful oval face. It was only for a moment that her smoky eyes met his, then she moved ahead of him to the long flight of steps. Byrne came beside her, smiling as she glanced questioningly at him.

"Are there always so many people?" he asked.

"No — not always."

They were on the sidewalk now and the girl said, "It was nice meeting you; but I've got to get to work."

"You must think I'm some kind of nut speaking to you without being introduced," Byrne said.

She smiled then. "There's no reason why we should be introduced."

"No — I guess not."

"Do you come every morning to Mass?" he asked.

She turned her head, smiling. "I do, yes. But I'm sure you don't."

He thrust his hands into his pockets. "I'm a stranger in Darrington — but maybe I'll get the habit."

He heard her mumbled good-bye as she hurried toward the intersection. "I'll see you," he said.

The conversation between Byrne and Julie Nealy puzzled Father Massimo. It was impossible to surmise the subject of their brief chat but it seemed apparent after a few moments that the red-headed young man was more interested in Julie than in questioning her about the monastery.

The superior wondered if the presumably chance meeting with Julie was the sole purpose of Byrne's visit to the monastery. As Father Massimo turned away from the window he felt that such an explanation would be much too simple.

After he had his breakfast Father Massimo went to the oratory to hear confessions, thankful for the occupation. It provided a reprieve he surely needed from trying to probe into the missions of the unexpected visitors — the man in the crypt and now the youthful redhead.

Father Georgio was unhappy about Father Largo's vision. All the while he was getting lunch he could think of nothing but how he would get the man out of the cellar before the poor Spaniard discovered he had been deceived.

Everyone knew that St. John of the Cross was a tiny man, and that he had been timid and submissive. On at least one occasion the Lord had to take a hand to see that John got established. When the archbishop of Granada refused to allow John to establish a convent in that city, lightning struck his house, knocked the archbishop out of bed, and set his library on fire. The archbishop, who apparently could take a divine hint, readily agreed to allow the saint to have his way.

Father Georgio, of course, knew that he had no thunderbolts at his command, but there ought to be a way to get this rather enlarged and improbable vision of St. John out of the house before disillusionment set in.

Perhaps Father Dmitri would have some idea how it could

be accomplished, the Croat thought. He gave his stew another stir and hurried out to the corridor. A quick glance into the library assured him that Father Dmitri was still there trying to find something in the encyclopedia. He came into the room and closed the door.

Father Dmitri closed his book. "Lunch is ready?"

The big Croat laughed. "Not yet. I've been too busy thinking. We've got to help Largo."

"He needs no help from us!" said Dmitri. "Adventurous as I am, I'm a little afraid of going down to the basement. What if he actually did see something down there? It has made me wonder if I am not too worldly for a priest. If I ever had a vision I would fall dead from fright."

"No," said Father Georgio, "I think you would be too interested in the mechanics of it." The Croat had seen a good many examples of the Moravian's mechanical genius since he came to the monastery.

"I think it is up to you and me, Father Dmitri, to get this man out of the house," Father Georgio said.

"Man? He is real then?"

"Yes — thank God! I ventured to the crypt an hour ago. I talked to him — poked a finger in his stomach and gave him some pickles to eat."

Father Dmitri laughed heartily. "It's a good thing for you it was not the real Spaniard!"

At dinner that night Father Massimo was pleased to see that the other exiles had settled down either to enjoy or ignore the visitation of St. John of the Cross. Only Father Georgio had spoken of being down to the crypt and had explained that he had ventured down to make sure that Father Largo hadn't forced any primitive penances on the visitor.

The suggestion of the commissario that San Juan be invited to the refectory for dinner was greeted by a scowl from Father Largo. He thought it was a remark without feeling or sensibility.

"Would you remind him of his tortures? Don't you know it was in the refectory of the Toledo priory that he sat on the floor for his bread and water. And it was there that the friars scourged him."

The Spaniard's look, and his angry words, alarmed Father Georgio and he said no more. As they left the refectory Father Largo came to the superior, a pleased look on his face.

"Do you think it is good theology to say that the saints get soft in heaven, Father Superior?"

Father Massimo was sure most of them had earned it, but he hadn't heard any authoritative comments one way or the other. "You evidently have an opinion, Father."

Father Largo smiled. "I have evidence. But I'm making a good Carmelite out of him once more. This afternoon I was very insistent that he leave off his shoes. I saw that he wondered why I didn't do the same until I explained that our Venerable Founder, Father Bruno, never prescribed it. He did as I suggested without complaint. I'm sure he feels more at home. And he will be even more pleased when he lies down tonight. I put some boards under his mattress. I thought I might even try it myself. We're living too comfortably here."

Father Massimo smiled placatingly. "It's good to be comfortable for a change."

"San Juan doesn't like it," said Father Largo crossly. "Don't you think that's why he chooses to stay in our cellar? He disapproves of our soft living. And while I'm speaking on the subject, I hope you will remind Father Georgio that San Juan is my guest. Who has been his devoted client for more than forty years? Yours truly! You bet your life!

"He told me what Father Georgio sneaked him down for dinner. Why, I don't think that even in Paradise they have such portions! Father Georgio should remember that San Juan doesn't want to be pampered. From now on I bring all the meals to him. I don't know how much longer he will stand to be scandalized by our worldly lives."

CHAPTER FIVE

FRANCIS HICKEY was up at his usual early hour Saturday, surprising one of the housekeepers, Sister Eulalia, with a request for coffee and a roll. He explained to her that he wouldn't be celebrating Mass until 10:00 when he would drive out to Lancet to officiate at the dedication of St. Bernard's. Father Andrew Sweeney, the pastor, had selected the day, June 11, since it was the feast of St. Barnabas, who he thought was a much-neglected Apostle — having brought St. Paul to Antioch where they spent a year and probably was the first man to use the word "Christian."

On the drive to Lancet the bishop glanced through some of the mail his secretary had brought along for his attention while Father Redmond kept his eyes on the road.

As usual the bulkiest letter was from Bishop Bryan McAuley, who wrote: "I have a great favor to ask of you, Francis, and I'm sure you will comply with it in good grace. As you know Oliver Newman is to arrive in your see city Saturday (and perhaps by the time you read this you will have already met him). Now that he is so widely known in this country for his good works — his tireless activity for souls — I find myself taking much too much credit for his conversion and I have to remind myself that I was no more than the poor instrument of God's grace.

"His current project will be a book on the exiled priests to whom you have been kind enough to give shelter. I assume that his main interest is in Stefan Dworjanski, but I understand the other priests have suffered some discomfort as well and, as Oliver Newman said to me, it is his desire to get it all down on paper — every drop of blood, every tear — as he phrased it."

Francis Hickey squirmed uncomfortably. When McAuley first began writing about Newman the bishop hoped he would never have to face the issue of the convert squarely. Until recent months his uneasy feeling about Newman was based on nothing more than vague distaste for this loudly militant layman who traveled up and down the country, lecturing, autographing his books, getting himself photographed with governors and cardinals, speaking to Catholic groups, even posing with his hands clasped at the Communion rail. His piety could not be doubted. He was, surely, a good though thoroughly professional Catholic. The happiest possible thought one could have on the matter was that the publicity hunger would wear off and he would settle down to being innocuous, as they had every right to expect.

What troubled Hickey most about Newman was his ruthlessness in telling on his friends when he confessed his Red ties. National columnists, notedly cynical, said that Newman had actually told the Congressional investigating committee no more than was already known by the FBI. At best he had confirmed only a few details that had long been suspected.

Deportations and prison terms followed the Newman revelations. It was known that several men returned to certain death in the Soviet Union.

The bishop's eyes returned to the letter and he sighed at the sight of Nicholas Shannon's name.

"Archbishop Shannon was my guest here in Utica last week for our spring conference (the Ecumenical Council's Liturgy Commission, you remember), and when he heard that Newman was to give a lecture in Darrington he said he hoped you'd have an opportunity to call on Newman and talk with him as everyone owes it to himself to observe that man's piety and conviction. . . ."

[103]

It appeared to be a remark without guile, and (out of context) Hickey might have taken it that way except that it was too much like Shannon. The Concord prelate was better known for other things than tact and had once remarked, when asked to pose for the photographers with the visiting Anglican bishop of Bath and Wells (who wore the traditional gaiters), that he would do so gladly if the good man would go back to his hotel and put on some trousers.

"Candidly, Francis," continued McAuley, "I have been trying for a rapprochement between you and Shannon. This estrangement distresses me. . . ."

Bryan McAuley had a long, colorful, and rather curious career in the Church. He had come from a celebrated Southern literary family and, with ample funds at his command, had studied for the priesthood in Rome, had been snatched up as a brilliant linguist for the staff of the Congregation of the Council by the English Benedictine, Cardinal Mortram. For more than a decade McAuley was the cardinal's secretary, friend, and protégé, but quite abruptly (in 1931) Mortram died and McAuley was sent home.

His career as a palatine prelate thus ended (without explanation as far as Hickey had ever heard), McAuley became the authority on Roman questions and a national figure as a spokesman for the Faith and suddenly (much to his annoyance) was named bishop of Utica.

Bryan McAuley had moderated the conversion of Oliver Newman, who had come down the labyrinthine road to Utica and found McAuley sympathetic; and the bishop had assured him that he would find equal sympathy in the public heart. His confession before the Congressional committee brought smiles to the senatorial faces; but sometimes Francis Hickey had the uneasy feeling that the absolution had been self-administered, most of all.

When Hickey thought of Newman he thought too of Mark Curtain (ambitious, undoubtedly, but his patriotism never doubted, only his methods) who had exposed so many other national enemies and was himself exposed by Newman. The country was shocked, and some were saddened by Curtain's suicide.

Newman wrote an eloquent obituary for Mark Curtain, making it clear that he had pitied him and had hoped Curtain would have the moral courage to repent and throw himself on the mercy of the Congressional committee.

Yet there were moments when Hickey thought he was too harsh in his judgment. If one doubted the sincerity of a man's repentance what was there left to believe in? Some things had to be accepted on faith alone. God was one and evidently Oliver Newman was another. Hickey had battled with the idea that McAuley was a learned and perceptive man. It was inconceivable that Newman could have deceived him — but his own vanity could have deceived him. He had thought of nothing but that Newman had been converted and had never wondered why, had never marveled at the prosperity Newman had reaped, the many copies of repentant books sold.

Francis Hickey sighed. This was the man he was expected to welcome. Still dismayed, the bishop set aside the letter, thankful that it didn't appear to require an answer.

The dedication of St. Bernard's Church was undoubtedly a success. It was a beautiful day for the outdoor part of the ceremony and a great crowd had gathered to watch the display of vestments and colorful robes and the dashing uniforms of the parish societies, which Monsignor Darcy McDonough, the vicar-general, described as too much "fuss and feathers."

Hickey remembered little of the ceremony. His mind was too filled with disturbing thoughts about Oliver Newman, thoughts that still preoccupied him when he got back to his desk in the afternoon. He fingered through the mail, hoping to find some distraction; and it was almost with pleasure that he came upon a letter from Father John J. Galvin, pastor of St. Smaragdus at Cohagansett who had asked for a curate with a strong back and a pliable disposition and got poor little Father Constant.

Father Galvin, in spite of his infirmities, was a capable and devout pastor and held a particular place in the bishop's heart as the last native-born Irish priest among the diocesan clergy. As a young priest almost forty years ago (fresh out of the seminary and still as hard as anthracite from his work in the Scranton coal mines) he had joined in the building of his church at the resort, scampering up the ladder with a hod of bricks on his back much to the consternation of old Bishop Foley, who frequently stopped by to watch the work.

Bishop Hickey wondered at times if the priest's apparent kowtowing to the socially conscious Doolans was not a tongue-in-cheek masquerade; for he certainly took no particular joy in looking forward to the "tea and tedium season."

"Your Excellency," wrote the Cohagansett pastor, "it is high time, I suppose, that I write to thank you for the curate, such as he is. My sister Clara has nearly recovered from the shock of realizing we would have a foreigner with a beard in the house. I think you should have warned me that his English is far from elegant and he has the most disconcerting habit of tiptoeing about as though he was afraid he'd scratch the layers of varnish, which a blowtorch couldn't remove.

"Incidentally, he started off on the wrong foot with me by playing the bearded medico. When I told him he'd have to do most of the legwork he insisted on looking at my feet and brazenly informed me that I have gout. Then, just this afternoon, he gave me the fright of my life when he came dashing downstairs shouting at me to get my pistol. 'There's a rattler in my room,' he cried, 'nesting on my bed.' Well, Bishop, all I could think of was the two-bit carnival that had happened this way a week ago. I have no pistol or any other firearms, but I seized my cane and dashed up the stairs (my arthritis notwithstanding). When I threw back the coverlet there was the vacuum-cleaner hose which Clara had left behind. Bishop, your poor Lithuanian had never seen a vacuum-cleaner hose!"

"Perhaps not in bed anyway." The bishop chuckled aloud.

Father Galvin boomed a good deal but he had a kindly heart and would probably end up leaving his old 1932 Lincoln to the frightened curate. The bishop was determined to be realistic about the exiled priests, to absorb them into the diocese, Americanize them, and help them forget their unhappy experiences. His plans had been delayed for more than a year by the venerable processes of the federal government. Although they were not aware of it, the exiled priests had been thoroughly scrutinized by a number of interested bureaus of the government and had, as far as Hickey knew, been cleared.

As he concluded the letter, Hickey was a little surprised that Father Galvin made no mention of Cardinal Gasquet. There was a typical comment about the hazards of resort life "the tourists with their tomato-colored convertibles and hideously blackened torsos," and he concluded with the comment that he would be able to endure it in spite of his arthritis, "not gout, which I understand is the product of overindulgence, intemperance, and sundry dissolute habits."

A brief knock on the door preceded the appearance of Paul Redmond's impish, freckled face. "Mr. Doolan is on his way. I thought I'd warn you. I just saw him trying to park his Sherman tank." It was the secretary's way of describing Doolan's custom-built Cadillac.

A few minutes later Doolan popped his head around the partially opened door. "Cheerio, Bishop! Busy?"

It wasn't one of Francis Hickey's favorite greetings but he acknowledged it temperately while he tried desperately to think how he could shorten this visit.

Doolan bounced forward, genuflecting and making a pass at the bishop's ring.

"I thought you were much too busy with the wedding plans to think of visiting."

"Daisy's taking care of that, thank goodness!" Dalton said

as he took a chair near the desk and sat down, leaning forward and rifling the papers on the desk with his elbow. "I suppose you've been apprised, Your Excellency?"

"Of what?" Hickey asked apprehensively. Doolan considered it his prerogative as a prominent layman to drop in on the bishop from time to time for a tête-à-tête.

"We found out all about the mysterious cardinal."

"Oh," said the bishop warily.

"Yes, he's an Italian. He's been getting letters from Rome. Mr. Dawson, the postmaster, tells me the chauffeur picks up his mail at the post office. His name is Sanodo!"

"You have it only partly right, Dalton. San Odo is probably the name of his titular church. The man himself is Cardinal Gasquet. He's a Canadian but a member of the Curia, secretary of the Congregation for the Fabric of the Archbasilica."

"How should I address him?" said Doolan blandly.

Bishop Hickey smiled. "Your Eminence, will probably do."

"Does he speak English?"

"I wouldn't know that. Do you plan to call on him?"

"I thought I might — "

"I'd wait until he seeks you out if I were you."

"Is that proper?"

"Apparently he wants privacy. He hasn't chosen to let me know he's in the diocese, and of course I have no control over dignitaries who wish to vacation here."

Doolan looked crushed, but then suddenly his face lit up. "We decided to ask Oliver Newman to be our guest at Cohagansett while he's here. That's partly why I'm in town. He wired this morning that he'd arrive on the 2 p.m. plane. He asked if I'd meet him at your office."

It was presumptuous of Newman to assume the bishop's office was available as a convenient meeting place, Hickey thought.

"I'm surprised that you'd entertain an ex-Communist," Hickey said with amusement.

Doolan gasped, "You make it sound like a dirty word, Bishop.

It's like calling a convert to the Faith an ex-pagan or ex-Protestant."

Bishop Hickey reset his scarlet skullcap with an amused grimace. He felt a bit sorry for Doolan. He didn't mean to tease him but it was too much of a temptation at times.

"I'm sure he won't mind being called an ex-Communist. He's made his sins a matter of public record. My concern is that he wants this to appear as some sort of official visit. Actually the man has no official capacity, civil or ecclesiastical, of which I am aware."

Doolan fidgeted nervously. "I hope I've done right in asking him to be my guest."

The bishop smiled blandly. "I hope so, too."

Father Redmond opened the door and announced that Oliver Newman had arrived. The man strode into the room, his quick eyes flashing around. It was a look that Bishop Hickey hadn't seen since seminary days when his prefect had made a surprise raid to his room and caught him gorging himself with a box of Crackerjack.

He was tall, his hair was thin, his gaunt intellectual face much too full of zeal. He wore a black suit and a string of black necktie.

A faint smile crossed Newman's face as he came quickly to the bishop, genuflecting as he kissed the ring firmly. Hickey drew the reluctant convert to his feet.

"I'd feel much better about it, Mr. Newman, if we simply shook hands. After all, I'm only flesh and blood."

"I've heard so much about you from Bishop McAuley."

"Not too much, I hope," Hickey said. "This is Mr. Doolan — J. Dalton Doolan. I understand you've been corresponding?"

The two shook hands and, as their eyes met, the bishop could see the look of dislike in Newman's face. It was a disappointment, but logical. Doolan represented everything Newman hated — or was it things that he had once hated? Now, of course, there should be no hatred at all in his heart.

Newman turned to Bishop Hickey. "I'm a perfect stranger here. I'm afraid I'll have to depend on you for everything."

"Oh," said the bishop, "I understood your lecture bureau had arranged *everything*."

Newman laughed. "That is rather incidental to my actual purpose, as you know."

"So Bishop McAuley informed me."

"Bishop McAuley is very kind, particularly with someone such as I . . ."

The bishop sat back, listening only vaguely as Doolan outlined his plans for entertaining Newman. The look of distaste on Newman's face was missed by the contractor, who blueprinted every move to the point of tedium.

"We still have no idea of your itinerary, Mr. Newman, other than the scheduled lecture," the bishop said.

"I thought Bishop McAuley informed you. I have a suite at the Essex, and will visit a few days later with Mr. Doolan. I plan to spend some time here interviewing the foreign priests — for my forthcoming book, you know."

"You include Bishop Stefan Dworjanski?"

"I think it would defeat my purpose if I couldn't obtain material from His Excellency."

Bishop Hickey smiled distantly, "You know the bishop? But then, you were in Europe about the same time the bishop was tried and imprisoned, if I'm not mistaken."

Newman's face was impassive, "Approximately the same time, I understand."

Francis Hickey looked at Newman searchingly. What had he hoped to discover? He had no idea. Most persons able to read would know of the mock trial before the Red puppet court, the outrageous charges brought against Stefan Dworjanski, his disappearance into the Soviet mesh of concealment, then suddenly his reappearance in Bratislava, his hairsbreath escape into the French consulate, and his eventual escape to Vienna and Rome.

Newman probably thought of this spectacular adventure as the climactic point of his book — and certainly Stefan Dworjanski would include it in his memoirs.

"My best advice to you, Mr. Newman, is to go to the monastery and let them know your plan. I'm sure your interest is something other than financial — and perhaps if you worked out some arrangement with them — "

Newman nodded, with a slight show of reluctance. "A fine idea, Your Excellency. I'm sorry I didn't think of it myself. I'll assign all royalties to the Order."

Bishop Hickey got up, a sign that he considered the interview ended. "Fine. I'm sure that under those conditions something can be worked out with the bishop and the good Fathers."

Newman took his hat. "I'll be looking forward to seeing you at the lecture, Bishop. Although I don't care for the term 'lecture.' My little talks are simple accounts of the journey of a man into the depths and out of the depths."

Bishop Hickey's expression was impassive.

They left, with Newman making a farewell genuflection that made the bishop distinctly uncomfortable.

Newman's parting shot had been to the effect that he would be seeing more of the bishop, but as he turned from the door Hickey thought, "It takes two to keep that kind of bargain."

In spite of Father Largo's imposed austerities Steve Halidon felt quite comfortable in the crypt. Father Columba had smuggled him down a radio which he kept under the cot. Its presence might have been difficult to explain to the Spaniard who would probably expect that he had more direct means of keeping abreast of the latest events.

Halidon had dusted out one of the burial niches and had stacked there the magazines the Irish missioner had brought down to him. It was apparent that it was a particularly painful penance for Father Columba to keep from asking questions, but he had managed to satisfy himself with the thought that

[111]

Father Massimo must know what he's doing.

Halidon had just lit a cigarette and was sorting over the pile of magazine when he heard the soft pad of footsteps on the cement floor and then the rusty groan of the hinges of the crypt door. Halidon quickly crushed out his cigarette and slipped out of his shoes before the smiling face of Father Largo appeared.

"Buenas tardes," said Father Largo. The priest came close to Halidon, his watery eyes probing and his nose sniffing at the unexpected odor of smoke.

"Are you smoking, Holy One?"

Halidon smiled and spread wide his hands to indicate he wasn't concealing anything.

"*Perdone*, I should trust you more," Father Largo said. "But why is it I never catch you at your prayers?"

"My praying days are over," Halidon said.

"Perhaps you need no prayers yourself. But you could pray for me!" The priest took the books from under his arm. "I thought if you are wearied with doing nothing you could correct this translation of your writings." He selected the book and handed it to Halidon.

"I would advise you to go over it carefully. I am certain some of your best thoughts have been lost. You, better than I, understand that these foreigners know nothing of true mysticism."

Halidon took the book, opening it cautiously as he motioned Father Largo to sit down.

The priest sighed, wagging a finger at Halidon chidingly. "I cannot sit in your presence. And if you continue to stand I will have to kneel."

Halidon smiled secretly. "And if I lie down?"

Father Largo laughed. "Ah, you are teasing me, Holy One! But I'm glad to see you can have some fun. I always thought your good friend Santa Teresa laughed excessively for a serious reformer."

Halidon closed the book and watched Father Largo thought-

[112]

fully. In spite of his protests of a moment before, he had sat down on the cot and was feeling for the boards he had put under the mattress.

"Can you keep a secret if I ask you something, Padre?"

"Secret?" the priest laughed. "I will tell you something! The Communists locked me up for months but I wouldn't confess to their lies. They told me I must admit that I had murdered the orphan babies brought to our mission — that I was a Vatican spy! Padre Largo a Vatican spy! My memory is so bad that I have trouble remembering the rubrics not to mention the plots these mad men imagined. But I would have been quite delighted if there had been a plot. I would like one time to play the cavalier!"

"Perhaps you will get your chance for revenge, Father."

Father Largo shook his head, "No — you should not tell me that. Vengeance belongs to God." The priest sat in thought for several minutes, then getting up, he came to Halidon. "You are going to tell me why you are here? Is this the secret you have for me?"

"At the moment I'm just curious. There's a man named Newman coming here — "

"Yes — yes. We are waiting for him — "

"Will you do me the favor of not telling him I am here? It's very important, Padre."

Father Largo nodded wisely. "I will do better than that, Holy One. I will see that he doesn't bother you. If he does he will answer to me!"

Father Massimo was surprised that the red-headed young man came for the lesson. It was irritating to realize that for the time at least he must keep up pretending he had accepted Byrne's excuse for coming, his masquerade. For a moment yesterday he had allowed the romantic thought to malinger in his mind that Kevin Byrne had taken an interest in Julie Nealy. But as they chatted briefly before the lesson the superior saw

[113]

that Byrne was much more interested in the monastery and its occupants.

The lesson went on pleasantly enough. Byrne took no time at all to memorize, and almost accurately pronounce "hello," "good-bye," and "thank you" in four languages.

As the redhead prepared to leave he returned momentarily to his probing. "I suppose you know other languages besides Italian, French, Spanish, and German, Father Massimo?"

"Only one other — Polish. I went to Poland many years ago with the Nuncio Marmaggi."

"But you remained longer?"

Father Massimo's eyes widened in surprise but he didn't answer.

Byrne flushed. "I was assuming that you stayed longer."

"You're excellent at guesswork, Mr. Byrne," the superior said, smiling blandly.

"Will you return, Father — to Europe?"

Father Massimo sighed. "Evidently you've heard that some of the exiles are planning a rather imaginative missionary campaign. I wasn't quite aware of their determination until I learned that Father Georgio has received information from the Russian embassy."

"Oh," said Byrne, as though the information surprised him.

Father Massimo laughed. "They were very helpful. They sent him maps and literature. He is still trying to digest the mass of material — and trying to puzzle out how much of it is deliberately deceptive. Father Dmitri is convinced that they have a diabolical motive in being so cooperative. But in spite of what you might have heard, several of the priests would like to remain here."

"But not you?" Byrne said. The superior watched him with an amused twinkle and Byrne went on: "I can't help thinking that you're in a different position from the other priests."

"I am an exile like the rest — a priest with the one purpose of teaching the Faith." Father Massimo rose. "We're straying from the purpose you have here, Mr. Byrne, or perhaps you've lost interest in our little lessons."

There was a clatter of wooden beads and Father Edmund appeared at the library door. "Excuse me, Father, but I've been wondering what you plan to do."

Father Massimo eyed the Englishman apprehensively. "I suppose I must do my duty — whatever it entails."

"I think you had better stop humoring Father Largo. He's now pestering visitors to the chapel with his claim that he has seen St. John of the Cross. You have no idea how he frightens people. Worst of all, some are curious."

The superior glanced quickly at Kevin Byrne. "It will pass. He's had visions before, so he says."

"This could be serious, Father," persisted Father Edmund. "If it gets out, it is bound to be embarrassing. I'm sure Monsignor Brady will say that we've contrived the whole thing to establish ourselves."

"I don't think this is the time to discuss poor Father Largo's imaginings — "

Father Edmund's receding chin took on the appearance of protruding. "It's got to be nipped in the bud, Father. He's determined he's going to convince me. When I tried to pacify him by saying that I'd reserve my judgment, he came near assaulting me. He insisted on dragging me down to the cellar for a look. But I will not make a fool of myself, as though I actually believe our guest is some sort of wraith."

Father Massimo looked up warily at Byrne, then put his hand on Father Edmund's arm as he led him to the door. "I'll speak to Father Largo as soon as I am free."

The Englishman went out, muttering to himself, and Byrne arose uneasily. "I'd better not keep you, Father. You have your problems, I can see."

As they walked to the door, Father Massimo said, "I hope this little tempest of Father's hasn't disturbed you, Mr. Byrne. He's quite excitable."

"These things don't bother you, Father?"

"One becomes used to it."

"I hope you don't mean that visions are a regular thing here. If I were Father Edmund I'd at least be curious to have a look."

"If you knew the background you wouldn't be the slightest bit curious. Father Largo has always wanted to see St. John of the Cross. And sometimes when you want to see something badly enough, you sometimes do see it."

The superior said good-bye to Byrne at the door and stood watching the young man stride away along the street, when he heard Father Maximilian calling from the top of the stairs, to tell him that "der Amerikanischen" bishop was on the telephone. Father Max always referred to Bishop Hickey as the American in a tone that implied he had never quite accepted him as a *bona fide* bishop.

The superior hurried to the office and picked up the phone. "Father Massimo, Your Excellency," he said warily.

He heard the bishop's familiar greeting. "I thought I had better inform you, Father. Oliver Newman is on his way over, Mr. Doolan is with him."

"Newman," Father Massimo said, hoping he didn't sound too dismayed.

"Yes. He's interested in interviewing you and some of the other priests. But you may do as you please about that. If you think some stories on the missions will be helpful to the Holy Father's mission program you may want to cooperate with him. But I made it clear to him that he is not to profit from the works of the Church."

"We will try to be helpful, Your Excellency," Father Massimo said, hoping his lack of enthusiasm would leak through. Apparently the bishop had nothing further to say. The superior went on, "Bishop, I wonder if I might bring to your attention a problem we have here — "

"Yes, Father — "

"It's about our guest — "

Hickey laughed. "You have no obligation toward him. None whatever. Do as you think best, Father."

Father Massimo stared at the phone incomprehendingly, "You know about this, Your Excellency?"

"I understand your problem perfectly, Father. If it makes you too uncomfortable I wouldn't put up with him. He's well able to shift for himself. Doolan would like to bring him down to Cohagansett."

"Oh," said Father Massimo, "you think I'm concerned about Mr. Newman?"

He heard the bishop's laugh. "I know you better than that, Father. Now, if you'll excuse me, I have a meeting. . . ."

The superior heard the hum of the dial tone and realized the bishop had hung up. But at least one thing was apparent. Bishop Hickey had not yet heard of Father Largo's vision.

At the sound of voices coming from the corridor, Father Massimo came out of the office to see Father Maximilian escorting J. Dalton Doolan toward him. Behind Doolan was a man Father Massimo recognized at once as Oliver Newman.

The smile of triumph on Doolan's face was indication enough that he regarded Newman as his prize. "Oliver Newman, Father!" His voice boomed unnecessarily as he introduced the man.

Father Massimo hoped his expression wasn't too reserved as he acknowledged the introduction and offered to take him to the other exiles.

"I'd like to meet Bishop Dworjanski first," Newman said.

Father Massimo tried to maintain his calm as he answered, "His Excellency hasn't been informed yet that you're here. He doesn't like to be disturbed. He hasn't been well, and as you know, has been devoting all his time to his memoirs. If we broke in on him now I'm afraid he'd be abrupt with us."

"But if the bishop knew Mr. Newman was here . . ." Doolan exclaimed.

The superior flashed him a look, then smiled blandly at Newman. "His Excellency is aware of who Mr. Newman is — fully aware. But the visit will have to wait."

He led the two men out to the cloister and made a general introduction while Newman preened himself. The reception was polite, aloof, and relatively indifferent. But if Newman was disturbed he didn't betray it. He devoted several minutes to apprising them of his recent activities including a speaking engagement at a regional congress of Catholic women at which Cardinal Moran had also said a few words.

"I thought I might get started today," he said.

"Started? Back to New York?" asked Father Columba, hopefully.

"On your experiences," Newman said impatiently. He looked at Father Massimo who stood at the door. "It might be best to start with you, Father Superior."

"I forgot to tell you. Today is Saturday, and most of us will be leaving in a while to assist in the City's parishes. Anyway. I'm afraid my activities were of an official nature. I would have to secure permission from the Holy See."

"Official?" said Newman. "I wasn't aware."

"I was with the diplomatic corps — briefly." Father Massimo smiled blandly. "Mine was a minor mission, of little consequence — "

"Father Superior absolutely refuses to talk about his mission in Poland, Mr. Newman," said Father Edmund. "Father Columba would be more helpful, and he's not bashful. He's battled more Reds in his time than any of us — with the exception of Bishop Dworjanski — and, it would appear, Father Superior."

Father Columba cast an annoyed look at the Englishman, then laughed, leaning forward with his big hands on his knees and his toes wriggling beneath the soft leather of his shoes.

"What would you like to hear, Mr. Newman?" he said.

"For a start, perhaps the prosaic facts, and then perhaps a

humorous episode or two."

"Have you heard the one about the Communist who died and appeared before St. Peter asking for admittance and was told that all the Communists were being sent to the moon?"

Newman looked a bit grim.

There was a commotion at the door and Father Dmitri bustled in balancing a bulky manuscript in his arms. He banged the dust from it and deposited it in Newman's lap.

"There, Mr. Newman, all for you!" He rubbed his hands together. "The story of my life. For $50,000 you may have it."

Father Massimo saw that Newman would be occupied for some time in explaining to Father Dmitri why he wasn't interested in buying the manuscript. The superior returned to the house and went up to Bishop Dworjanski's room. When he knocked and entered he found the old bishop seated at his desk. He put down his pen and closed the folio he had been writing in.

"I'm sorry to disturb you, Bishop—"

The old man's heavy jowls moved in a vague smile. He reset the violet skullcap on his head. "I have run my thoughts dry for the day, Father. It's pleasant to have a visitor." He rose heavily and indicated the chairs in front of the ponderous fireplace.

The large room had been made comfortable for the bishop with the installation of a gas heater in the fireplace. He turned it up and motioned Father Massimo to a chair.

The bishop stood warming himself and after a moment realized that the superior had no intention of making himself comfortable. He stood with his hands crossed, moving them nervously in the cuffs of his sleeves.

"You have something to tell me, Father?"

The superior's eyes narrowed thoughtfully. "Newman is here — the man whose books I gave you to read."

"Newman?" Then, quite unexpectedly, the bishop laughed dryly. "I read the books. I have read them and see quite clearly your intention in bringing them to my attention."

Then as Father Massimo tried to conceal his dismay the bishop continued. "This is a very holy man we have to deal with, Father Superior. We must be on our guard that we carry out all the specifications of Canon Law while he is here."

"He has asked to meet you, Bishop."

Stefan Dworjanski nodded slowly. "I am curious. But I think I will wait a time. How long will he be here?"

"I'm not sure," the superior said. "At least until a week from Sunday. He has a lecture engagement in the civic auditorium for that night."

"He has told you he wants to write a book about us?"

Father Massimo smiled. "Yes," he said.

When the superior came downstairs he was met by Father Columba who was laughing.

"Father Georgio took Newman out to the cemetery to meet Reverend Gillis," he explained to Massimo. "When the minister heard who he was, he asked if "in the red" was a proper bookkeeping term in Russia.

"Is Newman still here?" asked the superior.

"Father Edmund is showing him the oratory." Father Columba got up. "I suppose it was a bit sinful taking so much enjoyment at Newman's expense."

The superior went back to the corridor and Newman and Father Edmund emerged from the chapel. Newman hurried toward the superior.

"I was inspecting your oratory, Father," he exclaimed. "It's a gem! But the statue of the archangel seems quite out of place."

Father Massimo smiled cryptically. "St. Michael is here to protect us from the powers of darkness."

Newman shrugged off the remark; then, he said blandly, "I believe you remarked earlier, Father, that you had seen service in Poland. Isn't that unusual for a Brunite missionary?"

"It was a temporary assignment — many years ago."

"During the war?"

"Yes," Father Massimo said, his eyes narrowing. "In the city where I was stationed — Kzalineka. . . ."

"Kzalineka! I've heard of it. A railroad center. . . ."

The superior waited but saw that Newman was not prepared to say what sort of cargo passed through the great railroad yards at Kzalineka.

Newman smiled calmly, and said, "I'm afraid I cannot say exactly what the city is famous for or why there should be a railroad there."

"It is famous for nothing. But it was made infamous as the place where a thousand inhabitants were slaughtered because they had stopped a train, freed the prisoners, and executed the guard."

"But you were spared, Father?"

"Diplomatic immunity."

"Thank God for that!" Newman murmured. "You must tell me about these events sometime." He moved toward the door.

"When there is time I will tell you about Kzalineka," Father Massimo said. He gave an almost imperceptible nod to Newman's good-bye and closed the door.

CHAPTER SIX

MOTHER SUPERIOR EVARISTE-MARIE had come to the convent roof after Sunday dinner, hopeful she would find that one of her pigeons had returned with a message from Father Constant, but its cage was empty. She turned from the dovecote, looking away across the rooftops toward the river and the hills to the east.

Mother Evariste-Marie had named her birds for the popes, starting with Peter and over the years had got as far as the Avignon Captivity. Strangely, the troublesome ones were the ones she remembered best. Leo the Great (of whom much was expected) had turned out to be a great trial, had pecked some of his brother pigeons to death, tore the messages from his leg when dispatched on a flight, and rounded out the perversity by living to a ripe old age.

As the old nun stood at the edge of the roof wall, she was rewarded with the sight of one of her birds winging his way up from the bridge. He circled the bell tower of the convent, perching for a moment on the ridge, then swooped down to her. He waddled with a satisfied familiarity down the ramp and nudged the superior's hand.

She took the message from his leg and gathering up her skirts hurried down the circular stairs. At her desk she read the brief note from Father Constant, who had also enclosed a greeting for his fellow missioners.

Content that the little priest was comfortably settled at St.

Smaragdus, the superior watched for the arrival of the convent chaplain to give him the message.

Father Columba, a disconcerting confessor at times, had recently recommended squab once a week as a solution to her excessive interest in her birds. When she told him now that a message had actually arrived from Cohagansett by pigeon, he blushed apologetically. "I must confess, Mother, I never thought your pigeons would find their way back."

"We must have faith, Father," she said a bit severely. "We in religion should have more of an appreciation of the homing instinct than those in the world."

Father Columba, tucking the note in the cuff of his sleeve, laughed appreciatively. "If I must count on flying I'm afraid I'll never make it."

Father Georgio was taking his Sunday afternoon siesta in the cloister when his Irish confrere brought news of the greeting from Cohagansett. A bit disgruntled, he thanked Father Columba for waking him up and trusted he would have enough courage to arouse his English brother who, if the Croat was not mistaken, was dozing over a book in the library.

The commissario lumbered to his feet and vibrated down the hall to the kitchen, where he found Father Dmitri taking care of the dinner leftovers.

Father Georgio gave the Moravian a chastening look. "Our poor Spanish padre is going to be impossible to live with when he finds he's been deceived by this 'vision' in the basement. It makes me wonder — the terrible experience he's had — if he had a vocation for the priesthood."

The Moravian laughed, "If you had seen me when I was a youth you would never think I had the spiritual ingredients."

The superior had been waiting anxiously since Sunday dinner for Dr. Lambert to arrive. He was scheduled for a routine check of Stefan Dworjanski and the priest hoped he would have time to look at the head injury of the guest in the crypt — and, too, perhaps he could rescue the fellow for a few minutes from Father Largo. It had been hardly more than daylight when the Spaniard scurried off to the crypt with his paints and brushes to set down on canvas this apparition of John of the Cross.

When he was absent from the dinner table (the superior had been unable to persuade him to leave his work) Father Edmund, back from his Sunday stint of preaching at St. Peter in Chains, took note of the Spaniard's empty seat and commented that they had waited quite long enough to call a psychiatrist.

Dr. Lambert came when the afternoon was half spent. There was no need for apology, Father Massimo assured him, and besides, he wasn't sure Dworjanski wanted to be disturbed. He was back at his memoirs and more irascible than ever when interrupted.

But the task proved easier than expected. The intern gave a report as Father Massimo poured him a cup of black coffee in the kitchen. "Surprisingly, he was cooperative. But I hope he'll wrap up those memoirs soon. It's a terrible drain on his strength."

"He assured me he's nearly finished," said the priest.

Lambert drank his coffee in silence then said, "You mentioned another patient?"

"Yes — the man in the crypt."

"He's still here then?"

"He is — and still very much incognito. I'm at odds with myself about this situation. There are a number of reasons why I'm reluctant to send him away. For one thing, I'm sure Father Largo would fiercely oppose anyone who tried to take his saint away."

Lambert nodded.

"He's prepared himself for this event for many years," said Father Massimo smiling grimly. "From his actions this morning

[124]

it's apparent that he's determined to preserve his vision for posterity. Before I left for the hospital he was up and on his way to the crypt with his paints and brushes, mumbling happily to himself."

Lambert laughed. "Leave it to Father Largo. He'll drive the fellow out for you."

"I'm not too happy to have Father Largo dispense his particular brand of torture to the young man. . . . Come with me, Doctor. It will give me an excuse to get him away from Father Largo."

When they came to the crypt they saw Halidon sitting under the window, the old cassock carefully arranged by Father Largo. There was an air of impatience in the way he held a crucifix and an old book.

Halidon saw them and with quick embarrassment put down the crucifix. "We have visitors, Padre," he said.

"Pax tecum, Father," said the superior. "May we come in?"

"Certainly," cried Father Largo. "I'm used to interruptions! It's one of my crosses!"

Father Massimo tried to give him a pacifying smile. "I think you've done enough for today, Father. Posing is very tiring. Dr. Lambert is here to attend to our guest. We've forgotten, I think, that he's been injured."

Father Largo looked anxiously toward his guest. "I had no idea you might be suffering, Holy One! You're a good man, Father Superior, to think of him!"

Andy Lambert set his bag on the cot and nodded to Father Largo apprehensively. "How are you, Father?"

"Confidentially, Doctor, I'm in pain from head to foot!"

"Maybe you should have a general checkup, Father," the intern said.

"Doctor," replied the Spaniard, "just talking to you has helped, I think."

Father Massimo took the Spaniard's arm, conducting him gently from the crypt.

[125]

There was a mocking smile on Halidon's face when the intern looked at him.

Andy Lambert eyed Halidon calmly as he probed in his bag and prepared a new bandage. He came to Halidon and inspected the bruises on his face. "Any aches and pains?"

Halidon grinned. "Besides my head — no."

The intern removed the old bandage on Halidon's forehead and put on a fresh one.

"Thanks, Doctor," Halidon said. "Your out-patient clinic covers quite a wide area, doesn't it?"

Lambert returned his instruments to his bag before he answered. He looked at Halidon remotely for a few moments. "I came to look after Bishop Dworjanski. Coming down to check you was an extra favor to Father Massimo."

"Oh — " said Halidon.

Lambert folded his arms and leaned against the grille as he studied Halidon. "I'd be doing Father another favor if I found out why you're here."

"Didn't he tell you?"

"Yes. But I could see that even he doesn't believe your story. Your beard is convincing, but for a fellow who is supposed to have lived out of doors — on the road — your face and hands are much too unweathered."

Halidon grinned amiably. "I'm a new type. I sleep in the best motels and eat only at Duncan Hines approved restaurants."

"Then you should be able to pay your hospital bill," the intern said impatiently.

Halidon laughed.

"If Father Massimo refuses to do something about you, the police should."

"You're a hard man, Doctor. But I'd hate to ruin Father Largo's pleasant dream. I'll bet the poor old fellow is happier than he's been in years."

Andy looked at Halidon with annoyance. "And when you're gone he'll be back where he was — maybe worse."

While the superior was waiting for the intern to emerge from the crypt he had strolled into the oratory to see that the relic of Venerable Bruno was still in its place. The chapel was open for the afternoon and Julie Nealy was there changing the altar cloths.

He had thought about going out to the cloister but he knew Oliver Newman had arrived for another visit, and the superior was not anxious to face him at the moment.

Father Columba had greeted Newman affably, and much to the English priest's annoyance carried out his self-appointed role of vice superior, acting in Father Massimo's place when the occasion arose.

Newman was all business and wouldn't understand why they couldn't take him directly to Stefan Dworjanski. It had taken all the Irish missioner's diplomacy and a good hard grip to direct Newman out to the patio.

"Hasn't the bishop even given an indication that he is willing to see me?" Newman said impatiently.

"He finds it hard to get used to strangers," Father Columba said, "owing to his long imprisonment. You know almost as well as we do what those prisons are like. But I'm sure he'll see you eventually."

Newman sighed and opened his briefcase, raising his eyes to the English priest who stood staring at him a bit peevishly. He had not quite made up his mind about Newman. He sensed that even the laying on of nationalization hands hadn't appeared to democratize him much. The English missioner had no use whatever for intuitive feelings, and was sure that he had never trifled with any himself. They were too akin to superstition and, what was worse, impulse.

Father Edmund was satisfied that it was the superior's responsibility to give or withhold the freedom of the house to Newman. His decision to let him come was apparently backed up by Bishop Hickey, in whom the Holy See must have had sound reasons to deposit its trust even though they must have been fully aware that Hickey was of Irish stock.

Newman gave the Englishman a fixed smile. "Perhaps if we continued with your story, Father. . . ."

Father Edmund sat down. "I've forgotten where I left off — "

"We hadn't really started — except for one or two of your little anecdotes which I'm afraid I can't use," Newman said. "I'm going to have to probe deeply. I'd hoped to make this a serious work. Perhaps if we got directly to your mission station —"

Father Edmund's brows bristled. He should at least be given the choice of where he would start. At the moment he had the impulse not to start at all. Newman's arrival had disrupted his work on a lecture.

Newman glanced at the other missioners, a flick of annoyance crossing his face as he saw Father Maximilian tuning out his hearing aid cautiously.

Father Georgio and Father Dmitri had returned their attention to their maps, sticking their colored pins with unaccustomed zest into a new line of strategy they were mapping.

"There is someone missing besides your superior, if I'm not mistaken," Newman remarked.

"You're thinking of Father Constant," said Father Edmund.

"Bishop Hickey — quite unwisely — sent him to Cohagansett. His English is atrocious — a fact that makes me wonder if the bishop isn't playing some prank on Father Galvin, the pastor down there. But we're hoping he won't make Father Constant's life wretched. The poor young man has been through enough trouble. The Communists strangled him and threw him in the Nemunas. He's in an enviable position."

"Enviable?" said Newman, alarmed.

"I heard — or perhaps read somewhere — that those tortured for the Faith, though not fatally, are true martyrs and cannot be lost. The contention appeared to be that salvation was guaranteed."

[128]

Father Edmund saw Father Dmitri glance at him with a quasi-anathematic scowl, which only strengthened his belief that the theory might be a sound one. He was wondering if the same principle might not be applied to Father Largo, when he realized that Newman had slipped from his chair and was peering curiously into the corridor.

"Who is the young lady with Father Massimo?" he asked, his eyes wide with speculation as they turned to Father Edmund.

"You must mean Julie Nealy," said the Englishman.

"She comes here often?" asked Newman, his attitude hinting that he scented something irregular.

"I suppose it's improper of us to take such a human — even sentimental interest in the child — not me, the others," said the Englishman. "But we are very fond of her. We've sort of adopted her or she has adopted us. I'm not sure which. She works at the branch public library nearby and has been very helpful to me in my research. And she's been quite generous to Father Largo, keeping him supplied with paints, brushes, and canvas."

"Largo, you said. Have I met him?"

The British priest smiled cautiously. "We don't talk about our Spanish brother to strangers."

"You mean he's demented?"

"Perhaps that's too strong a word," said Father Edmund. "I prefer to think he's lost in God." He glanced quickly toward the German priest who appeared to be listening quite intently, a thing that disconcerted the Englishman because Father Maximilian was theologically conservative and thought everything that was to be said had been said centuries ago.

"That is a private opinion," he said hastily. "I hope I will never have to make a deposition concerning the Spanish padre for a papal commission."

"Why might you be expected to do that?" asked Newman.

"If he continues his claim to mystic experiences the Holy Office will want to look into it. But I think the local bishop has finally put the thing in perspective. He's suspended the poor fellow's faculties. He claims to have had a vision of St. John of the Cross while at a Buddhist monastery in Burma. Since then he's been pining away for another glimpse of the saint."

There was a scowl of distaste on Newman's face. "It should be clear to all of you then why the Church looks with suspicion on self-styled visionaries. Such claims are too apt to be psychotic lies."

Rather presumptuous, thought Father Edmund, for a man who was still quite busily engaged in disentangling himself from his own maze of pathological adventures. But the opinion shouldn't have been surprising. Church periodicals had been lavishing praise on his pithy opinions for many months. But it seemed strange that a man of such widely advertized faith placed such little faith in the things which faith alone supported.

"But we were talking about St. John of the Cross," Newman said. "I've always wondered why he gave so much credit to heavenly visions and so little to his own ingenuity at the time he was rescued from the Carmelites. As I remember the story, he made his escape from the Toledo priory after Father Maldonado kicked him awake in his cell but refused to allow him to say Mass on the feast of the Assumption, the following morning. According to his account he was given instructions by the Virgin herself to remove the bolts from the door hinges of his cell — a favored method of the priests since — "

Newman paused, smiling blandly at Father Edmund. "I understand that some escaped from the Nazis and Communists that way — "

"Indeed?" exclaimed Father Edmund.

"You heard this, Herr Newman?" asked Father Maximilian. "While I was at home — in Meissen — we heard very little about these things. They do not publicize their failures."

"Naturally," said Newman, "I was in on many of the details — the failures, as you call them. Gossip gets around — even in a police state. In addition to this, they trusted me. I assume it is something to my credit that while I was a Communist, I was a good one."

"We had no idea how *gut* a Communist you were!" said Father Maximilian.

Father Massimo said good-bye to Julie Nealy at the oratory door then turned to the altar, his thoughts flickering with fears and doubts like the votive candles before the altar. Perhaps the human happiness he desired for Julie wasn't the thing she herself prayed for. He had no way of knowing. She rarely talked about herself and never of her aspirations.

The Father superior genuflected and turned from the altar, content that he had more immediate problems to worry about. Word of the Spaniard's vision had been spread through the neighborhood and undoubtedly it wouldn't be long before the curious would come to probe and to have their reasonable doubts verified. Ever since Father Largo had decided he was favored with a vision, the superior had been making excuses to his conscience. But he knew that the excuses would have to make a good deal more sense when he tried to express them to the other priests and to Bishop Hickey.

Father Massimo went into his office, occupying himself with his bookkeeping until he heard Newman being edged toward the outside door by Father Columba, who was having trouble getting off Newman's conversational hook and was standing on the sidewalk with him.

The other priests had dispersed as soon as they could, and when the superior came out to the cloister he found the Englishman Edmund and the Moravian Dmitri occupied with their particular recreations.

Father Dmitri was watering his plants. In the Hebrew cemetery beyond the cloister fence Father Georgio was strolling with the Baptist minister, Harold Gillis. At the far end of the block, and separated from the cemetery by the token remnants

of a picket fence, was Gillis' parsonage, an unpainted ginger-
bread house, and next to it the equally weathered wooden church
with a rooster weather vane atop its steeple. Father Massimo
didn't know how appropriate the bird was for the denomination,
but it seemed a quite fitting symbol for Gillis.

The friendship between Father Georgio and the minister
puzzled the superior. From bits of their conversations repeated
by Father Georgio, they had little in common except a fondness
for Madam Gillis' cooking. For more than a year there had been
an unrelenting exchange of food going on between the monastery's Father commissario and the homey Baptist housewife, an
exchange that appeared to be impossible to consummate because
neither remembered who had made the first gift and each
seemed determined to outdo the other.

Father Edmund had remarked that charity was a fine trait
(and they certainly wouldn't miss the baked beans from their
ample larder), but the worst of it was that even the most
palatable dishes from Father Georgio's kitchen didn't appear to
sweeten the minister's acid tongue and there now seemed little
prospect that unremitting charity would relieve his evangelical
gauntness. Gillis wasn't content unless he was taking verbal
swipes at the foundations of Rome. Father Edmund had found
talking to the Reverend Gillis a provocative but hardly profitable
occupation.

To Father Edmund, who was, at the moment, perusing his
reference books, he said, "Would you mind a little interruption
in your work, Father?"

The Englishman smiled placidly. "I'm always at your command, Father Superior."

"I want to say a few things about Father Largo — and his
vision."

"Bones a' Becket! The less said about that the better,
Father!"

"That was my thought, Father Edmund. If you and Father
Dmitri would join me in the library in a few minutes. . . . And

[132]

I think you had better summon Father Georgio — or rescue him, perhaps."

They assembled in the library, Father Georgio hurrying to the table wiping his brow with his huge red handkerchief.

"We are all here, I see," said Father Massimo, noting with gratification that Father Maximilian wore his hearing aid and was adjusting the volume. "We are all here except Father Largo and I think we can rely on the probability that he will be occupied with his painting until the sun goes down. I wish I could tell you something about our *guest* — the man in the crypt."

"We thought that was why you summoned us," said Father Edmund impatiently.

"I wanted to assure you that he is here with my permission. But I'm not sure why he is here — unless it is the reason he gave, that he had no place to go. You, perhaps, will have your own guesses — as I have mine. But there are two things I want to ask you, that, for the time, you permit Father Largo to continue with his conviction that the man is St. John of the Cross, and that you refrain from discussing it with Newman."

CHAPTER SEVEN

THE next morning, Monday, found Halidon pacing in the chapel. The Spaniard had aroused him at six o'clock to inform him that he had decided he wanted to paint a clean-faced St. John of the Cross. He had brought along soap and razor as evidence of his decision.

Halidon turned in his pacing to come almost face to face with the girl he had seen several other times in the chapel.

He edged into a rear pew, suppressing a phrase that came to his throat as he banged his ankle on the kneeler. It served him right for not being more regular at Mass. He moved in against the wall, making a three-point landing that had been the bane of existence for the nuns years ago back in Jersey City.

The lame girl knelt in a front pew. She didn't look back as he thought she would, but he sensed she was wondering about him.

Halidon watched as the people moved to seats, scattering through the chapel. He noticed the redhead he had seen on the day of the procession and once at the hotel, coming down the aisle.

Maybe the young fellow had a romance going, but more likely he was using the girl as an excuse to hang around. When Halidon considered, he wondered if it might not have been a simpler device than passing himself off as a bum.

Seemingly satisfied that the lame girl was there in the chapel, the redhead returned to the rear of the church and, as though there weren't plenty of seats elsewhere, planked himself down in Halidon's pew. Halidon bowed his head, trying to look as though he were absorbed in prayer, aware that the redhead was staring at him curiously every few seconds.

The Mass started. From the red beanie on the head of the priest at the altar, Halidon gathered that it must be Bishop Dworjanski. Father Largo was assisting him, giving Halidon the satisfaction of knowing that he had plenty of time to get back to his dungeon.

There was something about the monotonous hum of the old bishop's voice that made Halidon feel drowsy, but he didn't realize quite how drowsy he had become until he glanced up with a start to see that the redhead had left. When he looked toward the altar he realized the Mass was nearly over. He got up from the pew and walked through the passage to the corridor of the monastery.

He was about to go down to the crypt when he heard someone coming up. Halidon moved swiftly to the refectory across the hall and when he looked out from his place of concealment he saw the redhead close the basement door carefully, then hurry back through the chapel.

The fellow would be surprised to see that Halidon wasn't still dozing in the back pew. That would give him something to mull over. But one thing was now clear. The redhead's main interest was not in the lame girl.

If the redhead was from a rival paper it meant that others were suspicious of Newman. When he slipped out of the monastery tonight to call Shanley, he would have to ask about that. But Shanley was quite pig-headed at times. He still insisted that Newman was after the relic. He somehow imagined the hollow-eyed convert putting on the old metallic undershirt and smuggling it out of the country, just as the German priest had smuggled it out of Meissen.

No one was more aware of the importance in Darrington of Wadleigh Thorne than Harlan Brissart, district attorney of Gilmore County. There were few committees that Thorne's portly figure hadn't graced and few editions of the rotogravure section of the Sunday *Gazette* that didn't depict him either passing or receiving a gavel or heading up a committee.

Thorne assured Brissart that he didn't drop into the county building to give him a hard time. He simply wanted to make it clear to Harlan that his good name must not be besmirched.

"I'm not sure what I can do, Wadleigh," Brissart said cautiously. "This is now a civil case — now that you've been cleared of the drunken driving charges."

Cigar smoke spewed from Thorne's apoplectic face. "Chief Tracy will rue the day he let his boys fingerprint me!"

"And took mug shots, too, I understand," Brissart said.

"Imagine having whisky forced down my throat!"

It must have been a new experience, being forced, Brissart thought. "If I didn't know better I'd say it was a plot to discredit you," he said.

"I'm sure it has turned into one!" said Thorne. "The police have refused to cooperate in rounding up that hobo fellow. They didn't even bother to get his name at the scene of the accident or afterward at the hospital. But I've done a bit of detective work on my own."

"You've located the fellow?"

Thorne shrugged cautiously. "Not positively. At the emergency ward in the hospital they told me there that he was last seen leaving the hospital with the foreign priest from the old monastery — the building that Hickey has been so stubborn about giving up to condemnation proceedings. But the point is, a police officer — a man I greatly respect for his integrity — informs me that a ragged fellow had been seen coming and going from the monastery at peculiar hours."

"Peculiar hours?" said Brissart warily.

"I think 4 a.m. is a peculiar hour, don't you?"

"Then this means — ?"

"I'm not claiming that someone is trying to make a mockery

of the law, Harlan. But there are a few technicalities that bother me. Identification may be difficult. It seems that one of the priests there claims to have a vision and has annoyed visitors by trying to drag them down to the cellar. But the man in charge has stopped them from getting a look at this fellow. A subpoena server could easily be foiled. Perhaps even the law itself could be circumvented if they should invoke sanctuary. But I want you to get the man out before my case comes up next week."

"Have a warrant issued, you mean?" said Brissart.

"No!" exclaimed Thorne impatiently. "Drop a few hints about the precarious position of resident aliens. I'm sure everyone in Darrington — in all of Gilmore County — is aware of your legal perspicacity."

"You think this information should have been made available to me? I'm sure it was never turned over to my assistant. It's common knowledge that Chief Tracy dislikes me."

"And he probably isn't the only one," said Thorne.

"I'm going to get to the bottom of this, Wadleigh," Brissart said with sudden determination.

"If I were you, I certainly would," Thorne said meaningfully.

District Attorney Harlan Brissart was aware that he couldn't stand for long in the rear of the monastery chapel without attracting attention. Even among these people, coming and going, dashing water in their faces and bending their knees, there might be someone astute enough to recognize the district attorney.

He viewed the scene with deliberate tolerance, quite happily aware that he was centuries removed from their rather barbarous customs and ritualistic symbolism.

Brissart saw the side entrance was opened and went to it, peering out into the cool-looking corridor. No one was in sight. He strode to the partly opened door, and knocked sharply. In the room he heard a chair move, and then a priest appeared at the door.

"How do you do, Reverend. I'd like to see the head one."

"Head one?" repeated Father Massimo, smiling with amusement. "Oh, I believe I'm the *head one*, at least no one has tried to overrule me yet. I'm Father Massimo."

"Oh, indeed," said Brissart, sticking out his hand. "It's a pleasure to meet you, Father."

"You are — ?"

"Harlan Brissart — the district attorney."

"Oh," said the superior. He was not quite sure what that was.

"I've been told that you have visitors here."

"All the time," said Father Massimo.

"I mean guests," said Brissart, narrowing it down.

"Guests?" said Father Massimo. He considered the man's inflection, which he feared he understood too perfectly. "It so happens that we have — yes."

Brissart smiled. "I'm surprised that you say so."

"I'm a little surprised myself," said the priest.

"Could I talk to him?"

"Him?" said Father Massimo, wondering how Brissart had pared it down so rapidly to one. "I think I had better turn you over to Father Largo. He's in the cloister. If you'll come this way."

The superior led the way along the polished hall to a door which opened on the lattice-enclosed garden. At the wooden bench in the center Father Edmund sat typing furiously, and near him, his silken brown skin shining brightly in the full light sat Father Largo cleaning his brushes and mumbling cheerfully to himself.

Father Dmitri looked up from his gardening, rubbing the soil from his hands, then got up and flexed his knees. He came over curiously, waiting to be introduced.

"Mr. Brissart — Father Dmitri." said the superior. "Mr. Brissart is a government man."

[138]

"Oh," said Father Dmitri, "you want to ask me some questions?"

"No."

Father Massimo smiled at the baffled look on Father Dmitri's face. "Perhaps you'd like to meet Father Edmund, Mr. Brissart?"

The Englishman looked up, nodding as Brissart turned his head to get a look at what he was doing on the typewriter.

"I'm preparing a lecture on the Copts," he said.

"Oh," said Brissart in surprise, "you're an authority on police work?"

Father Edmund frowned. "The Coptic Church. The one that Hailie Selassie belongs to."

The superior moved to Father Largo. "Father, could I disturb you. I want you to meet Mr. Brissart."

"I heard," said Father Largo, "a government man." He drew the fine hairs of the brush through his fingers as though it were a stiletto.

He looked up at Brissart. "I thought I was done with the government. I got the full treatment. They did everything but punch holes in my ears."

Brissart laughed uneasily. "I'm from the county government. Father Massimo said you could tell me something about your guest."

Father Largo smiled reflectively, then his looks changed to mistrust. "What can I tell you? Everything has been said about him. Even some of these doubters now admit he is actually here."

"But I would still like to see him."

"Well, as long as you have come to verify that I am not imagining things —"

"Yes —" said Brissart, but not so certain now that he knew what he was expected to verify.

"I'm not sure he will see you," said Father Largo. He placed his brushes in a jar, then, looking mistrustfully at Father

[139]

Edmund, gathered up his equipment and turned to Brissart. "But I must warn you, he is much occupied. At my request he is writing an account of his imprisonment and he dislikes being interrupted."

"I'll chance it. Now — if we may."

Father Largo, unable to detect any disapproval on Father Massimo's face, led the way into the house. "I would not have you miss this chance to meet the holy one."

"Holy one?" said Brissart in dismay.

"Oh, dear," said Father Largo. "I thought you were better prepared. Well, I won't have you haggling over his identity when I present you. He is San Juan de la Cruz. You are certainly familiar with the great sixteenth-century mystic. He is less well known by the name Juan of St. Mathias, his name in the Carmelite Order before he accepted the reform and cast off his shoes."

Brissart looked at Father Largo in annoyance. What in heaven's name was the man talking about? He turned to look in vain for Father Massimo.

"Come," said Father Largo, opening the cellar door. "You must be respectful. Are you of the faith?"

"You mean Roman Catholic — no."

Father Largo shook his head sympathetically. "Well, God is merciful — watch your step!" he added quickly as he started down the steep stairway.

Brissart followed along the darkened area, surprised as the priest stopped before the grille that looked like a cell door.

"This was once a crypt for the burial of nuns," Father Largo whispered.

Brissart gasped inadvertantly.

Father Largo looked at his companion's ashen face. "What's troubling you?" he whispered.

"I was thinking of those poor women," Brissart whispered back.

Father Largo shrugged. "I'm sure they didn't complain."

He pointed to the man asleep on his cot. "He's sleeping right now, as you can see. He needs much rest. His wounds are not yet healed from the treatment he received from the good Carmelites of Toledo."

Brissart looked at the priest nervously.

"This is unfortunate for you," continued Father Largo. "He once knocked the archbishop of Granada out of bed. I dare not waken him. He may get angry and leave us. He will soon anyway. He's due at Almodover for a convocation of the Discalced —"

"What nonsense are you talking?" said Brissart.

"Nonsense!" cried Father Largo. "Reform must come! I would indeed be careful, unless of course you are on the side of the Inquisition."

Brissart wiped his brow in bedevilment. This skipping back and forth through the centuries, as though time was nothing, baffled him. It was apparent he could get nowhere with this nimble-witted priest who somehow seemed to be a survivor of a specter-ridden age.

Harlan Brissart found Father Massimo in the library with his two bearded colleagues whose names the district attorney hoped he'd have no need to remember.

The superior got up, mumbling something foreign as he closed his prayer book. The enigmatic smile on his face was no surprise to Brissart.

"Is there anything further we can do for you, Mr. Brissart?"

Brissart stared at the priest petulantly. At the moment he was certain only that he had no intention of continuing this farce. But they didn't have him buffaloed. This man in the cellar was undoubtedly the one the FBI was hunting. Brissart was sure of it even though no information had been sent out yet. It was a technicality that convinced him he should be cautious for the moment.

"I think I have the information I need," he said.

The priest nodded, immoderately calm for a man who must

know how precarious it was to attempt to conceal a wanted criminal under the guise of a long-dead monk.

"Then we will see you again," Father Massimo said.

"I'm sure you will," Brissart said. "But I have one more question. Is there some law you can resort to, Reverend, at the appropriate time?"

"Law," Father Massimo said. "I'm not sure. If there is one, I'm inclined to think it will not work to my advantage."

Brissart went out and strode to his car where it was parked halfway along the next block. It paid to be cautious. He jiggled his keys in his hand nervously as he jerked open the door.

He had begun to slide under the wheel before he realized that someone occupied the passenger seat.

"I hope I haven't alarmed you, Mr. Brissart." It was Kevin Byrne.

Brissart glared at him as he tugged at his coat that had become entangled under him. "Have you been following me?"

Byrne laughed. "Hardly. We haven't anything on you, that I know of. I'm just a little disappointed in you. I thought you would have been here long ago."

Brissart glowered at Byrne. "All this appears to mean that you've been watching my moves."

Byrne smiled cryptically. "When I observed that you had a man tailing me I had no alternative but to find out what you were up to. I was relieved to see that you got sidetracked by the man in the cellar."

"You knew the man was there all the time?"

Byrne nodded, his smile repressed.

"You should have informed the police or my office."

Byrne laughed. "I was sure the local police could unravel what was basically a simple disappearance."

"Who is this man?" Brissart said peevishly. "I demand to know."

"I thought you did know. I observed that after you were

in the monastery a few minutes you had Father Largo take you to the basement."

Brissart grunted with annoyance. "It's easy to be smug about it when you have all the facts."

Byrne laughed, "The man you saw in the basement has nothing to do with our case. But his presence worried me for a while."

"You know who he is then?"

"I know at least as much about him as you do," Byrne said.

Brissart sighed impatiently. "Then you probably know I'm being pressured to get him out of there. But I want to be dead sure of my procedure before I invoke the wrath of the Catholic Church."

"Then you must be about ready for a suggestion or two," Byrne said.

"I'm not going on in the dark any longer," Brissart said angrily. "A few days ago you came to me with the blunt statement that you are here on a case and wondered if you could count on my cooperation at the appropriate time. I should have demanded then what I demand now. Why are you here?"

Byrne smiled calmly. "All I can tell you is that we are very near solving a long-drawn-out case. We will need your help eventually, I'm sure."

Brissart's eyes brightened. "I knew you would."

"But the help will be somewhat negative. All I ask is that you make no move to get the man out of the cellar. Since even those who know he's there have no idea who he is, seems to simplify things. No one in your department knows who he is?"

"No — but I don't understand," Brissart said.

"I think you understand more than you pretend to. It's hard for me to believe that you don't suspect something when you know I've been keeping my eye on the monastery — being fully aware that several of the priests there are from Communist countries."

"You mean one of them — perhaps several of them!" Brissart

[143]

gasped suddenly. "I don't think I'd care to be involved. My constituents are more than 90 percent Catholic —"

"Well said." Byrne laughed. "But you have the wrong impression. We think one of the priests may help us resolve a case that has international implications. It might be helpful for you to know, Mr. Brissart, that any local official who assists us will have his name splashed on front pages all over the country."

Brissart licked his lips, "Oh."

That night, Julie Nealy was placing magazines back on the library racks when she realized someone had got up from a table in the corner and was now standing behind her. She turned and saw Kevin Byrne, grinning at her.

"When do you close?" he asked.

"Nine o'clock."

"It's almost nine now," he said.

Julie glanced at him impatiently, then looked quickly toward the head librarian, Mrs. Avery. "It's against the rules to carry on unnecessary conversations."

"The old gal was worried about you," he said. "I saw her look at the clock at least a dozen times."

Julie smiled in spite of her determined annoyance. "For you and for Mrs. Avery — I had an errand at the post office and then stopped for a visit at the monastery."

"Visit?" he asked.

"It's an expression. If you're a Catholic you ought to be familiar with it."

"Guess I was thinking about something else."

The minute hand of the clock moved up toward the hour and Mrs. Avery began her discreet rounds, closing the windows with the long pole, turning out the lights at the unoccupied tables. The few elderly people took the hint and left. The redhead was the last to go. He looked back from the door, grinning suddenly when Julie glanced at him.

[144]

Mrs. Avery, her hat and coat on and key in hand impatiently motioned Julie to the door. Julie pulled on her coat outside the door as Mrs. Avery turned the key.

"Good night, Miss Nealy," she said as she strode off up the hill.

Byrne was waiting, smiling at her. "Can I give you a lift home?"

"I always walk," she said.

"Then may I walk with you?" he persisted.

"But you'd have to come back for your car."

"You don't give me much choice."

Julie smiled in spite of her determination not to. "I don't want to cause you trouble. I'll ride."

"Are you sure you trust me?"

Julie wondered why his bemused eyes disturbed her so. He directed her to the car.

"You know Father Massimo so you can't be too bad."

"But I don't know him very well."

"Did you ask Father Massimo about me?"

"No — one of the others." He opened the car door and assisted her in, then stood with his hands on the open window. "It was Father Columba. He told me you worked at the library. He told me more than I expected — everything good — everything I expected to hear."

"If there was anything you wanted to know I would have told you." She stopped suddenly, aware that she had let him know more than she intended. He knew that she had been thinking about him since the other morning when they'd met in the oratory.

He laughed indulgently. "When would you have told me?"

"I meant if I knew you better — if there was ever some reason that you should know me better."

There was a quizzical smile on his face as he turned and strode around the car. As he got in under the wheel he said, "My name's Kevin Byrne. That's a start toward knowing me."

"And you're a stranger in Darrington?"

He nodded, "I work in Boston — mostly. I'd like to come up here more often. I'd like to have a reason to come."

"Why?" Julie asked.

He laughed. "To see you!"

Julie drew her hands together in her lap, glancing at him in spite of her determination not to. "But that isn't why you were at the monastery?"

"Father Massimo is giving me language lessons. I thought I told you that."

"I hope you're paying him."

"I'll pay him," Byrne said. "But I have the idea he'd do it anyway."

There was a thoughtful look on Julie's face. "They're very kind."

"And rather mysterious," Byrne said. "One of them — the odd one — is having visions —"

"Father Largo?"

"I'm not quite sure why they chose this way to conceal the fact that they have someone in the cellar."

There was sudden anxiety in Julie's eyes. "I saw him — this man — in the chapel. He's very strange."

Byrne watched her face thoughtfully. "He didn't look much like the vision of a saint, I'd be willing to bet." Then at Julie's questioning glance he averted his face and started the car. As he drove down the hill she wondered if she had done the right thing in telling him she had seen the man at the monastery. But somehow she felt better that Byrne knew about him.

CHAPTER EIGHT

Monsignor Lawrence Brady approached the monastery the next afternoon with trepidation. He looked on the exiled missioners as poachers who had won the affection of some of his parishioners and, as a result of it, were siphoning off some of the normal parish revenue. But he was (unfortunately, he thought) a tolerant man, and one way or another they would have had to support the exiles anyway.

But they had gone a bit too far now — fostering spurious apparitions. And as it was, it was humiliating to hear it first from the Baptist minister.

The disclosure had come to Monsignor Brady today at the Tuesday noon Chamber of Commerce luncheon when the rector found himself placed between the Baptist preacher and the rabbi, Julius Silver. The Chamber chairman seemed to think of this particular luncheon (the last of the season, he said, and everyone seemed gratified) as a sort of interdenominational agape. Harold Gillis was an open-minded fellow and invariably began his conversations by saying precisely that.

After the entree it had become apparent to the rector that the preacher's pliable mind had been kneaded even a bit more in recent weeks by the clever foreigners with whom he had become excessively chummy. He said he was beginning to feel now that Roman doctrine and discipline, if democratically diluted with Yankee heterodoxy, might be more palatable to a wider public.

The rabbi, fully aware of the esoteric distinctions that Gillis painfully disregarded, winced while the monsignor cleared his throat uneasily.

"Some things simply cannot be sacrificed for the sake of popularity, Mr. Gillis. Eternal truths, for instance."

"You'll never get anywhere that way," Gillis chuckled.

"We will get the one place that is important," the sober rabbi countered.

The rector would have sided with the rabbi but he was always wary of biting into clinkers.

Suddenly Gillis was off in another direction: "There is one thing that I can't go along with you on, Monsignor. That's visions — reincarnation —"

Brady looked at the minister apprehensively. "They're not the same thing — not the same thing at all."

But Gillis wasn't to be sidetracked by hairsplitting. It was then that he told about the Spaniard's vision.

The monsignor had always been a little bit embarrassed for the Church, and for himself, by phenomena of this kind, even the purportedly authentic ones. But as long as they had been remote in time and locale, he felt secure. But this was too close for comfort. He couldn't get away from the luncheon fast enough and even though he dismissed everything the minister had said as nonsense, he still had the queasy feeling that it could be a troublesome bit of nonsense.

His mission firmly in mind, the monsignor hurried up the oratory steps and after a quick genuflection in the chapel he hurried through the passage to the house. Father Georgio greeted him in his usual blustering manner, escorted him into the library, and hurried off to the kitchen to fetch what he had called "a special treat for our patron."

Waiting to see what the treat might be, the rector sat uneasily in the library wondering how he would bring up the subject of the vision while dark-faced Father Dmitri strode up and down with his breviary, stroking his beard like a conspirator.

There was the clatter of wooden beads and the cook lumbered into the room with a tray containing a bottle and one glass.

"A special wine for a special friend, Monsignor!"

"Madame Gillis presented this to me in exchange for my recipe for feeding ten people with one chicken. But I'm sure the wine is better than the chicken. She wasn't always a Baptist. At home back in West Virginia her daddy was a bootlegger."

"Am I to drink alone?" asked the rector, accepting the glass.

"You must — certainly. Venerable Father Bruno, our founder, forbids us to touch wine, except of course at Mass, and then it isn't wine — is it?"

As he sipped the wine the rector asked casually about Father Largo. He saw the Croat's eyes shift nervously to Father Dmitri and felt sure they were keeping the Spaniard out of sight since the rumors had got around.

"These Baptists miss much, don't you agree, Monsignor? Another glass of blackberry wine?"

It was fortunate that the wine came from Gillis' wife. It provided an opening to tell them of his chat with Gillis at the luncheon — and an opportunity to bring up the alleged vision.

"We talked his brand of theology for a while," said the rector. "I'm afraid the good man thinks I'm a stuffed shirt for adhering so blindly to doctrine. He's now convinced that God isn't going to be so mean as to damn anyone no matter what He promised. His own sect, he says, is now soft-pedaling hell."

Father Dmitri came close to the rector and looked down at him curiously. It seemed the visitor was getting a bit flushed about the jowls.

"Have you seen the vision yet, Father?" the monsignor asked.

"What vision is that, Monsignor?" asked the Moravian.

"This disturbing rumor about Father Largo — "

"Think nothing of it, Monsignor — just a little more wine?" said Father Georgio, bottle in hand. There was no point in protesting and, anyway, it was poured before he could think to nod.

[149]

Monsignor Brady, though unsatisfied with the little chat as he got up to leave, finished the short walk back to the cathedral rectory in a more pleasant mood than he had been in before his visit.

After he had taken two aspirin and relaxed for a few minutes the monsignor came downstairs. It was only then that everything was clear to him. The foreign priests had deliberately diverted him, plied him with wine, and kept him from inquiring about the visions. They couldn't have used a better method to convince him that something was amiss.

The monsignor found Francis Hickey exploring the outside of the cathedral, quite obviously thinking again about the major repair job he mentioned every few years.

Puffing a bit as he circled about the beds of flowers, Monsignor Brady came up to the bishop. "I knew those priests would bring us notoriety, Your Excellency — "

"Notoriety?" the bishop said, wondering if a sandblasting job was the thing needed for the granite trim on the façade.

"I'll be specific — if one can be specific about such things. One of them — the Spanish one — has had a vision and is broadcasting it far and wide."

"Oh, come, come, Monsignor."

"I repeat — Father Largo has had a vision."

Bishop Hickey chuckled. "I'm sure no one will take such a report seriously."

"Those priests are encouraging him!"

The bishop shook his head compassionately. "We all know that the poor fellow has never recovered from his terrible experience in China. Let us be charitable toward him — humor him if we must. I say, let him have a vision. I'm sure it's a devout one — very probably a vision of the Venerable Father Bruno making a good deal of noise getting into his sleeping hardware."

"But it isn't Bruno! It's a St. John — the Spanish St. John, naturally."

The bishop looked discerningly at the rector then clasping his hands behind his back he strode toward the west entrance to the cathedral. There was a musing look on his face as he turned once to look at the still perturbed face of the monsignor. St. John of the Cross, hmmm? Well, he was a doctor of the Church! Not many of the saints had achieved that eminence. One couldn't go too far wrong in having communion with the mystical doctor — or even dreaming that he did.

Francis Hickey was suddenly aware as he strolled the darkened nave of the cathedral that Monsignor Brady was ready to dismiss his renovation plans with a hasty bit of housecleaning. A few hundred dollars he said should take care of washing the walls and putting a fresh coat of paint on the statuary.

The rector was within a few weeks of striking out on his summer vacation and already his suite in the episcopal residence was littered with steamship folders and brochures of shrines from Knock to Oberammergau. He had signed on with Bishop Aime Thibeault's pilgrimage, but if the monsignor followed the pattern of his previous holy romps through Europe he would soon cut loose from the restrictions of a guided tour to seek out some gems of architecture in remote villages. Perhaps it was his predilection for decay that led him to accept the status quo at home.

Monsignor Brady rubbed his finger on the dusty toe of St. Gregory the Wonderworker as he said he hoped it could all be done while he was off on the pilgrimage.

Francis Hickey stared at him in exasperation. "Monsignor, I am not talking about hiring ABC Cleaners. This must be a thorough renovation — crypt to rooftree. The baroque balconies must come down and the army of statues must be dispersed to the mission parishes. All the plaster must be torn out and replaced with brick. I see the entire attention focused on a plain liturgical altar with dear old Bishop Foley's Resurrection window as the only backdrop."

"I presume you have an estimate of the cost, Your Excellency," said the rector stiffly. He always used the formal address when he was raging inside.

Costs of course had to be counted, but the rector was always overcautious. Hickey had spent most of his nearly thirty years as bishop of Darrington in paying off the excessive debts incurred by his predecessor, Finbar O'Boyle. When Hickey had returned from Chicago that hot summer day of 1926 with the body of Bishop Foley in its coffin he found that the diocesan consultors had already met and had made Father O'Boyle apostolic administrator until a bishop was nominated.

Hickey found that he had been linked too closely to Leonard Foley's administration and with the advent of O'Boyle he was exiled to the poverty-bare parish of Porter from where he saw the Holy See confirm O'Boyle in the bishopric. With inordinate haste O'Boyle entered on a regime that set the diocesan wheels spinning. His wildly ambitious building program astonished his brother bishops, who advised prudence. But the advice was ignored and the impulsive Finbar O'Boyle failed to see financial disaster until it was on him. One calamity fell upon another. The bishop suffered a stroke and the remaining few years of his life were spent in the isolation of his room, where he refused to receive Francis Hickey who had been appointed coadjutor bishop and apostolic administrator.

Hickey had the right then to undo all O'Boyle's heedless projects, but it was not as simple as that. Banks were merciless corporations which had to be paid measure for measure, and interest over and above. But the irresponsible projects were saved, even "O'Boyle's Folly," the rural St. Finbar's Basilica at Stonehill. But O'Boyle never knew that all ended well. When visitors came he would lie with restless apathetic eyes, fingers tearing at the threads of the coverlet.

His pitiful last request was whispered to his housekeeper. He had always deplored the custom of burying the deceased bishops in the cathedral crypt. "Don't let them bury me in that damp cellar," he had pleaded.

[152]

As he wished, he was not interred in the crypt of the cathedral under the altar where his predecessors lay. One morning, amid the unexpected storm of late March, 1934, the bishops of the province of Boston gathered to make their absolutions over the remains of the unhappy bishop. Afterward the procession of black cars turned north through the bleak hills and there in the town of Hammon, in the family plot, he found peace at last.

Francis Hickey hoped that he was a compassionate man, and, now with so many years gone, he found it easier to be charitably disposed toward Bishop O'Boyle who had left an angry, troubled, but somehow successful chapter in the diocesan annals.

Leaving the rector to ponder on the unaccountable vagaries of jurisdictional prelates, Francis Hickey returned to the rectory. He disliked upsetting the even tenor of the monsignor's life but there appeared to be no alternative. He had hinted for years that the cathedral needed a face-lifting.

Francis Hickey was frequently troubled by the position of tyrant his duties imposed on him. He always deferred giving orders until no other resort was left him. There were many times when he longed for the relatively simple life of a parish priest, but even there the scale of business that must be transacted could be onerous, as the monsignor's complaints verified.

The bishop had found it impossible to cast off the feeling that he was merely the administrator of a huge financial enterprise. Perhaps it was because he was, in law, a corporation. But at least he was solvent. The people had grumbled about his practical approach to the financial problems of the diocese, but in time they saw that he had done what he had to do and had let the contumely fall where it would.

Only during his annual retreat could he escape the vast financial problems incidental to operating the diocese. At times he wondered if he had been oriented away from the sign of the cross to the dollar sign. And now it seemed Monsignor Brady felt the financial burdens every bit as much as he did, the bishop realized.

[153]

Perhaps he had been too severe with the rector. Certainly his words had been more biting than he intended. In fact, it had been an altogether bad day. He felt the need for confession — not to the monsignor, of course, under the circumstance. And, in any case, this was the hour when the rector got in his best licks at being a priest. After a half hour of meditation before the Blessed Sacrament, he had formed the habit of visiting among the parish families.

There appeared to be no one in the house. Undoubtedly the curates were busy with their parish organizations, all but one who should be on duty for sick calls or unexpected visits. The bishop consulted the chart in the hall and saw that it listed Father Gorman for duty. He was the junior among the rector's assistants and as skittish as a deer where the bishop was concerned, although he was flip enough with Father Herndon and Father Asherbrand, the other two curates.

Father Gorman's skittishness had in turn made the bishop uncomfortable with the young man, particularly when he remembered his long talks with James Gorman during his seminary days. He was eager to please then, even though his conversation was more about the misadventures of Leo Durocher than the reforms of Leo XIII.

The bishop found Father Gorman in the library watching a six-gun melodrama on television. "Father, I'd like to make my confession if you have a few moments."

"Confession?" said the startled curate, looking as though he were a Hotentot who had never heard of the sacramental system.

"Certainly. Confession. Bishops confess, you know."

Father Gorman sprang out of the chair as though the TV hero had challenged him to a gun duel. "I'll see if I can find Monsignor."

"But I asked you," the bishop said patiently.

"Oh —"

Francis Hickey chuckled understandingly.

The bishop was at peace when he had been shriven, although

[154]

he felt a bit rueful at the thought that Father Gorman had surely taken advantage of their temporarily transposed positions to admonish him to be more charitable, and also to cut down on the cigar smoking if he was morally convinced that it was injurious to his health.

Francis Hickey came to his study, switched on the green-shaded lamp on his desk, and fingered through the afternoon mail Father Redmond had left for his attention. It was opened and sorted — and, sometimes he suspected, censored too by Father Redmond. At least there had not been any scurrilous, annoymous letters brought to his notice lately. The circulars were always at the left of the desk, handy to the wastebasket.

He took up a letter from the middle pile, amused to see that it was from Father Galvin and quite convinced that it contained another request to try to make it for the Doolan-Wood wedding.

" . . . The Doolans inform me," wrote the pastor, "that they now have their sights on Cardinal Gasquet for the wedding, and are closing in on him. Your Excellency's loss seems to be His Eminence's gain, if I have interpreted them correctly.

"While I'm at it, Bishop, there's another matter that galls me. Doolan has asked me to give them the use of the parish hall for a talk by this Communist fellow. If the request had come from someone other than J. Dalton Doolan I'd have given him a quick 'no.'

"As to this Oliver Newman — undoubtedly Catholicism needs new blood, and that it was blood that has been reddened by political views need not make it unacceptable. But I would like very much to hear my bishop's opinion on this pinky. Is it true that he has swallowed the catechism and is now spouting theology with our top divines? For myself I don't take to Englishmen (no matter how naturalized they've become) who have hopped across the hedgerow. Let us not forget Cranmer!

"Looking forward to your forthright appraisal of this noisy fellow and a judicious concurrence with me, I remain . . ."

CHAPTER NINE

It was almost five o'clock when Father Massimo came downstairs the next morning. As he passed the Spanish padre's room he heard him breathing contentedly. He was happier these days with the flesh-and-blood vision to haggle with and browbeat. But at times there had been a momentary glimpse, a twinkle in the old man's eyes that made the superior wonder, giving him the impression there had been moments of lucidity when the artist had faced the fact that his model was more than a wraith.

The priest came to the sacristy, noting that the vestments were prepared for the day, Wednesday — red for the triple feast of the early martyrs Vitus, Modestus, and Crescentia.

One accepted so placidly the fact that the youth Vitus and his companions died for the faith, giving up the life that was as sweet and dear as it is to the men and women now living.

Still musing over the courage of the saints, Father Massimo switched on the lights and walked out into the oratory, always a bit uneasily these days with the holy relic on display in the sanctuary — the relic that had been the object of such bitterness.

"Buon giorno, Padre," Halidon said and the priest glanced down, momentarily startled at the sight of Steve Halidon slouched comfortably in a pew. The superior nodded a greeting and saw that his guest was glancing around to see if any early visitors had entered the chapel.

"You needn't be concerned yet, Mr. Halidon. I haven't unlocked the doors."

Halidon grinned as he rubbed his grizzled chin. "I'm sorry to be giving you so much trouble, Father. I couldn't sleep. I came up here. The last thing I knew I was sitting here — meditating." He laughed briefly. "Is that the correct word?"

"I'm not sure what you would call it, Mr. Halidon," the superior said wryly.

"If you promised you won't laugh — I was thinking about angels — if they exist — and what they look like. I'm sure they don't look like that plaster statue of St. Michael."

Father Massimo smiled. "What is your theory?"

"I wouldn't want you to get sore at me."

"I'm a priest and have heard all sorts of theories about angels. I think I could stand another."

Halidon raised his eyes to the irresolutely ponderous statue. "The artists always depict them as men — at least the angels I've heard of. I'm sure there must be some females floating around up there."

"You have what Americans call a one-track mind, Mr. Halidon. And while I'm on the subject — you should know that you haven't performed a kindly service in teaching Father Largo some of your crudities in the guise of Americanisms."

"I don't think I said anything obscene."

" 'Hunky-dory' is a poor substitute for 'excellent.' "

Halidon laughed. "But it sounds so funny coming out of him!"

Father Massimo shook his head sadly. "You are not a very serious man, Mr. Halidon. I had hoped you'd take advantage of this time — "

"To improve my soul?"

"I'm not even sure that you believe you have an immortal soul."

Halidon smiled uneasily. "Father Largo seems to see some good in me."

"Yes — there is good in you or you would not have been so patient, so tolerant, with poor Father Largo."

"He's very unhappy that you won't allow him to say Mass. Is there some reason why you haven't had psychiatric treatment for him?"

Father Massimo sighed. "He's very much against it. And I've been reluctant to have his mind probed for the terrible things that happened to him in China. He seems to have no memory of his tortures. But we have learned from a mission Sister who was with him that he suffered terrible degradation. What would his reaction be if he remembered he had confessed to the crimes they charged against him? When they were done with him they drove him through the streets of Chien-Chio while the people spat on him and cast dung at him. At the mission they staked him to the floor of the mission tower and left a guard to ring the bell above him. It was tolled throughout the night and when the Communists came in the morning they found Father Largo gone and their guard hanging by his neck from the bell."

"His people rescued him?" Halidon asked.

Father Massimo nodded. "And in reprisal every known Christian in the town was shot or bayoneted to death."

Halidon watched the superior's troubled face. "I see," he said.

The superior's shoulders moved apprehensively. "Perhaps I am wrong. A doctor might be able to make Father Largo see that those murders are a part of the universal pattern — a cleansing process. But sometimes I think the scientist is more concerned to find a word to describe a condition than he is in curing it. The psychiatrist prescribes for the soul — sometimes without admitting that the soul exists — and, more important, that it is immortal."

"Psychiatry is the function of the priest in the confessional — is that what you mean?"

"It always has been. *Ab immorabile!* It took science, medical science, a long time to find out that much of the world's ills are spiritual."

"And now they've usurped your work?" Halidon said.

There was a disturbed smile on the priest's lips. He shook his head slowly. "They could never do that, Mr. Halidon. The priest's function is to reconcile the soul to God — to fix satisfaction for sins. In the confessional the penitent cannot hide his sins under the pleasant euphemisms employed by the psychiatrist."

Halidon nodded, smiling grimly. "You must call a spade a spade. I guess that's why I always found it so hard to go to confession."

Father Massimo looked at his watch. "I wish I had more time to talk to you, but if I don't get to the hospital for Mass they'll be worried."

Halidon got up from the pew and walked back through the passage with the superior. "Do you mind if I help myself in the kitchen. I'd like a cup of coffee."

Assuring Halidon that he was perfectly welcome to make himself at home, the superior took up his coat from the long bench and drew it on as he reentered the oratory. He was passing the pew where Halidon had been when his eyes were caught by a folded piece of yellow paper on the floor. Father Massimo picked it up hurriedly. He unlocked the chapel door and in the brighter light outside he opened the telegram.

"Steve Halidon, Hotel Phoenix, Darrington, Mass.," it read, "Steve: Stick with it. Your man sure to make his move soon. He has reservation on flight out of country for Monday. Old man has OK'd double time and bonus. Good luck, Shanley."

Father Massimo folded the telegram and slipped it into his pocket as he strode up the hill. He didn't know quite why he felt relief to know that Halidon hadn't come to the monastery by chance. The superior didn't wonder that Halidon had found confession difficult. Perhaps when he returned from the hospital he could help to ease the confession — at least to the point of asking Halidon for an explanation of the telegram.

Father Massimo's work at the hospital took longer than he had expected that morning. When he returned to the monastery he found Fathers Columba and Edmund awaiting him with anxiety on their faces.

"The grand inquisitor is here," said the Englishman.

Father Massimo smiled. He could mean no one else but Newman. "I hope you made him welcome, Father."

"He made himself welcome!" roared Father Columba. "He's already trying to run the house. He told poor Father Max that it's undignified for a priest to be answering doors and cooking meals."

"Where is he now?" asked the superior.

Father Columba shrugged. "Somewhere in the house. The last I heard, Father Dmitri had him cornered in the library and was giving him the details of how an African tribe he knows of treats its enemies. They are staked out in the sun and devoured alive by ants."

"Father Dmitri can be painfully blunt at times," said Father Edmund. "But at least he distracted this meddler. He was quite curious about our guest in the basement. But he appeared to understand when Father Columba told him he couldn't go down there. I'm sure the fellow must have black and blue marks on his arm from the grip Father Columba clamped on him as he conducted him away from the cellar door." The Britisher nodded to his Irish brother. "But you did make your point, Father."

"I thought we had scared him off for a minute," said Father Columba, "when he said he had accepted an invitation to spend a few days with the Doolans at Cohagansett. But from the questions he asked about Father Constant, I have the idea he's going to put our little Lithuanian brother through an inquisition."

The superior looked at the two priests with distress. "I wish we could spare him from this prying."

"Exactly what we have in mind," said Father Edmund. "We

[160]

are going to Cohagansett — with your permission, of course, Father Superior."

Father Massimo smiled wryly, quite aware that they didn't take the Father superior business very seriously. "I thought if anyone went to visit Father Constant it would be Father Georgio. He's always looked after him."

"We talked that over," said Father Edmund, "and agreed that another beard at the resort would only stir up misunderstanding and resentment against our order."

Father Massimo waited while the two priests hurried away whispering together like conspirators. Waiting these long months for Newman to move had put him on edge. But until this morning he didn't realize how impractical he would be. Only when he at last had full knowledge that Halidon had plans for Newman, too, did he become aware of his jealousy at the intrusion. He had been the hunter, waiting patiently for the killer beast to come within his sights.

But what weapons did he have? During the months of waiting he had tried not to think of that. There were times when he tried not to forget that he had the duty to pray for Newman. He had forced himself to his knees and had prayed that when Newman knew his game was finished, the man would pour out his heinous crimes and bend his head for absolution. But the priest was a dreamer to think it would be so easy.

His only weapon then would be the one that Holy Church permitted him to invoke, to withhold absolution if he believed the repentance insincere.

Newman would laugh at such thoughts as these, Father Massimo felt sure. He and his kind wanted the world, not the world to come.

Fearful that Newman had gone alone to Bishop Dworjanski's room, Father Massimo had started up the stairs when he saw the cellar door open and Newman's face appear, with a startled look on it when he saw the superior watching him.

Newman dusted his hands fastidiously and smiled calmly.

"I'm surprised at you, Father Superior, permitting this farce in a religious house."

The priest studied Newman's face reflectively. He drew the heavy beads up from his belt as he walked toward the library, snapping them through his fingers as he motioned Newman ahead of him into the room.

"I'm sorry you found it necessary to disturb Father Largo at his painting," said the superior. "If you had asked me about our guest I would have told you — perhaps with some hesitation — but I would have told you. He is a homeless fellow — hobo, he calls it."

Newman breathed out through his nose impatiently. "How do you know he is what he claims? He could rob or murder you!"

"It is hard for me to believe a man would repay kindness with violence, Mr. Newman. I suppose you will be shocked when I tell you that I am shielding him from the police. He is wanted in connection with an accident in which he appears to be an innocent party. Perhaps it was a sentimental impulse — "

"Will that be your excuse when they charge you with shielding this man?" Newman asked.

Father Massimo repressed a smile. "I would ask for a definition of my position. I'm not at all sure that the ancient law of sanctuary does not apply."

Newman gasped. "What can this worthless fellow mean to you?"

"Society, in fact, would be served by his liquidation — is that your meaning, Mr. Newman?"

Newman stared at the priest, suddenly drawing a hand across his mouth in frustration and confusion. "I didn't mean that, Father Massimo. Even his kind may hope for salvation."

"But nothing else apparently."

Newman smiled, a touch of repentance on his lean face. "Thank you, Father, for reminding me. Sometimes I forgot my own regeneration. There are times when the full flow of the

[162]

grace of God makes me forget that I am only a poor sinner."

"The grace of God is not a toy, Mr. Newman. It's my sincere hope that you have that grace, but it is not becoming to boast of it."

Newman bowed his head, somewhat abjectly. "The extraordinary circumstance of my conversion has led me to the sin of pride."

Father Massimo looked at Newman cautiously. "My problem is not quite as simple as you imagine, Mr. Newman. There were a few possibilities I failed to take into account when I allowed this man to stay here. It is never wrong to be merciful. But as to observing the law, I believe I have been influenced more by the spirit than the letter. The county prosecutor made it clear to me that he has no particular regard for the clerical collar. He was angry, but not quite sure that he understood all the technicalities of my position in law."

Newman sighed in exasperation. "I know these politicians, Father Massimo. They'll probe into it a few days to make sure of their ground. And when they are, they'll crucify you."

"You're much too sanguine, Mr. Newman," Father Massimo said calmly. "But if they do I'll ask for it head downward like St. Peter."

Newman laughed nervously. "You take me too literally, Father, but you could be expelled from the country."

The priest stared calmly at Newman. "My position here is tenuous at best. My mission will soon be finished."

"Mission?"

"Yes. I started to tell you the other day. I was recalled from my work as a librarian in our Order's institute in Rome to pursue a matter that had its beginnings many years ago in Poland."

"A secret matter, of course," Newman said.

"I'm not at all sure that it is very secret anymore."

Newman laughed as he fidgeted with the groove of the table. "Come now, Father, you don't need to be secretive with me!

I suppose it is one of these canonical processes that Rome is forever conducting to uncover new saints."

"A canonical process?" the superior mused. "Perhaps you are right, Mr. Newman. Perhaps it is a canonical process of some sort. But Rome never knows when it begins these investigations whether it will uncover a saint or a devil."

Francis Hickey had had a busy morning. During the drive back from Portland where he had the sad duty to preach the eulogy at the funeral of his old friend, Bishop Ambrose Heenan, he had time to dwell on the uncertainty of his own mortal span. Life was sweet; he realized anew how sweet when he saw Father Asherbrand's heavy foot on the accelerator and the speedometer vibrating nervously at 85. Until that moment he had never taken seriously Martin Asherbrand's reputation as the Barney Oldfield of the diocesan clergy.

Back at his desk Francis Hickey flipped through the pages of his appointment book which was packed solid with confirmation engagements through the rest of June, the whole of July, and much of August.

The deceased Bishop Ambrose Heenan had retired to Portland after forty-five years in the Solomon Islands, most of them spent as Vicar Apostolic of San Cristobal and the Isles. Bishop Hickey, who had known him well in his active missionary years, was asked to deliver the funeral sermon. The nonogenarian Bishop Blaise Wallenburger was there, solemnly predicting that he would be next as he vested for his role as one of prelates to give the final absolutions over the body along with the cardinal archbishop who officiated. Blaise Wallenburger had already delivered absolutions over three generations of bishops and no one was about to contradict him that his own time was approaching.

Francis Hickey saw that Father Redmond had been efficient as usual. The mail was opened and sorted.

The bishop was about to tackle the mail when his secretary

popped his head in the door. "Father Galvin on the phone, Bishop. Are you in?"

Not being in was an easy out, but the bishop had never been able to convince himself that it was a thoroughly honest one. Only Father Redmond knew when the bishop was in a mood to get away with such a suggestion.

"Put him on, Father," he chuckled. "I need some cheering up."

The buzzer sounded and the bishop picked up the phone, "Good afternoon, Father," he said.

Father Galvin boomed back the greeting: "Mrs. Doolan is still after the Canadian cardinal. She's been unable to get in touch with him, though, and is in a pretty nervous state."

"I don't envy you, Father," the bishop said. He was sorry Daisy Doolan had ever heard of Cardinal Gasquet, and probably the cardinal would be too before Daisy got through pestering him. The bishop was grateful for his own reprieve from her annoying insistence that he officiate. Daisy Doolan seemed more concerned about rounding up a first-rate dignitary for the wedding than she did about assuring herself that her daughter was making a good match. Everything was being made regular enough with the Wood boy getting in under the baptismal wire, Catholic in name at least, even though he probably didn't know what sanctifying grace meant.

"It frightens me a little, Bishop," said Father Galvin. "For my own part, I'm mighty queasy about courting a cardinal. I've never had much truck with princes of the Church."

Hickey laughed outright. "I'm told they put on their pants one leg at a time, just as you and I, Father. But it appears now that making contact with Cardinal Gasquet is getting to be quite a project in itself. I understand that no one at Cohagansett has seen him yet."

"Daisy is confident anyway — and she usually gets her way. But you may be sure, Bishop, that I'll be prepared. You always told me I had native ingenuity."

"There's one serious point for you to consider," the bishop said. "While Cardinal Gasquet is free from our point of view to officiate at this wedding, I hope you haven't forgotten that he is a Canadian and must meet with the civil requirements."

"Good Lord!" exclaimed Father Galvin. "I can just picture myself advising His Eminence to trot up to Boston and get himself a notary's license if he wants to perform a bona fide marriage."

Long after the Cohagansett pastor hung up the bishop paced in his study wondering if it might have been wise to urge on Father Galvin the necessity for bypassing the cardinal. But he couldn't quite bring himself to it, not when he was so curious himself to see what Gasquet's reactions would be when they eventually flushed him from his retreat. If afterward apologies were needed, they could be made with the properly contrite demeanor. But if Gasquet was the aloof and shy fellow he was reported to be, nothing might ever be known of his reaction.

The Cohagansett pastor's parting remarks were of his rheumatism which he said was no better and which might (perhaps fortunately) have him abed the day of the wedding. The priest might even be of a frame of mind to appreciate his affliction by that time.

The bishop was on the point of applying himself to his desk work when Father Redmond announced the arrival of Mr. Brissart, the district attorney.

Francis Hickey arose expectantly, watching as Harlan Brissart hurried warily along the hall, probably a bit apprehensive that some of dear old Bishop Foley's ponderous statuary and busts might fall on him from their niches.

The bishop would have known Brissart without being informed of who he was. He had made it a point to acquaint himself with the faces of public officials so that he need never be embarrassed at civic functions if accosted by one of them who assumed he would be known to the bishop.

He greeted the district attorney in a friendly manner, and

the man immediately established his conformity to pattern by commenting that it was a beautiful day.

"Some of them are bound to be," Hickey said with an amused smile. He drew a chair to the side of his desk for Brissart and they sat down.

They talked of a number of things of mutual disinterest and finally Brissart leaned forward and said, "As you may suspect, sir, I've come to ask a big favor of you."

"Oh," said Hickey uneasily.

"But I'd like to establish something in my own mind first. I know very little about the extent of your authority. In my own church we are very democratic. No one has authority over anyone else. It works out very well."

"Except when you want to speak to someone in authority, I imagine," Hickey said.

Brissart gave an abashed but appreciative laugh. "But I understand that you are somewhat autonomous, sir."

"If you mean my word is law, you're somewhat right."

"Does that mean that you have authority over the foreign priests at the monastery?"

"To a degree. They have put themselves at my disposal while in the diocese, and must observe the rules."

"Then you can be of service," Brissart said.

"Police work is a little out of my line," said the bishop.

Brissart's face tightened with a poorly concealed impatience. "I'm talking about the man they have hidden out in the monastery cellar. I'm sure you've heard of it by now."

The bishop nodded apprehensively. He hadn't expected a confirmation from this source though. "Is it someone you're interested in?"

"I'm caught in the middle, sir," Brissart said grimly. "The man is wanted as a witness in a case. But I'm not too sure this whole thing isn't some scheme to invalidate any testimony he might give. Certainly if the man gets on the stand and claims that he is this, this dead Spaniard. . . ." Brissart glanced quickly at the bishop. "But that isn't the point. The point is, could we ever get the man out — legally, I mean. This sanctuary business bothers me. I'm not prepared to debate with theologians on immemorial laws."

Bishop Hickey looked placidly at Brissart. "If you're looking for immemorial laws — and possible loopholes — I have the vague recollection of one that requires the Church to turn criminals over to the secular arm."

Brissart stared at the bishop in dismay. "The man isn't a criminal. I'm not making any charges. I wouldn't want to do anything that would make him testify — the wrong way."

"The wrong way? I thought all testimony was to be truthfully given whether it proved to be favorable or not."

Brissart smiled sardonically. "Let me put it this way, sir. If the truth is unfavorable it is sometimes better not to hear it."

Bishop Hickey arose from his chair, his face disturbed. He was quite sure he had missed entirely the objective of Brissart's visit. He should have known better than to assume that the district attorney had a straightforward request to make: to provide a witness for a hearing. He should have guessed that Brissart had an angle.

"I had hoped to secure your cooperation, Bishop," Brissart said calmly. "I have been requested to leave the man where he is for the present."

"Requested? By whom?"

"By its nature it is more than a request. The FBI has stepped in. But I'm not sure of their purpose. I suppose you don't know, Bishop?"

"Good Lord!" exclaimed Hickey. "Why should they tell me?"

Hickey was almost pleased that he was unable to answer the question the district attorney had put to him. He was reasonably sure now that to get such an answer was the true objective of Brissart's call.

Father Massimo was relieved to hear the bishop's voice when

[168]

he answered the phone. His Excellency was pleasant as usual but unusually mysterious. He knew it was very near to the dinner hour but he wanted to come over to the monastery for a talk on a very important matter.

The superior put down the phone anxiously. He really had his choice if he wanted to guess what the bishop might have on his mind — Rome's concern for Bishop Dworjanski — the disquieting presence of Oliver Newman — the other somewhat ubiquitous presence in the crypt — some unexpected problem with Father Constant at Cohagansett. . . .

But perhaps he worried needlessly. The bishop might simply have had a sudden impulse to inspect the house. If it was that he had only a few minor discrepancies to worry about, such as the complaint of the nearby supermarket manager that Father Georgio had tried to exchange two cases of Les Dames du Bon Secours baked beans for a better variety of canned goods.

The Father superior sat down at his desk and opened his record book. He had kept a strict accounting, he was sure, but there might be no harm in again auditing their good works and their failures to make sure.

He was still at his desk when he heard the doorbell, and, in a moment, Father Maximilian's steps hurrying to answer it. When the superior came out of his office he saw Bishop Hickey striding toward him as though he was anxious to get away from Father Max.

The last time the German priest had an opportunity for a chat with the bishop he had made quite an issue of the fact that Hickey had no cathedral chapter, and had wondered if he might be so presumptuous as to suggest that the exiles might serve as canons. The bishop's only comment had been that he didn't want to be the one to cause Monsignor Brady to have a stroke.

When Father Massimo had heard the reason for the bishop's visit and had explained how the stranger had come to the monastery, he saw that Hickey was content that there had been no deliberate intent to foster a bogus apparition.

"And you haven't any idea who this man is or why he is here?" the bishop asked.

"I have some idea — yes," said the superior calmly. "His name is Steve Halidon. I'm convinced that the accident outside the monastery wasn't a part of his plan."

"But he has a plan?" the bishop asked. "It isn't a coincidence that he is here at this particular time?"

Father Massimo smiled. "I'm sure if he were a hobo, as he claims, he would not endure the monastic discipline imposed on him by Father Largo."

"I have the impression that you feel more secure with this man in the house, Father."

The Father superior's eyes widened at the knowing look on Bishop Hickey's face. "We have ample protection — St. Michael the Archangel in the sanctuary and San Juan de la Cruz in the cellar."

Bishop Hickey smiled cryptically. "And a Don Quixote in the guise of a Father superior."

The superior was just as pleased that the bishop had declined his invitation to stay for dinner. He had been tempted to urge him to stay as he sniffed the aroma of Father Georgio's favorite meat loaf with noodles. It was amazing how many different ways the Father commissario could disguise hamburger, Father Massimo thought pleasantly as he inspected the tray Father Georgio had prepared for Bishop Dworjanski. The cook was in the habit of slipping pickles or something equally indigestible onto the bishop's tray.

Father Massimo had started up the stairs with the tray when he heard Newman's voice behind him. The priest was surprised that he was still in the house.

"If you are going to the bishop's room, Father, perhaps we could brush aside some of the protocol now so I could speak to him."

The superior paused, studying the man's anxious face for a moment. "Well . . . perhaps an introduction will do no harm. Come along."

There was a muffled response to the superior's knock and when Father Massimo opened the door he saw Stefan Dworjanski at his desk before the large window overlooking the street. The old man arose and closed the folio before him when he saw the stranger.

"I brought your dinner, Your Excellency — and a guest who has been quite anxious to meet you. Mr. Newman."

Father Massimo put the tray down on the table near the fireplace where the bishop was in the habit of taking his meal.

He wasn't surprised when he turned and saw a grimace of forbearance on Stefan Dworjanski's heavy-jowled face as Newman bent his knee before him and put his lips to the episcopal ring.

"So," Dworjanski said slowly, "you are Oliver Newman. I have your books here," he said, motioning toward the shelves beside the window.

"I hope you enjoyed them," Newman said.

"One does not always enjoy tragedy, Mr. Newman," the bishop said blandly, "but I'm sure your message was understood."

"I had to reveal the terrible mistakes I made . . ." Newman said, his voice unexpectedly shrill.

"It takes courage to condemn oneself," Bishop Dworjanski replied as he watched Newman's face, "and something more than courage to condemn one's former friends, the men later deported. For this bit of work, Mr. Newman, I assume you have been excommunicated by the Communists?"

"I hadn't thought of it in that way, Your Excellency."

Father Massimo turned from the window where he had been standing, letting the heavy curtain fall into its accustomed folds. His reserved eyes studied Newman's face for a moment.

"One excommunicates himself. But the more cautious of men have always felt it is a little foolhardy, although possibly

[171]

courageous, to court excommunication. Yet, throughout the centuries, there have been a few who braved social and economic suicide in the name of conscience. Most of them have suffered cruelly, in one way or another."

There was a smile of abnegation on Newman's face. "You overestimate my importance, Father. I was always a very small cog in the Communist machinery. I'm afraid my life hasn't been nearly as adventurous as Bishop Dworjanski's." He glanced quickly at the bishop. "The world was amazed that you survived so much torture and so many years in that prison. I'd be honored to hear your account."

"And disappointed if you don't," the bishop said. "Perhaps you shall read my account some day, Mr. Newman, when it is finished." He turned his eyes to the manuscript, running his hand over the thick folio. "I have it all here, or nearly all."

He sat down at his desk, and a glance from Father Massimo indicated that they should leave.

Newman was at the door when Stefan Dworjanski spoke again, his voice rather loud and quivering.

"One question, Mr. Newman. I'm surprised that you yourself survived. How did you accomplish that?"

"One learns how to survive. It wasn't too bad for me. I believed in the Communist ideal."

"And worked for it?"

"Yes," Newman said, impatience in his voice. "But all of it is in my autobiography."

Stefan Dworjanski laughed coldly. "Only a fool tells everything, Mr. Newman — and you are no fool."

"I'm not sure what Your Excellency means."

"There are things a man cannot tell about himself, perhaps not even to his confessor — moments of cowardice, moments when we are afraid that we cannot be the thing we are driven to by circumstance."

"There's much I have to learn about self-examination, Bishop."

When they were gone Stefan Dworjanski sat down to his

dinner but he was unable to eat. He got up and crossed the room to his desk, and opened the folio, turning the handwritten pages absently. The account of his stewardship of the See of Grajewo that the world seemed to prize so much, was here, almost all, but for a few unfinished chapters that neither he nor time had resolved.

Now, unexpectedly, he recalled with disturbing clarity the face and the voice of his inquisitor as they prepared his trial. The old man waved his hand before his face in bafflement. He was deceiving himself. He had spent too much time dwelling on his torments. Faces and voices had come to him before out of the circle of darkness.

He had wondered sometimes if his imagination was not fired as much by the unexpected interest there was in him when he reached this country. It was enough to make him lose his equilibrium when he saw how anxious the publishers were for his memoirs.

But as he wrote, he was troubled with the thought that it would not be wise to reveal the inhumanity he had seen and known, the bodies and the souls that had been destroyed.

He alone of all the priests imprisoned at the Fortress of St. Ladislas had survived. It had made him wonder if he had been preserved by God for some purpose, but at other times he thought the survival was a punishment. His great dismay was that he had encouraged, even demanded, superhuman courage of poor Father Zwiecki.

His young secretary had tried gallantly to keep his reason and his faith, but at length they broke him. He had died moaning at his fate and his betrayal, crying to his bishop and his God whom he believed had abandoned him.

It was a degrading way to die, confessing to heinous crimes that his simple and steadfast mind had never dreamed of.

The bishop had tried to resist the fierce hatred he had for the murderers of Father Zwiecki, but fight it as he would, he had found himself praying for the time when he could avenge

[173]

the crime that tormented him. Then, after months alone in his dark cell, messages came by a mysterious hand telling him that his enemies were being destroyed one by one. General Skobshek, commandant of the fortress, died after drinking a portion of acid and had run into the courtyard screaming for his guard to shoot him down. But they were afraid of reprisal and had let him die a slow, tortuous death. The judge who had sentenced Stefan Dworjanski had hanged himself when he heard that he had fallen from favor and was doomed to Siberian exile. Others of his accusers and his guard had met terrible deaths, some of them on the day that Polish patriots had stormed the fortress, ramming the ancient gate with a vegetable cart loaded with explosives.

When the firing ceased and the door of his cell was opened, Stefan Dworjanski was hurried through the dark corridors into the courtyard, and he saw the price that his captives had paid. All were dead and his rescuers dispersed except for the man who would speed him south toward the mountains.

But there were days when he lived again through the brain-washing. He knew from the beginning that they dared not murder him and knew how much mental and physical torture he could endure. What bones were broken, he never knew. Pain deadened pain, defiance deadened fear, and hate deadened love. It was only when he forced himself to make a formal avowal of forgiveness for his enemies that he felt justified.

He had forgiven them, yet justice pursued them and would find them out to the last one.

There was one face, one name, he had nearly forgotten. The revival of that memory made Stefan Dworjanski's mind stir with excitement as that face emerged distinctly.

The pulsing in his head was such that the bishop had to rise from his chair. It was strange how that voice rang clear above the others.

Stefan Dworjanski laughed harshly, and after a moment he sat down and began to write quickly.

[174]

CHAPTER TEN

FATHERS COLUMBA AND EDMUND set out early Thursday morning for their visit to Cohagansett. They boarded the bus at the downtown depot, trying to ignore the stares they attracted with their contrasting white and black robes. They were in no particular hurry to get to the beach and were a bit nervous as the driver barreled down the middle of the highway, at times forcing his foot down rather hysterically on the accelerator when another vehicle loomed up ahead of him.

The Britisher's prayers, however, brought the bus safely to the Cohagansett depot; and Father Edmund recovered his equilibrium on the sidewalk while his companion got the directions to St. Smaragdus parish, and thanked the unhappy-looking cab driver for his expression of concern that they would have quite a walk. They set out, guided by the slim, slate spire in the distance.

St. Smaragdus rectory was an ornate many-gabled white house adjoining the blunt Norman-Gothic church on a craggy ledge perilously close to the yawning ocean.

A large-boned woman stood on the front porch, drying her hands on her apron as she watched them approach. But as they came up the steps and before she could speak, Father Constant appeared.

Father Columba clamped his arm about him in genuine delight and his companion extended his usual reserved greeting.

"We've been expecting you, Fathers," Clara Galvin said. "I'll tell the pastor you're here."

She went inside and the Irishman looked down affectionately at the diminutive Lithuanian. "Well, you look happy. Are they treating you all right? Enough to eat?"

Father Constant shook his head, a bit too eagerly, the Englishman thought. "If you're unhappy you can come back to the monastery. The atmosphere here is somewhat like Brighton — our British Brighton, of course. I could fancy myself making out quite well here — "

They heard the pastor's booming voice on the stairs inside the house and Father Constant, sudden alarm in his eyes, dashed inside, mumbling that he was already late for the Doolan wedding rehearsal.

Father Galvin was a lumpy, uncomfortable-looking man with large, unhandsome features and curly, unmanageable hair. He greeted them with a quivering jaw and directed them to follow him into the house. He took a shuffling lead, appearing to move without lifting his feet, which were propelling loose, worn carpet slippers ahead of him. He had sent Clara off for iced coffee, if they went for that sort of thing, when he realized quite abruptly that they were in dead earnest about refusing any sort of drink.

The pastor cracked his enlarged knuckles. "I may as well be frank with you, Fathers. I'm unhappy with your fellow Brunite. I was in a fair way of getting used to his beard and his peculiar eating habits — since he's been here his faith embraced only soft boiled eggs. My sister Clara is almost compelled to believe that he thinks she's trying to poison him. On Sunday last my rheumatism was so painful that I was forced to ask Father Constant to stand by me while I offered my Mass, though I prayed with might and main that I wouldn't collapse. He kept smiling at me strangely during the Mass and afterwards in the sacristy he complimented me on my courage in enduring the pain. Then he asked me if I thought the pain of rheumatism could be compared to the anguish of being slowly strangled with a garroting wire."

Father Columba chuckled. "We are sure Father has no

[176]

intention of throttling you and your sister in your beds unless it be for some purely domestic reason."

"I'm sorry to see you look on the matter with levity," said the pastor. "I wish I could have had the same feeling about the terrible harangue he delivered against wealth in our parish hall the other evening. Frankly, I feel betrayed — and I dare not think what effect the talk will have on my Sunday collection. . . ."

The visitors eyed each other uneasily. Father Galvin gasped cholerically as he got up, trying to locate the opening in the side of his soutane so he could get at his hankerchief. "When your good brother does open up with us, it's about how fine things were in the old days in his own country. I understand perfectly his wish to return to the homeland, and no one prays harder for that glorious day than I do — unless it's Clara."

The two priests started to get up. "We're imposing on you, Father Galvin. You must be busy . . ." said the Irishman.

The pastor blew his nose vigorously as he waved them back into their chairs. "No sense going to look for your little chum. He went off to sub for me at a premarital tea at Daisy Doolan's. I'm having a final conference this afternoon with Huntley Winslow Wood the Third, the young buck who's marrying Maryanne Doolan. Daisy considers the match quite a triumph for what she calls our side. To state it simply, the Woods are first-class elite. The Doolans will be rubbing noses with people their parents didn't even have enough status to scrub floors for a generation ago. The late Mr. Wood made his social reputation in yachting, but his widow is delighted at the turn of events."

The visitors looked at each other, wondering why the widow was so delighted.

"Mrs. Wood has been here a few times to discuss religion with me," Father Galvin continued. "She was at first opposed to having her son baptized — over again — our way. I couldn't get it through her head that administering the sacrament is more than a mere social occasion."

[177]

"I hope you explained to her about original sin," said Father Edmund.

"I tried," retorted the pastor sourly, "but she told me she didn't think there were any original sins left. The lady has no sense of humor. Her family's been Boston Brahmins for generations. It was only after some weeks that I got through to her that her son cannot take *temporary vows* as a Catholic."

"We were invited to the wedding ourselves," said the Irish missioner, "but we have to get to the parishes on Saturday. I hope the Doolans will understand."

Father Galvin chuckled. "They're after bigger game than you foreign missionaries. Mrs. Doolan thinks she can get Cardinal Gasquet — he's summering here — to officiate at the wedding. His Eminence is a palatine cardinal — the very best kind, Daisy has remarked."

The discussion was interrupted by the bong of the doorbell. "That would be the young man now," the pastor said and shuffled from the room to return shortly with a sandy-haired, rosy-cheeked young man, who came toward them and was introduced as the lucky fellow who was going to marry Maryanne Doolan.

They saw that the pastor was anxious to get on with his conference with Woody and edged toward the door, saying good-bye and noting with some disappointment that it never entered Father Galvin's head to offer them the hospitality of the house — dinner, anyway, if not a place for the night.

They walked on in silence, until they found themselves outside the town, trudging in the weeds beside the road. Father Columba bent down and plucked a blade of grass, running it through his teeth as he looked up at the sky.

"Do you realize, Father, that it's almost sunset and we have no idea where we're going to spend the night?"

"Not with Father Galvin, it seems," said his companion. They had counted on that hospitality.

They were dwelling silently on their plight, quite aware of

how foot weary they were, when a black limousine pulled up alongside them. The window of the back seat was being rolled down and they saw that the occupant was a priest — actually somewhat more than a priest — perhaps a bishop — no, a cardinal — undoubtedly Daisy Doolan's palatine cardinal. There was no mistaking the ring or the princely red of the piping on the aged man's cape, or his Roman hat.

"Please get it," the cardinal said as his chauffeur hurried around the car and held the door open. He slid to the far end of the seat to make room; then he leaned over to observe their faces.

"One of you is the pastor here?" he asked.

"No, Your Eminence," they said in unison. "Simply travelers — on a pilgrimage of sorts," added Father Columba.

Cardinal Gasquet put a thin finger to his cheek thoughtfully, "Oh, I had thought this would be my opportunity to speak to the pastor privately."

"We know the pastor at St. Smaragdus — if that's any help," said the Irish missioner.

The cardinal drew his hands together reflectively. "I hope I shall not cause him an inconvenience. I had been approached, by a letter, to officiate at a wedding. . . . But this is no concern of yours. You are visiting here, Fathers?"

Father Edmund explained who they were and what they were doing at Cohagansett. The cardinal seemed somewhat pleased with himself that he knew a good deal about them. He told them what he knew of the monastery in Darrington.

"If you would care to be my guests for the night, Fathers, I would be delighted to have you. We could talk about your work in the missions — "

At Father Edmund's incredulous stare a faint smile moved the cardinal's lips: "That is — if the rules of your order permit."

"We have wide discretionary powers," said Father Edmund.

[179]

CHAPTER ELEVEN

ON FRIDAY night, the eve of their ordination, the nine young men were gathered in St. Mary's Cathedral for a rehearsal under the direction of old Monsignor McDonough, the vicar-general. The rehearsal was always the vicar-general's show and Francis Hickey took his own part philosophically. No priest had been ordained in the diocese of Darrington in fifty years without first undergoing a dry run under the ritualistic eye of Darcy McDonough.

Year by year the young men who presented themselves for ordination looked more youthful but, disturbingly, more sophisticated. Perhaps it was just as well, Francis Hickey thought. To be so utterly worldly-wise might be one of their best defenses as they went out into the world and had their faith tested rather perilously.

When the rehearsal was over, Monsignor McDonough came toward the bishop, his frame trembling with age, his head completely denuded of even a wisp of hair, shaking dismally as usual.

"I'm sure there'll be blunders galore tomorrow, Bishop! But I've done my best . . . and I'll be with them every step of the way."

Francis Hickey smiled kindly at the old man and helped him to a chair. "We'll manage somehow, Monsignor. We always have."

After the vicar-general had rested for a few minutes they walked back to the house. The old man, who had come sixty-five miles from Granby, would be the bishop's guest for the night.

The bishop had said good night to the monsignor and was pacing in the hall with his breviary when Sister Patricia told him there was a visitor — a man named Kevin Byrne.

"Send him on to my office, Sister," he said. He was at his desk a few moments later when a red-haired young man appeared at the threshold, smiling at him.

"Please come in — "

Kevin Byrne came to the desk and handed his identification folder to the bishop. He studied it closely then raised probing eyes to his visitor. "You're from the FBI?"

"If there is any doubt in your mind you can call Boston."

The bishop drew off his glasses and massaged the bridge of his nose thoughtfully. "I have been in trouble before — but never with the FBI."

Byrne grinned, looking more like a freshly scrubbed athlete than an investigator. "We thought we had better warn you — and perhaps secure your cooperation — in connection with Archangel Monastery — "

"I thought all the priests there had been thoroughly investigated — their identities cleared."

"It isn't one of the priests, though Father Georgio did give us some concern a few months ago when he began corresponding with the Russian embassy. But it turned out that he had simply written them for maps for his hobby."

"I wondered if they might not run into trouble about that," the bishop said. "But if it isn't one of the priests you are concerned about it must be someone else there."

"You're thinking of the man in the crypt, Bishop. That bothered us only for a short while, until we discovered who he is. He's not a hobo. I'm surprised Father Massimo didn't guess that. He's a reporter — from one of the New York papers.

[181]

We were quite disturbed when Brissart wanted to get him out of the monastery. He'll be useful to us — "

"Then he is not there just to take refuge from the litigants in the accident suit?"

"If it will ease your mind, Bishop, I think it is a good idea to allow the reporter, Steve Halidon, to stay at the monastery. Brissart was quite disappointed that the man in the crypt didn't turn out to be a most-wanted criminal. When we came to Darrington and notified him that we were working on a case and might eventually need the cooperation of the local police, he went to the trouble of having one of his assistants tail me. I suppose when they saw me go to the monastery a few times they began to tally things up. And when they heard Father Largo was telling everyone who visited the chapel that he'd had a vision, they really got excited."

Bishop Hickey chuckled as he remembered his talk with Brissart. "Apparently you stopped him in time."

"We'd never have contacted him at all if we knew he'd try to jump the gun on us. He probably envisioned grabbing some publicity for himself. If he descended on the monastery with the police he might have muffed the whole thing. He was pretty disappointed when he heard who Halidon was."

"And Halidon is rather unimportant when there are other fish to fry — is that it?" the bishop asked.

"We expect favorable results — quite soon. But there are some things which still puzzle us — and one that greatly concerns the Bureau. They are wondering about the official attitude of the Church in this matter — " Byrne moved uneasily. "How would the Church feel if a Communist should be exposed in her midst?"

"Rather surprised, I should say. Whom do you have in mind?"

Byrne smiled. "I hope you'd understand that the question was merely theoretical."

Bishop Hickey laughed. "I know you didn't come here to

Darrington to theorize with me, particularly when you must know that I have a reputation for being blunt, a rather painful reputation. If I were a diplomatic man, I'd pretend that I didn't know what you were talking about." The bishop leaned forward. "But I'm in earnest and much concerned — and I won't mind a bit if you arrest this *theoretical* person."

"I was instructed to sound you out on it," Byrne said. "As you say, you do have a reputation for getting to the essence of public controversies — and you've been outspoken about ex-Communists. Wasn't it you who said the 'ex' stood for expedient?"

Hickey chuckled. "I've held that a man who comes over from that camp must prove himself — and not necessarily by enriching himself."

Bishop Hickey stood up and adjusted his scarlet sash evenly across his abdominal equator. "Let us stop the pussyfooting, Mr. Byrne. You are talking about Oliver Newman, and if I am not mistaken, you are closing in on him."

"He's a clever operator," Byrne said.

Hickey grunted. "He was able to deceive our Congressional investigating committee — "

"And Church officials," Byrne said.

The bishop sighed. "You mean Bishop McAuley. But you forget, Mr. Byrne. The Church ordinarily accepts men on faith alone. If we probed for hypocrites our ranks might be thinned a bit. It is the Christlike thing to accept on faith alone. The cheater deceives himself most of all. Stripped of all the accouterments of sacraments, liturgy, dogma, and other holy aids to salvation, a man stands alone before God. Deceits avail little then."

"I don't believe we want to wait for judgment day in this case." Byrne grinned.

Francis Hickey glanced uneasily at Byrne. "I'm not quite sure why you've chosen to confide in me. Perhaps you had no choice?"

"We could have arrested Newman several weeks ago. But then we discovered, through his correspondence with your friend, Bishop McAuley, that he had a rather fierce determination to come here to Darrington, one that couldn't be accounted for by ordinary standards. It was a fixed idea. We knew you had resisted his wishes to interview the exiled priests. We were frankly relieved when you finally consented."

"I'm not happy about it, not a bit," Hickey said.

Byrne thrust his hands in his pockets thoughtfully. "Do you remember Mark Curtain?"

Hickey nodded. "He died under peculiar conditions. I believe the final word was suicide."

"Murder," said Byrne. "You remember the case. Curtain wrote the first stories about Newman, his firm decision to tell all to the Congressional committee, his exposure of other Communists. Curtain was famous for his scoops — his firsts. Maybe for that reason he wasn't particularly beloved by other newsmen. He was ruthless in exposing gangsters, business frauds, and traitors. When he stopped writing about Newman it was assumed he was off on another crusade. He'd left it to others to record Newman's triumphs as a convert to Catholicism."

Bishop Hickey looked sharply at Byrne, then strode to the bookshelves across the room. He selected a book and flipped through the pages.

"What you appear to be implying, Mr. Byrne, is something that has nestled in the back of my mind since the Congressional hearings. I had often wondered why the friendship between Curtain and Newman turned frigid. And I was never fully convinced of the solution Newman offered."

"You're one of the few then," Byrne said.

"Are you familiar with the account of Mrs. Anna Bolt-Pierce, who covered the hearings for the *Times*? I think her doubts about Newman's veracity are rather thinly veiled at times. Let me read this passage:

" 'I attended the opening session of the resumed Senate

hearings on Communist activities in the United States this morning in Washington. The sensations promised by Oliver Newman were fulfilled. He began by telling the committee chairman that he had hoped another repentant Communist would be with him. Newman said the man had reneged on his promise to talk and that he had been unable to get his erstwhile friend on the telephone.

" 'At the chairman's insistence Newman named the man. But before he did so, it seemed that he wrestled overlong with his conscience. He sat slumped in his chair, his face contorted with conflicting loyalties as the TV cameras bore down on him. He was a man in agony, or so it appeared.

" 'When he finally spoke it was a long harangue on the demands of patriotism, terminated only by the comment of the Senator chairman that Newman's oratory was just delaying the hearing. "But even then there was a considerable preface before the name of the alleged traitor was given. Newman described him as a man who had been reared with every advantage of our precious American heritage — a free man who freely chose to betray.

" 'When he concluded his accusations with the name of Mark Curtain there was chaos in the hearing room. It was incredible to hear named as a traitor a man noted for his ruthless pursuit of traitors.

" 'Mark Curtain a Communist! It was preposterous. Yet, I could see, as I watched the faces of the committee, the newsmen, the spectators — that many of them were willing to believe it. And as I walked sadly from the room I was dismayed to hear the exclamations of delight at the revelation — at the downfall of Mark Curtain.

" 'As I flew back to New York, I felt sure that Mark Curtain would vindicate himself. He had been defamed and villified before because of his ruthless exposés. But he emerged triumphant, a dedicated citizen, an ink-splattered patriot, a blood-red crusader.

[185]

" 'Only when I got to my desk, a few moments ago, did I hear the news. Mark Curtain is dead — a suicide. I wonder. Is self-destruction the answer he wanted to give to these accusations?' "

Bishop Hickey closed the book. "Anna Pierce never did accept Newman's accusations. I'm surprised so many others did."

"You must have been an admirer of Mark Curtain," Byrne said.

"I was — even though I didn't always agree with him. His greatest weakness to my mind was his constant theme that the Soviet is impregnable. I think the politicians and writers have convinced the Communists that they are invincible."

Byrne nodded. "Curtain did sound on the verge of panic at times. But I don't think that drove him to suicide. He was found, as you know, that same day, at his retreat in upper New York, a bullet through his head and his automatic under his body."

"But he had been murdered?" Hickey said.

"We have evidence that Newman was at the camp a few hours before he appeared at the hearings in Washington. He knew when he testified against Curtain that Curtain was dead. We know from notes left by Curtain in his New York apartment that he never believed in the sincerity of Newman's conversion. Through contacts he'd made during the war, Curtain was able to trace Newman's activities during the period that he calls the 'hidden years.' We know that he was with the secret police in Poland and that he served under the code name of Lieutenant Bransk. It was under that name that he actively participated in the brainwashing and murder of countless Polish patriots. Curtain was apparently close to winding up his case against Newman when he was murdered."

Francis Hickey turned with a puzzled expression to Byrne. "Then why haven't you arrested him?"

"Unfortunately Curtain's notes were not complete, at least not on paper. Undoubtedly he had much more data in his head. We have been left with the impression that Curtain wanted very much to make one of his typical grandstand plays, perhaps pictured himself on his news broadcast, with Newman beside him, revealing through Mark Curtain's questions that he had deceived the Congressional committee.

"The way it has been pieced together, Curtain apparently invited Newman to his retreat, told him what he knew, and perhaps tried to secure some final bits of fact to wrap up his case. It was then that Newman shot him. But Curtain left us without these final facts. From his notes we have only the hint that Newman's fate is linked tightly with one of the exiled priests."

"Linked?"

"He knew one of them — Father Massimo, Bishop Dworjanski, Father Constant, or Father Maximilian. We believe that's why he's here — to determine if the priest is aware that Lieutenant Bransk and Oliver Newman are one and the same."

"It appears he would be safer not to come and show himself at the monastery."

"Not if he thought that Curtain had already talked to the priest."

There was genuine alarm on the bishop's face. "But you don't know which of the priests is aware of Newman's true identity?"

"We still have very little to go on in that connection — only that Newman has been interested — rather persistently — in them since their arrival in this country. Our surmise is that he must, that he has been ordered, to find out if any of them revealed facts about him to federal officials — perhaps to immigration men when they were processed. None of them did, but he has no way of knowing this. He will have to make his play tonight or tomorrow —"

"His lecture is tomorrow night," Hickey said.

Byrne smiled humorlessly. "A lecture takes little more than an hour. By 10 p.m. he will be on the plane to New York and a few hours later he'll join the pilgrimage for the flight to Mexico City, that is, if he was going to Mexico City."

At the same hour Friday, Father Massimo sat in his confessional in the oratory. The later afternoon and evening hours had been busy but as nine o'clock approached, the flow of penitents had dwindled, and for the past half hour the superior sat in the box with the light on, reading his breviary.

At least he thought he had been reading, but he must have dozed for there were disturbing overtones to the most mundane details of the report Fathers Columba and Edmund had given him at supper of their trip to Cohagansett. Why had he been disturbed at the account of the genial pastor's forebearing attitude toward Father Constant? Or perhaps it was the unexpected encounter they had had with Cardinal Gasquet and his invitation to spend the night at his palatial residence?

When the cardinal heard that the priests were to visit the Doolans before their return to Darrington, His Eminence had gone to great lengths to explain the many reasons why he could not officiate at the wedding of Maryanne Doolan and, strangely, concluded his remarks by recounting the story (with which they were perfectly familiar) of the Magi, who after finding the Messiah, were warned by an angel to return by another route to their own countries rather than report back to wicked Herod. But they had failed to see that a slaughter of innocents would inevitably follow and had brashly exposed themselves to an encounter with Mrs. Daisy Doolan by returning to St. Smaragdus for another visit with their little Lithuanian confrere.

The superior was aroused from his reverie by the voice of Father Georgio coming from the confessional across the aisle. The Croat was a popular confessor, though at times he was a bit loud in exhorting his penitents to amend their lives and then (after granting a hearty absolution) he frequently engaged the penitent in conversation about the time of day.

[188]

Father Massimo looked at his watch. It was 9:30 p.m., a bit later than the usual hour of closing the oratory. The Croat had lumbered out of his confessional and was locking the doors as the superior went to the front of the chapel, his eyes suddenly widening in dismay at the sight of the glass door of the reliquary standing open — the Holy Shirt of Mail gone from its place. It had been there after supper when he returned to the confessional.

There was only faint hope in the possibility that Father Columba, who had a mania for cleaning and polishing things, might have taken the relic. But he would certainly think about it twice if he was at all conscious that their German brother considered the accumulated dust of centuries quite as holy as the relic itself.

The superior walked on to the sacristy, undecided what action he would take about the missing relic. On the press the white vestments were laid out for the morning, the feast of St. Ephrem, bishop, confessor, and doctor of the Church. The ordo was opened to the place prescribing the Mass *In Medio* for the Syrian mystic: "In the midst of the church he opened his mouth: and the Lord filled him with the spirit of wisdom and understanding. . . ."

Father Massimo wished it had been so with him, but if he opened his mouth now it would be with dismay. Still baffled and wondering if he should notify the police, he was walking thoughtfully in the corridor when he saw Father Edmund and his Irish companion standing in the library doorway.

"We've been waiting for you, Padre," said the Englishman. There was something apprehensive in the way they ushered him into the library and waited for him to turn at the fireplace.

"We talked it over while you were in the confessional and decided there is something we ought to tell you," said Father Edmund. "Our Lithuanian brother is under surveillance!"

"He's being watched," added the Irish priest. "There was an FBI man at Cohagansett — the federal police. You may remember that we mentioned encountering Mrs. Doolan when we went to say good-bye at St. Smaragdus. We didn't see this FBI agent but Mrs. Doolan said he was there in the church during the wedding rehearsal. She's convinced he's there to watch Father Constant."

"Absurd," said the superior, making a bad job of concealing his uneasiness. After a moment he raised piercing eyes to them. "Are you sure of this? Do you know if the man talked to Father Constant?"

"We didn't see him afterwards," said the Englishman. "Apparently the federal man was there to observe him at the wedding rehearsal and undoubtedly has been skulking around the parish church there for days — if what Mrs. Doolan says is true."

The superior averted his troubled eyes from them. "I assume it was a guess — a thoroughly bad guess on the part of Mrs. Doolan."

"She was quite angry at the FBI," said Father Columba. "Her report must have been true. She said she encountered the man in the church and saw the gun under his armpit. She said when she jokingly addressed him as Mr. Hoover he told her firmly that she should not mention to anyone that she'd met him."

Father Massimo smiled grimly. There was no doubt in his mind that Kevin Byrne was the man in question. It was, he thought, somewhat more than coincidence that Byrne didn't show up for his language lesson today. He would have done better to keep his eye on Newman. While the priests had talked, the Superior decided against telling them the relic was missing. There was only one answer. The artfully forced lock convinced him of that. Newman had taken it — perhaps as a diversionary move — to conceal his real purpose.

More than an hour later in his room, the superior paused in the recitation of the Divine Office, feeling a bit apprehensive for Father Constant. Undoubtedly he would be uneasy about answering Newman's questions. But perhaps Newman would have little time for it, if, as seemed probable, Daisy Doolan had told him that the FBI man was at the seashore resort. But unfortunately the FBI had betrayed its hand and Newman now knew he was being scrutinized.

This fact might make him more dangerous, but the superior was certain it wouldn't frighten Newman away. He was there for a purpose, and come whatever danger, he couldn't leave his work undone.

Father Massimo knew that he was not alone and now he wondered if it might be time to confide in someone. If something should happen to him suddenly, unexpectedly, no one would know why he was here, and his mission would end futilely.

Newman's iron will had evoked the superior's admiration. He was tense, and betrayed it; yet he had not betrayed his purpose in coming. It was difficult to understand why he tempted fate by coming to the house when he could be reasonably certain that Stefan Dworjanski would recognize him.

The news that the FBI man had followed Newman to Cohagansett convinced Father Massimo that the government was unsure of Newman's purpose in coming to the monastery.

But if the government was uncertain, the Father superior was not. Newman wanted very desperately to know the contents of Bishop Dworjanski's memoirs. He surely knew that the old bishop was one of the few men living outside Communist Europe who could identify Lieutenant Bransk.

Under that name he had assisted in the prosecution of Stefan Dworjanski and was among the officers assigned to question the old bishop during his imprisonment at the Fortress of St. Ladislas.

Father Massimo felt little surprise that he himself wasn't remembered by Newman. But the priest had the advantage. The name of Lieutenant Bransk was well known in the Polish underground, and equally hated. Unlike so many others, he was a Communist by choice. He had been born in England, was graduated from an English university, and in the 1920's had become an American citizen. He said in his autobiography that he became a Communist early in the war when he was an exchange professor at the University of Cracow and after the Nazis swept into Poland.

Later, when the war was over, he said that he had soon become disenchanted with Communism but had kept up the masquerade to save his life. Escaping, according to his account, he returned to the United States with the story that he had been a prisoner of the Communists since 1939. His repentance was sincere, he had written, and he believed he was safe until he was approached by Communist agents who threatened him with exposure if he refused to work for them.

Someone reading Newman's confession would be inclined to sympathize with him. He had no choice but to become a Soviet agent. But, according to his testimony later, his soul rebelled, and after several years of self-searching torment he became a Catholic convert and confessed his treachery.

Father Massimo put aside his breviary as disturbing memories returned to him. It was appalling to realize how Newman had deceived everyone he had wanted to deceive.

And it was strange too that somewhere in his maze of lies he hadn't blundered. For a man who had claimed he was a prisoner of the Nazis during the war he had been surprisingly free and unusually active. He had taken quite readily to the brutal technique the godless employed.

Father Massimo had seen Lieutenant Bransk several times, always at the side of the chief of the secret police whom the people had named "the hairless one." In spite of the fascination of the bald dwarf, Father Massimo had a more distinct memory of his aide — a particularly vivid memory of the day Bransk had eyed him coldly as he accompanied the general along the line of persons who had been brought into the old palace for questioning.

[192]

The chief, obviously a Georgian, had been unable to bridge the linguistic gap, and Bransk was always at his side to interpret.

They stopped before Father Massimo, Bransk's face empty of everything but contempt. "They have rounded up another Vatican spy for us, General. He fits in well with the saboteurs and the English capitalist Jews."

The Polish official who accompanied them laughed coldly. "They will leave with their lives — and that is all! We know all the secret places on the anatomy where a phial of valuables may be concealed."

Newman continued to stare at the priest as he answered. "An enema may be needed for the stubborn ones . . . what is your business, priest?"

Father Massimo answered him moderately. If he was lucky he would be safely out of the country in a few hours, but retaliation would be made against his people in Kzalineka if he provoked them to anger.

"Ha, administrator of Kzalineka!" Newman exclaimed. "This one handled the money!"

The search Newman ordered was thorough and degrading. But even then they were not sure that he carried nothing when he crossed the frontier. Their suspicions were right, for he carried, imprinted indelibly in his mind, the picture of a man he hoped he would never meet again.

And now he was here. He didn't remember the priest he had degraded — but perhaps he would remember.

A sound in the hall distracted Father Massimo from his unpleasant reverie. He laughed quickly. It was strange what things crossed one's mind. He had thought for a moment that it might be Newman in the house. But that was impossible. He was at Cohagansett.

Perhaps it was Father Largo going to see if his saint was still in the crypt, or more likely to attempt a clandestine Mass, or even Halidon stretching his legs while the priests slept.

But most likely of all, at this hour, it would be the yet undetermined prowler on his way to Father Georgio's kitchen for a midnight lunch.

Father Massimo, coming to the decision to warn the kitchen raider that Father Georgio was onto him, left his room and came down the darkened stairway and along the hall to the kitchen. There was almost a feeling of disappointment when he pushed open the door and saw that the room was in darkness. He turned on the light and stood shaking his head for several moments. He's been so sure it was Father Georgio's nemesis that he had heard.

Well, he had evidently been mistaken — unless there was some evidence that he had been here already. Father Massimo opened the refrigerator. It was alarmingly bare, with a few bowls of leftover vegetables and some staples that looked far from appetizing. The Father superior sighed. The unfortunate midnight prowler would have little to choose from when he did come. Further probing revealed two rather shriveled frankfurters. He would prefer liverwurst or salami, but, then, beggars couldn't be choosers.

Father Massimo put the frankfurters on the table and opened the bread box. Half a loaf of raisin bread, hardly the companion pieces for hot dogs. Well, it would have to be raisin toast.

He had the bread in hand when the kitchen door swung open and Father Dmitri's startled face blinked in the light.

"Oh —" he exclaimed, backing against the still swishing door.

"Come in, Father," the superior said calmly. "Come in and stop that door from banging before you wake someone."

The conspiratorial tone intrigued Father Dmitri and he came toward the superior with a curious look on his fierce, hawklike face.

"Do you like cold frankfurters, Father Dmitri?" asked the superior. "That seems to be about all there is. It's after midnight and Friday is past."

The Moravian took in the meager contents of the table.

[194]

Then he smiled slyly at Father Massimo. "You too, Father? I had been wondering who got the last piece of Madam Gillis' blueberry pie two nights ago." He slapped Father Massimo's arm. "But you don't know all the tricks. I am careful to note what has been left after dinner. Father Georgio thinks he is very crafty. If there is meat left he puts it in tinfoil in the oven. It cannot spoil overnight and in the morning he has a nice feed for himself while he makes us a breakfast of cereal or hot cakes."

Father Dmitri went to the oven and took out a baking dish containing several slices of beef. From another hiding place on the top shelf of the cupboard Father Dmitri took a loaf of rye bread, and they sat down to milk and sandwiches.

The superior ate his sandwich in silence, feeling uneasy about the lunch until Father Dmitri remarked that the Father commissario could do with a little self-denial.

The Moravian finished his sandwich in another bite and got up, rubbing his hands together. "Now for something to top off this little snack," he said with a wink at the superior. He hurried off to the storeroom in the rear. The door had no sooner swung shut behind him than the door from the hall flew open, revealing the red and wrathful face of Father Georgio.

"Aha! I have you now!" the Croat sputtered, his beard waving ominously. "I caught you red-handed!" He blinked in the light, then there was a look of dismay on his face and he grasped his beard. "Father Superior! A thousand pardons!"

The superior shrugged. "As you say, Father, you have me."

Father Georgio blustered in confusion. "I had no idea you were the thief. I cannot reprimand my superior. Even though I am Father commissario. . . ."

The superior tried to look contrite, difficult as it was. But poor Father Georgio had to make some excuse for his magnanimous heart. For a moment it even looked as though he would make the superior feel entirely at home by joining him.

[195]

The thought, if it was there, was dashed away by the return of the Moravian. He burst through the door from the store-room. "Success, Father Superior!" Then his eyes widened in dismay as he saw Father Georgio. He drew the box of cookies behind his back.

"Two of you!" cried Father Georgio. "Two of you!"

"Well, we are apprehended, Father Superior," said the Moravian jovially, tearing open the box of cookies.

Then, as the cook went to see if they had found his left-over cache in the oven, the Moravian bent his bearded face close to the superior's and whispered, "I cannot help commenting that if you hadn't cut in on my territory I might never have been caught."

Feeling better after the snack, Father Massimo, in his room, had prepared for bed and was opening his window when a strange charade met his gaze in the no-man's-land between the cloister and the Jewish cemetery in the rear of the house. In the full flush of moonlight he could see two policemen approaching the garden gate from either end of the alley. Then, looking down closer to the house, he saw another figure moving stealthily toward the back door.

In a moment he realized it was Halidon, undoubtedly returning from his hotel. Halidon was near the door when another figure emerged from the shadows of the lattice. At the movement Halidon swung around and there were mutual exclamations of surprise, quickly submerged in the commotion as the two policemen broke through the gate simultaneously.

There was the flash of police automatics and the guest who had started to bluff his way out of the predicament quickly submitted, extending his hands for the cuffs.

The other man proved more of a problem, thrashing about with considerable obstinacy as the policeman tried to handcuff him. It was only when he'd been subdued and his face lifted momentarily to the moonlight that the superior realized it was the Baptist minister, Harold Gillis. Whatever explanation he had to give left the officers unmoved. They led the two men away to the police car at the end of the alley.

Father Massimo hurriedly got back into his clothes, quite certain that he would be summoned to police headquarters. Fifteen minutes later when he entered the station house he saw Reverend Gillis and Halidon sitting on a bench in the corridor. Gillis jumped up excitedly, jerking Halidon with him.

"Father Massimo!" Gillis cried. "Thank God! Now you can explain to them who I am."

"Possibly," the superior said, "but I'm not at all sure I can explain what you were doing when they apprehended you."

"What I was doing!" Gillis exclaimed. "I was protecting your interests! I knew this fellow had you all hoodwinked so I was keeping an eye on him. I'm sure he's been stealing things from your monastery and pawning them. I watched him the last few nights — the same pattern — going and sneaking back. Why, I was about to summon the police when they came. If they'd just waited a few more minutes — "

Father Massimo glanced quickly at Halidon. The man was amazingly calm. "I'll do what I can for you, Reverend Gillis — " the superior said. He looked toward the policeman standing at the end of the desk. He had apparently been assigned to keep an eye on the prisoners. "What are they charged with officer?"

The policeman shrugged indifferently and continued to massage his knuckles. He appeared about to make some laconic remark when the door of the inner office opened and Chief Walter Tracy came out.

The chief's eyes brightened as he saw the priest. "I've been ringing the monastery trying to get you, Father. When I heard they'd arrested Reverend Gillis I came right over." He looked at the minister apologetically. "Sorry, I didn't know they had you handcuffed." He motioned the officer to take the handcuffs off. "You can go now, Reverend. The fellows who picked you up had no way of knowing that you were a minister. If you go out the side you'll find one of my men waiting to drive you home."

When Gillis had gone, Tracy said, "But this fellow is something else, Father."

"I'm sure I can explain, Mr. Tracy," Father Massimo said.

Halidon shrugged. "Better let it go as it is, Father. I guess the jig is up."

"Why should the jig be up? You're still my guest."

Tracy pushed back his cap in perplexity. "You mean he's staying at the monastery?"

Father Massimo nodded. "It would appear that you have no charges against him — entering where he has a right to enter."

Tracy shrugged, still puzzled. "He can go, Father. I'll have someone take you back in a cruiser. Sorry for the inconvenience."

Halidon sat thoughtfully during the ride back. Father Massimo had the feeling he was anxious to talk but not too anxious to have the policeman hear what he had to say.

It wasn't until they were inside the monastery and the superior had locked the door that Halidon spoke.

There was a sardonic expression on his face. "I don't get you, Father — doing this for me."

"Where would you go at this hour of the night?" Suddenly the priest smiled curiously. "Of course there is the Hotel Phoenix — "

Halidon could not conceal his surprise.

"I neglected to tell you, Mr. Halidon. I found the telegram you dropped, some days ago. I read it."

Halidon grinned. "In a way I'm relieved. I think I should explain to you — "

The priest put up his hand. "I'd be just as pleased if you didn't. You have your work to do — and I have mine. If it is done alone it is free, at least, of the odor of conspiracy."

CHAPTER TWELVE

THERE was high excitement in the morning when the loss of the relic was discovered. Father Edmund wanted to call the police at once but the superior calmly told them that he'd take care of it. Alone in his office, he phoned the Essex Hotel and got Kevin Byrne. He told him of his suspicions, and concluded: "Perhaps you can see that Newman's room is searched. He has a room there, as I'm sure you know."

Saturday was always a busy day for the exiles. After lunch they would disperse about the city to the parishes they were assigned to hear confessions through the afternoon and evening.

Shortly before noon, when Father Massimo came to look in on Bishop Dworjanski, he found the old man buttoning up his best violet-piped soutane. He smiled pleasantly as he told the superior he planned to come downstairs for lunch.

"I'm pleased you're feeling well, Your Excellency. Perhaps you could keep an eye on Father Largo this afternoon. I'll have to spend most of my time in the confessional, and there will be no one else in the house — except our guest."

"Newman?"

"No, the other fellow — Mr. Halidon. But I suppose Newman will be back. I'm surprised that he hasn't returned already."

Bishop Dworjanski laughed briefly, "We mustn't be impatient, Father. He will come."

As they left the refectory after lunch Father Massimo saw

[199]

a brown briefcase and hat on the bench in the hall, resting rather precariously as though they had been set down hastily. Newman was standing in the door of the library. Apparently he had slipped in through the chapel. There was a momentary smile on his thin face. He came forward quickly and bent his knee as he kissed the ring of Bishop Dworjanski.

There was a reserved look on the old bishop's heavy features. "There is no need of this homage, Mr. Newman. We all know of your devotion to your faith."

"Your faith and my faith, Your Excellency."

The bishop made a disapproving sound and began to walk away, but then turned quickly. "Mr. Newman! You will forgive me if I remind you that you once prostrated yourself toward the east. I have wondered about your oath as a Communist."

There was a twitch in Newman's cheek, but beyond that he remained composed. "I repudiated all that. There never was an oath — not as we understand oaths."

A dry sound, too grim to be laughter, came from Stefan Dworjanski's throat. "But then, Newman, an oath would have been meaningless, would it not? The atheist fears only one thing and that is the God he refuses to recognize."

The bishop turned from Newman and went into the chapel. Newman stood uncertainly, aware of the hostility that surrounded him. He said suddenly to the superior, "If I could speak to all of you in the library for a few minutes — "

Father Massimo nodded. "We have a busy day ahead of us — but perhaps a few moments." He led the way into the library and waited while the others seated themselves.

Newman stood at the head of the long table. "I hope all of you will be pleased to hear that I've made reservations for you at my lecture tomorrow night. You'll be my guests. Many questions will be answered for you, I'm certain. I hope at that time that I'll be able to explain to you how the wretched poverty of my youth led me inevitably to Communism."

"Christ our Lord was wretchedly poor too," said Father Columba.

"You know that is apocryphal, Father. I believe that Christ lived a parable for us." Newman saw their dismayed faces and added hastily, "I mean, of course, that everything He did was an example. He needn't have been poor. But a rich young man preaching at us wouldn't have been very effective, would it?"

"The preachings of rich men seldom are effective," said Father Edmund sourly.

Father Maximilian leaned forward in his chair, taking a moment to adjust his hearing aid. "Yesterday, Herr Newman, you were telling us about the high-ranking Communists who secretly practice their ancient faith. This cannot be a sincere faith, or they would be willing to come out in the open and die for it. It is apparent, they are more willing to die for Lenin than for God."

"You can't imagine the persecution that would follow," Newman said.

The superior looked at Newman blandly. "None of us here has to imagine it. We have seen it."

Father Georgio tugged at his beard thoughtfully. "How does it happen, Mr. Newman, that these big-shot Communists told you their secrets?"

Newman's eyes flashed, then calmed quickly. "I presume they had an instinctive feeling that I wouldn't betray them." he said.

"Ha!" grunted Father Dmitri loudly. "They did not look at your record, Mr. Newman!"

Father Massimo gave the Moravian a disapproving look. "You mustn't mind Father Dmitri, Mr. Newman. In his homeland there were many who switched from cause to cause. I'm afraid he thinks as most of us do, that you have painted too happy a picture of life inside the sinister Soviet. But your intentions are worth considering. All is not hopeless. I have no doubt that many Russians still make the sign of the cross."

[201]

Newman looked at the hostile faces with more courage than they expected to see. "I still maintain that the Russian government will soon allow God to be worshiped."

"What interests me, Mr. Newman," said Father Edmund, "is how much longer God will allow the Soviet to be worshiped."

"That will change," Newman said, "perhaps after much persecution. And the persecution will bring forth the martyrs — the saints."

"Every cause has its martyrs," said the English priest.

"They are no longer willing to die for the gods of the Kremlin," Newman said, a bit shrilly. "I am an example of that for you to see."

Father Dmitri waved his arms angrily, as though to drive a devil from him. "I will not listen to this man. He is trying to get us into some trap." The Moravian strode out of the room.

There was a dry, humorless chuckle and the priests looked from the tense Newman to their superior who stood with his strong hands tensed in the cuffs of his sleeves. A dark vein throbbed in his temple, but his face was otherwise calm.

"We are surely trying your faith, Mr. Newman; but you must put up with us, remembering that we have been on only the receiving end as far as the new paganism is concerned — the unpleasant end."

Obviously unhappy at their hostility, Newman left immediately.

Steve Halidon arose restlessly from his cot. The slanting oblong of light from the crypt window told him it was late afternoon. He hadn't been in touch with Shanley for two days and he was certain his editor was getting more tense as the time neared when Newman had to act or run. But he wouldn't be able to get to the hotel to telephone Dev Shanley until after 9:30 p.m. at the earliest, when the priests were in bed and he could slip out unseen.

It had been fifteen minutes since Father Largo had left his easel and had hurried upstairs, muttering to himself. Judging from his angry tone, he was not praying. Halidon stood regarding the painting of himself — dark beatified eyes staring back at him from the canvas, the eyes of a saint, the Spaniard thought them.

Halidon laughed, a bit dismayed at the realization that his face — as the padre saw it — didn't look too much out of place on the canvas.

Posing for Father Largo had exhausted Halidon. He hadn't realized how weary he was as he sat through the afternoon while the artist worked feverishly as though he feared that at any moment his saint would disappear.

After a while, when it was apparent that Father Largo wasn't coming back, Halidon opened the door of the crypt and hurried through the cellar to the stairs. He went up, ducking his head. He stood for a few moments in the chapel door, the drone of a voice from the confessional giving absolution, assuring him that Father Massimo was there.

As Father Massimo emerged from the confessional later that afternoon he saw Julie Nealy and Kevin Byrne leaving the oratory together.

Father Massimo walked down the aisle, dismayed anew at the empty reliquary. As he genuflected before the Blessed Sacrament his eyes strayed for a moment to the statue of St. Michael the Archangel at the left of the altar. The statue glowed in the circle of votive candles lighted around it, some of them undoubtedly candles lighted by Julie Nealy.

"He seems like a nice fellow, this Mr. Byrne, Caro Santo. I would like to see her marry someone who would be good to her," the superior said.

He would have felt a good deal more secure, Father Massimo realized, if he could be sure that Byrne was giving as close attention to his work as he seemed to be giving to Julie.

Halidon stood leaning against the kitchen door a few minutes later when Father Massimo came into the corridor. He studied the absorption on the superior's face.

Father Massimo smiled. "Well, Mr. Halidon, I suppose we must get a supper for ourselves. Father Georgio is at St. Andrew's and won't be back until after nine."

Halidon laughed as they went into the kitchen. "I've always been pretty good at opening a can of beans."

"Beans!" laughed the superior. "When there is nothing else we can have beans." He opened the refrigerator and scrutinized the contents. There appeared to be the possibility of a salad with cold cuts. Halidon made the coffee while the superior fixed trays for Bishop Dworjanski and Father Largo, who always ate in his room on Saturday night.

As he prepared the salad, Father Massimo glanced warily at Halidon. "I suppose nothing happened while I was out hearing confessions, Mr. Halidon."

"I'd like it better if you called me Steve."

"I will — of course — "

Halidon lit a cigarette and leaned against the table.

"Did you expect Newman back tonight, Father?"

Father Massimo's eyes flicked up for a moment. "Should I expect him tonight? He knows Saturday night is very busy for us — that most of the priests are away."

"I thought that might be when he'd come — when hardly anyone would be here."

Father Massimo kept his eyes on his work. "You have some very strange questions, Steve."

"It wasn't a question."

"You seem to have an extraordinary interest in Mr. Newman."

Halidon shrugged. "I'm after a story. It's my job."

"But you don't know what the story is that you are after?" the priest asked.

"Only suspicions — founded in a deeply rooted cynicism," Halidon said. "He's a desperate man, I know that much. And

I know there's something to the suspicions when the FBI has men here watching him. You've seen only one of them, Padre, but at the hotel there are more. My room there was searched. I'm sure it was they. I suppose they had to know who I was when they found out I was here."

"What will they do?"

"You mean about Newman?" Halidon asked. "I'm not sure they know what they're going to do, anymore than you know what you are going to do, Father." Halidon was amazed at the calmness in the priest's eyes.

"I hadn't thought that anything like this would happen, with the federal officers here, and you to record it all. When I knew that this time would come, I thought it would be different. I thought it would be a matter between Newman and myself."

Halidon laughed. "If it came to battling out the moral issues involved, Padre, you might certainly win the theological arguments; you might convince Newman that his sins have found him out; but I'm afraid your adversary would carry the day."

Father Massimo looked at Halidon in alarm.

"Newman is armed, Father. He has a gun in his briefcase."

"A gun? How do you know this?"

"He left his briefcase on the library table — yesterday," said the reporter. "It was locked, naturally, but I felt the shape of an automatic through the leather."

The superior smiled calmly. "And what about you, Steve? Are you armed also?"

"Only with justice, Father, like yourself."

The trays had been taken to the bishop and Father Largo, and the reporter and the superior were sitting down to their supper when the doorbell sounded. Father Massimo hurried to answer it and returned a few minutes later to the kitchen with twinkle in his eyes.

He sat down and unrolled a small piece of paper. "A message from Father Constant by homing pigeon," he said. "Mother

Evariste-Marie sent one of the Sisters over with it."

He read the note through quickly, then said: "Would you like to hear it?" Halidon nodded and the priest read:

"Dear Father Superior: This has been a busy week and a sometimes confusing one for me. I enjoyed seeing Father Columba and Father Edmund again and I hope you will tell them I'm sorry that I had so little time to talk with them. Then came a man who told me he was authorized by you to secure information from me. I'm sorry that I was unable to help him other than to tell him that all my movements have been recorded by the government of the United States and that he could secure it there more accurately. Father Columba had warned me not to talk to him.

"But after a time I saw that this Newman was not so much interested in me as in what he could learn about Stefan Dworjanski. He asked me if I had been given the privilege of reading the bishop's memoirs. I told him that I had not, and that I hoped he could contain his impatience and wait to read the memoirs — as a book.

"But there are pleasant moments too. This morning I had the privilege of officiating at the marriage of the daughter of our good patrons, the Doolans. With our beloved pastor laid up with the gout and the failure of another priest to show up at the last moment, I was summoned to perform the service. As all mothers, poor Mrs. Doolan cried profusely during the ceremony, somewhat more than was reasonable, I would say. But perhaps only a mother can understand a mother's loss.

"Obediently yours in J. C.,
Constant, O.V.B."

"Well," Halidon exclaimed, releasing his breath through his nostrils. "There need be no further doubt that Newman is interested in Dworjanski's memoirs."

"But not to publish them — I don't think," said the superior.

CHAPTER THIRTEEN

As so many other things, Father Largo's portrait of St. John of the Cross stood unfinished on its easel the next afternoon. In spite of the Spaniard's fevered and frantic application the painting was hardly sketched beyond the face.

Father Massimo turned from the somber canvas and looked questioningly at Steve Halidon. The priest had been surprised and a little amused when he came to the crypt Sunday afternoon to find Halidon reading St. John's *Ascent of Mount Carmel.* The more practical of men, even among the clergy, had at times found the Spanish mystic's ascent of the holy mount a bit heady, and, once there, if they ever managed to make it, giddiness was apt to overcome them in the stratosphere of thought.

"Perhaps you will return some day and allow Father Largo to finish the portrait," the superior said, "not of St. John of course but of a good friend just the same."

"Thank you, Father, but I don't deserve it," Halidon said. He got up from the cot and groped for his cigarette in the folds of the old soutane, which he continued to wear to keep Padre Largo happy. He lighted one as he strode to the window.

Father Massimo wondered that he had permitted Newman to carry out his masquerade. Yet the possibility that he might be mistaken about Newman's motives disturbed him. Byrne had reported that the relic was not in Newman's room at the hotel. The man, in spite of the prods to his memory, gave no indication that he remembered the talk he had with the apostolic administrator of Kzalineka so many years ago. The superior couldn't even be sure that Newman remembered Bishop Dworjanski, if the evidence since his arrival was considered.

The superior was thankful for the added duties of Sunday that had kept him occupied to a late afternoon hour. But he couldn't keep the thought from his mind that it would be today, or tonight at the latest, that Newman would make his move.

Halidon's telegram had said that Newman planned to leave the country Monday — tomorrow.

"Have you heard anything, Father?" Halidon asked.

Father Massimo raised his eyes, nodding slowly. "We are all going to Newman's lecture — all except Bishop Dworjanski and Father Largo. You will look after them. . . ."

"You think now that he will come?"

"He is making very sure that we attend the lecture. He telephoned a few minutes ago to inform me that he is sending taxicabs to take us to the auditorium. Seven-fifteen exactly, he said."

Halidon turned from the window. "You go to the lecture, Father. He seems to have his plans too perfectly laid for us to disrupt them."

Father Massimo went up from the crypt, thinking apprehensively of Stefan Dworjanski.

The superior went to his office and looked out the window. It was reassuring to know that Byrne was across the street watching for Newman's arrival.

Bishop Bryan McAuley had telephoned that afternoon from Cohagansett to assure Bishop Hickey that he would be in Darrington in time for Newman's lecture. The bishop was sure McAuley's arrival would be at the last possible moment, forbidding any discussion of the merits of the lecture before they sped away to the auditorium.

Bishop Hickey felt he had no alternative but to go unless he confided in McAuley that Newman's machinations were closing in on him. He didn't want to be the one to tell McAuley that Newman had deceived him. He hoped the bishop wouldn't be too stunned when he learned of the deception.

The bishop was watching at the door of the rectory when the big black car spun the driveway gravel and Bryan McAuley waved his hand out the window in an effusive greeting to Francis Hickey.

McAuley appeared to be in no hurry to be off to the lecture hall and made no protest when the bishop invited him in to his study. McAuley was remote as he sat down and lighted a cigar. He savored it for a few moments, commenting amusedly that Hickey's desk was, as usual, piled high with work that he could very well have parceled out to an assistant. He was afraid that the bishop of Darrington had never learned the fine points of delegating authority.

"I hope you won't be annoyed with me, Francis, but I took the liberty of paying my respects and yours to His Eminence."

"Gasquet?"

"He was delighted — even though we'd never met before. Of course we have mutual friends. I was dismayed to hear that my old Hebrew professor, Cardinal della Ganga, is near death — but he's eighty-nine." There was a smile on McAuley's face as he leaned forward with a confidential look. "You'll be pleased to know that Cardinal Gasquet has heard of you — particularly concerning your generosity in inviting the Brunite Fathers to your diocese. He had a number of questions about them."

"I hope you were able to answer them," Hickey said, a little annoyed.

McAuley laughed pleasantly. "I told him what I knew, quite frankly. He appeared to be impressed with the news that they are content here — so impressed that he has an invitation that he asked me to extend to you. He'd like you to visit him at the beach. I assume he'll put forward his proposition at that time."

[209]

"Proposition?"

"The cardinal is quite aware that he is not here in an official capacity," he said. "What he will suggest is merely an impulse of the heart. He has in mind offering the exiled Fathers the use of his home at Cohagansett as a permanent residence."

In his mind Francis Hickey tried to put in order all the ramifications of such an offer. He would dislike seeing Father Massimo and his company leave the city, but some, including Monsignor Brady, would be pleased.

"I'll have to think about it," Hickey said.

"You're much too conservative, Francis," said McAuley indulgently. "Why not accept the magnanimous gesture in the spirit in which it's offered? Gasquet is a lonely man. I'm inclined to be sociable myself and know when another finds it difficult. I know my man, Francis, and I assure you that the cardinal has no hidden motives."

Hickey sat back thoughtfully, fully aware that McAuley, in spite of his remonstrances, did not always perceive that mature men seldom acted on impulse.

"We're forgetting the lecture, Bishop," Hickey said abruptly.

McAuley raised his eyes ruefully. "I have far from forgotten it. I'd hoped that you'd rush me off to it without giving me time to think. I wanted you to hear him. I wanted very much to get your impression after his talk."

"You already know my impressions," said Hickey patiently. "I thought it would be enough for you to understand that I was opposed to his visit here."

"But you never said why."

"In the beginning it was my natural suspicion of anyone who profits — financially — from a disreputable past. Later, in his writings, I noted a pattern. He harps continually on the theme that the Communist world is weak, rotten to the core. He disdained their power and predicted imminent collapse of the Soviet system. I cannot trust a man who tries to lull us to sleep. Those were my impressions until recently."

There was alarm in McAuley's eyes. "Now you have a change of heart about the man?"

Hickey laughed. "My heart is not involved. I've been uneasy about Oliver Newman's success, especially since it was raised over the corpse of Mark Curtain."

McAuley sat back, putting his hands reflectively to his florid face. "You have been thinking earnestly about this, I can see. It almost makes me think you have some extraordinary power of perception."

"I have a good deal more than that. I am convinced that Mark Curtain was murdered."

"Then you must know how wretched I feel at this moment," McAuley said. "My good friend Carmine Bonomi, the district attorney of Ross County, indicated to me that the grand jury would be presented with certain evidence against Newman Monday. I think he was trying to prepare me — for some rather bad news."

"There was no hint that a murder indictment would be sought?"

McAuley shook his head. "Of course it was a hint, if I had been sharp enough to take it. It only dawned on me afterwards why he would be indicted in Ross County. That was where Curtain died. If these — indications — are true, I've been deceived — "

"I think you were in a receptive mood to be deceived," Hickey said.

"I accepted the man on faith — "

"But what you couldn't know was that he is inherently faithless. Fortunately, there were some who mistrusted him. At the moment you would probably like to confront Newman. But it would defeat the plan of the federal authorities. From all indications, they are here to arrest him."

"You think there will be no lecture?"

"There will be a lecture of some kind, I'm sure," Francis Hickey said.

[211]

Father Largo was thankful that he was, as he believed, the first to observe that the monastery was under surveillance. "Viene la policia!" he gasped as he pulled aside the curtain of his room and released it as quickly. A police car was parked across the street. Suddenly, he chuckled. The search for the Holy Shirt would keep them busy enough!

The Spaniard stroked his chin thoughtfully, the suspicion in his mind growing that Jeronimo Tostado had at last sent for the secular arm to seize San Juan de la Cruz. Tostado felt safe now that Nuncio Ormaneto was dead and Madre Teresa had no one to appeal to for her friend. The new Nuncio Sega, may God forgive him, had proved himself a tool of the Inquisition.

Father Largo blessed himself fervently. There was no one else to watch over San Juan except himself. He hurried from his room and down the stairs, trying to be as soft-footed as possible. Tostado would be watching for him.

He opened the cellar door cautiously and went down. When he came to the crypt he wasn't sure he was relieved to see that Blessed Juan was still there.

The saint looked a bit out of breath but he smiled pleasantly, "What time is it, Padre?"

Father Largo looked about the crypt as if hoping he'd see a clock somewhere. Finally he shrugged. Once Juan had too many clocks and now he had none. When he first determined to follow Madre Teresa and had cast off his shoes, he and his companion, Father Antonio, had with them at the little house at Duruelo five clocks but little else.

The priest shook his head impatiently. "It is the time you've been waiting for. They are up to something but we will strike first! Escape will be quite simple. I'm surprised that you thought you had to wait for the Holy Virgin to give you instructions." Father Largo waggled a finger under Halidon's nose. "You wondered what mysterious hand it was that helped you over the wall! Well, my dear holy one, tonight it will be mine!"

[212]

Halidon nodded and Father Largo went on. "If you doze I'll wake you. Leave your clothes on — but I should know better than to tell you that. You've had on those same rags for nine months, thanks to the miserable Tostado! I know how this happens. Those strange monks in Burma did the same to me. But they were gentlemen compared to Tostado. They were never angry when I wanted to say Holy Mass. In fact, they appeared to appreciate that I hadn't perverted the liturgy as they had, poor unfortunate devils! I still don't know to this day what order those peculiar men belonged to. I must make another inquiry to the Congregation of the Oriental Church."

Father Largo moved to the door. "Tonight then, Blessed One! I hope you will remember me if I fall into Tostado's hands!"

The Spaniard came up from the cellar, peering out cautiously into the hall before he closed the door. When he looked in the library there was no one, nor in the sacristy or kitchen. He hurried to the superior's office, saw it was deserted, and when he looked out the front window he saw the priests getting into taxis.

There was a smile of triumph on Father Largo's face as he turned from the window. This was the time he'd been waiting for. He must inform San Juan at once. He almost danced as he came toward the basement door.

It opened before he reached it. The priest drew back in alarm.

"Senor Newman!"

"Yes, Padre, it is Senor Newman." He gripped Father Largo's arm firmly, a satisfied smile on his face. "I've been looking for you. I've come to help you."

"Help me?"

"Escape. Isn't that what you want?"

"No — no, not me! But the Blessed One must escape from Tostado tonight!"

"Don't worry. I've taken care of that. I was watching — like you. I came in through the chapel, disguised of course, as your enemies were leaving. I've seen to it that your friend has been taken care of."

"He has made his escape?" cried Father Largo.

Newman laughed, "Of course. But I see you don't believe me. Come!" He led the priest down the stairs along the basement to the crypt. Father Largo stared at the worn black soutane thrown across the cot.

"They will blame you for this, Padre. You must make your own escape now."

Father Largo turned, a calm smile on his face. He shrugged. "Now that San Juan is gone, I am safe enough. They never believed he was here. I will deny everything."

"I wouldn't try to be clever, Padre. They wanted you to believe that you saw this saint. Now they will make you confess that you are a fraud — "

The priest's face was suddenly alarmed. "Yes — Tostado would do that! That is why the secular arm is waiting! Another *auto de Fe!*"

"You are thinking clearly now, Padre. They want only to save your soul! They will make you confess that you are looking for sainthood for yourself." Newman flicked his fingers at the discarded robe. "This will be their proof that you dressed up some wretch — this and the painting that you have been doing!"

"You are right, Senor!" Father Largo exclaimed. "I should have discovered this trap myself!"

Newman took his arm impatiently. "We haven't much time, Padre, and there is one other thing that must be attended to. The old man upstairs — if he sees you go he will give the alarm."

He propelled Father Largo along the basement to the wine shelves, smiling secretively at the priest as they paused. "Perhaps a bottle of wine for Dworjanski. We will go in to his room, very casually, as though nothing is wrong. Take a bottle, Padre. You know which is the best wine."

Father Largo took down a bottle from the shelf, brushing

it carefully with his sleeve. Then his eyes were raised in a startled glance at Newman. "What was that? Someone is moaning — "

"You are on edge, Padre. I hear nothing. Come." He led the priest to the stairs. "Go up to Dworjanski's room. Don't let him trick you. As soon as I see that the way is clear, I'll be after you."

Stefan Dworjanski raised his head slowly at the sound of a knock at his door. The green-shaded lamp on his desk before him cast jagged shadows on his austere face.

The knock was repeated and the bishop closed the folio before him and lifted himself up heavily from the chair.

"Come," he said, his voice expectant.

The door opened slowly and Father Largo entered, the bottle of red wine cradled carefully in his arm.

"Oh, it's you, Padre Largo. Pax tecum."

"Et cum spiritu tuo, Senor Obispo."

The bishop came toward the Spaniard, his eyes going questioningly to the bottle of wine that Father Largo held out to him.

"Wine? You have wine for me?" He took the bottle, smiling understandingly. "It is pleasant to be thought of, my son, but this is sacramental wine. It should be reserved for Mass and nothing else."

At that moment Newman glided into the room. And pushed the door closed with his foot. There was a grim smile on his thin face.

"I sent Father Largo with the wine, Stefan Dworjanski, to remind you that you are a priest and should keep your secrets like a priest!"

The bishop studied Newman's face, a slow perception narrowing his eyes. He backed toward his desk, not turning as his hand found the edge of the desk and moved slowly toward the folio. "It is finished, Mr. Newman. . . ."

"Then the wine is appropriate," said Newman. "We can toast the completion of your work."

The bishop drew his fingers along the chain of his pectoral cross. His face was still reserved. "My mind has already had the stimulant it needed, these past few days. But this wine — it has been a prod to my memory too. I had nearly forgotten the bottle that was placed in my cell at Fortress St. Ladislas, the bottle that remained untouched because I could never be sure it wasn't poisoned."

"I didn't realize, Your Excellency, that wine had such a sinister memory for you."

"It was an unnecessary reminder," said the bishop wearily. "I have already recorded here in my memoirs the death of another priest who could not believe that his enemy would be so heinous as to poison the wine that they offered him for Holy Mass. This was the kind of thing they did at Fortress St. Ladislas!"

"You seem to think I know of this place — "

Stefan Dworjanski laughed coldly, "You know it better as Krostok Fortress. It was the Soviet name — you would be faithful to that!" The bishop's hand clenched over the cross at his breast. "You know this place. You know what happened there. There is much in the sound of your voice — the fear on your face — that tells me I am not mistaken. Only those who were there, those who died and those who made them die, know how Father Radynz was murdered at the altar after they had deceived him — a blasphemous deceit! That was your Krostok Fortress!"

"I never knew of such a place," Newman said.

"You lie! You sent the wine here with this poor priest because you had to be sure that I did remember."

"I had to be sure that you did remember, Dworjanski. None of this would be necessary if you didn't."

Stefan Dworjanski's heavy jowls shook; there was almost satisfaction in the sound that came from his throat. "What

[216]

memories do you want to hear — Lieutenant Bransk?"

Newman moved backward nervously as Father Largo came close to him, staring up into his face. He pushed the priest aside impatiently.

"You have been so very stubborn, Dworjanski! We never wanted to make a martyr out of you. But now you are determined to tell the world about Krostok Fortress."

"And about you, Lieutenant Bransk! It is too late to change my mind — even to silence me! You are here in the pages of my manuscript. That's what you wanted to know, is it not? You are here — your life — your true confession that would have made you very great if you had been able to confess and repent. But then, you would have died instead of being enriched! You would have died for the murder of Father Zwiecki. For that foul crime I would execute you myself, but I am a priest and my hands are consecrated!"

"You are broken at last, Dworjanski, if there is murder in your heart!" Newman shouted.

The bishop shook his head. "Not murder — execution. Man thirsts after justice. There are some who will be damned. It is a sad truth of history. Their necks must be broken because they cannot bend them. They will not serve God, but they will serve his justice. You have received Christ into your godless soul, Lieutenant Bransk, but there is no grace from these sacraments you have defiled."

Newman's hand moved and, as he stepped toward the bishop, there was a gun in it. He waved it impatiently. "Back — back from that desk! I've got to finish up my work here and get to my lecture."

He pushed the bishop's hand from the manuscript and stepped to the fireplace and dropped the folio on the gas grill. The pages curled into a crisp black as the flames leaped around them. Newman laughed and swung the gun toward Dworjanski. He backed to the door, feeling for it with his hand.

The Spaniard threw himself in front of Stefan Dworjanski

as Newman fired, the blue flame lighting his face for an instant.

Halidon, roused from unconsciousness, remembered that he had heard a sound at the farther end of the cellar, had walked into the darkness. He was chagrined at the realization that he had been knocked on the head.

He was on the stairs to the second floor when he heard the shot. He finished the last few steps in a bound and was at the door of Stefan Dworjanski's room when it was flung open and Newman backed out.

Halidon was upon him knocking the gun from his grasp. Newman staggered against the wall, then plunged past Halidon down the stairs, at the bottom of which Father Massimo was standing, blocking his way to the rear door. Newman, now thoroughly confused, hurtled himself past the priest and toward the door.

He jerked it open, and stood tense as he saw the police car in the street and Kevin Byrne hurrying up the steps toward him.

They carried Father Largo to his room and placed him on his bed. While Father Massimo felt his pulse he listened to Stefan Dworjanski's account of what had happened. Newman, as they expected, believed the stack of worthless papers on the desk was the bishop's memoirs.

Father Largo moaned as he regained consciousness and his hand moved to his chest, fingers fumbling with the buttons of his soutane.

The superior unbuttoned the robe and the shirt beneath, his hand probing in wonder as he heard Father Largo's choking laugh. "My saint was with me, Father Superior — "

Father Massimo drew the shirt wider, his amazed eyes staring at the Holy Shirt of Mail, the relic of the Venerable Bruno.

He found the place below the heart where the bullet had lodged and the slug came away in his fingers.

The superior held the bullet up for Stefan Dworjanski and Halidon to see. "Thanks to the holy relic of our founder, Father Largo has only been stunned."

"I suppose you feel that you had a miracle coming, Father," Halidon said dryly.

Father Massimo shrugged. "Father Largo, when he realizes what has happened, is apt to be very annoyed with San Juan de la Cruz for leaving him to the ministrations of Venerable Bruno."

It was several days before Father Massimo ventured to put down on paper an account of the conclusion of the Newman affair. Even now he was by no means sure what he would write to Cardinal Vincenzo Amalfi. It was dismaying to have to record that the final minutes had nearly been bungled, almost causing Stefan Dworjanski's death.

In spite of Byrne's vigil outside the monastery Newman had slipped past him, entering the oratory in the disguise of an old man. The evidence of the disguise was later found in the chapel.

Halidon was gone. He had left that same night and had been the first to inform the world of Newman's attempt to murder Bishop Dworjanski. Halidon had made Father Largo the improbable hero of the hour and the relic of Venerable Bruno his equally improbable armor. The Spaniard said he had taken the relic to wear in the event Tostado caught him and subjected him to a beating. It was enough to make Father Largo forget all about the imagined visit of San Juan de la Cruz.

Father Massimo arose from his desk, certain that whatever he wrote to Cardinal Amalfi would be anticlimactic. All the world now knew what had happened, and some were even surprised that Newman had run true to type.

The house was quiet and only when Father Massimo came along the hall toward the cloister did he hear the voices of the other priests coming from the garden. In the excitement of the past few days he had failed to realize what the conclusion of

[219]

the mission Cardinal Amalfi had assigned him would mean. When the letter was dispatched to Rome his work would be done. There would be no further need for him here.

That was the quixotic thing about this exile. Coming to Darrington he had thought himself an exile, and now, going away from this place he had come to love, he would be even more the exile. But at least he had the satisfaction of knowing at last that the others would remain to establish a seminary for the Order through the generosity of Cardinal Gasquet who had given them his house at the seashore.

Father Massimo's reverie was interrupted by the appearance of Father Georgio who bumped the kitchen door open with his elbow and sallied into the hall, his face afire with perturbation. "Father Superior, just the man I wanted to see!

"Pax tecum, Father," said the superior.

"Et cum spiritu tuo, Father. I have a complaint — "

Listening to the grievance, Father Massimo smiled peacefully. He had never quite appreciated Father commissario's complaints before. He would miss them.

HOUSE OF EXILE

By Joseph E. Coyne

THE scene is the "House of Exile," a run-down monastery located in a quiet section of the city of Darrington, Massachusetts. Once deserted and slated for demolition, it recently was opened to a veritable tower of Babel's-worth of priests, missionaries of the Brunite order seeking refuge after escaping from behind the Iron and Bamboo curtains.

Besides being of various nationalities and cultures, these priests have all shared persecution and torture at the hands of the Communists. And they all, in varying degrees, possess knowledge the Commies would rather have them forget.

Chief of these priests is Stefan Dworjanski, former Bishop of Poland, a man whose very escape from the Reds was close to miraculous and who is now determinedly engaged in writing his memoirs, naming names, citing specifics; a man far too dangerous for the Communists to let alone.

To protect the Bishop, Father Massimo, the Italian, is assigned